THE BARRIER

SHANKARI CHANDRAN

Pan Macmillan Australia

First published 2017 in Macmillan by Pan Macmillan Australia Pty Ltd
1 Market Street, Sydney, New South Wales, Australia, 2000

Copyright © Shankari Chandran 2017

The moral right of the author to be identified as the author of this work
has been asserted.

All rights reserved. No part of this book may be reproduced or transmitted
by any person or entity (including Google, Amazon or similar organisations),
in any form or by any means, electronic or mechanical, including photocopying,
recording, scanning or by any information storage and retrieval system,
without prior permission in writing from the publisher.

Cataloguing-in-Publication entry is available
from the National Library of Australia
http://catalogue.nla.gov.au

Typeset in 12/15 Birka by Midland Typesetters, Australia
Printed by McPherson's Printing Group
Map illustration by IRONGAV

The characters in this book are fictitious and any resemblance to real persons,
living or dead, is purely coincidental.

The paper in this book is FSC® certified.
FSC® promotes environmentally responsible,
socially beneficial and economically viable
management of the world's forests.

To Amma and Appa, who gave me faith

There have been as many plagues as wars in history; yet always plagues and wars take people equally by surprise.

Albert Camus, *The Plague*

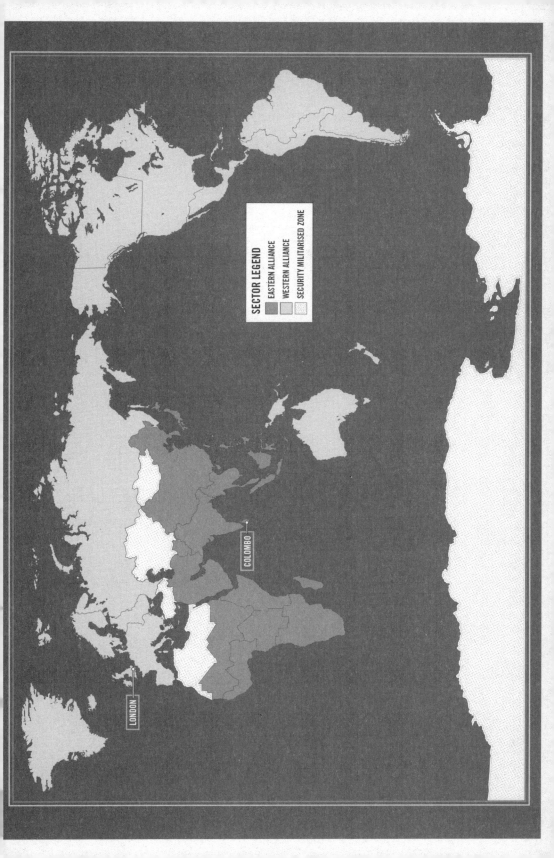

Armistice Accord

signed at the end of World War Righteous

On this, the ninth day of the sixth month of the year 2025, we, the surviving children of the human race, declare that World War Righteous is over, five years and more than three billion deaths after it began.

We each acknowledge our role in the destruction of our citizens and cities and solemnly vow that we will never allow our philosophical differences to lead us into war and to the point of extinction again.

Out of the funeral pyres, we will create new institutions, laws and mechanisms that will protect us from ourselves and all known biological threats.

The first mechanism is the Immunity Shield. We declare that immunisation is the right and obligation of every citizen. In 2021, the Great Ebola Pandemic swept across our world. It wrought unprecedented devastation until it was finally controlled in 2025. We must always be vigilant against its rise and recurrence. The Global Vaccination Programme will provide the vaccine, EBL-47, to maintain herd immunity against Ebola. The programme will be administered freely by the World Health Organization (WHO) and enforced by a new public health agency, the Department for Biological Integrity.

The second mechanism is the Information Shield, a barrier between the countries of the Western Alliance and the countries of the Eastern Alliance. The purpose of this barrier is to ensure that only approved information and people may move between these two new governance zones.

The final mechanism is our resolve to learn from the past and do whatever is necessary to ensure the security and stability of our world.

Prologue

A voice cut through the turbulence and ricocheted inside Noah's helmet.

'Hard landing, soldiers!' the pilot shouted.

Noah braced himself as the plane shuddered and listed to the right. He coughed, a charred smell catching in his throat. The soldier next to him jabbed him in the ribs, reminding him to turn on the air filter in his mask. The sudden movement of the plane threw him against a window and he looked down. It was night-time and for a moment the cloudy haze below cleared. What had looked like hundreds of thousands of streetlights were actually fires. Sri Lanka was burning. Buildings, vehicles, homes and people.

He pushed his feet into the floor of the plane, his hands across his chest, threaded into the straps the way he'd been taught.

Deep breath. He was only a few months out of the academy but he wouldn't let Commander Hackman down.

The plane dropped and dropped again, tossed like the ash swirling around them. His stomach somersaulted. He bit the inside of his cheeks.

Brace for impact. Trust the pilot. Trust your unit. Trust yourself.
The plane slammed into the ground, hard but controlled. It skidded, turned and stopped. The impact shook him violently but it didn't shake him loose. Noah laughed and cheered with the others.

*

Noah and the Western Alliance units boarded a military convoy and headed straight to the Sivanadana Cave at the northern tip of the island.

They passed the smouldering remains of towns and villages, and the massive refugee camps that had replaced them. World War Righteous had started in this quadrant of the South Asian Sector. Sri Lanka had a greater mix of religions than most countries – and a greater propensity towards carnage.

There were quarantine camps with large 'No Entry' signs at the front and smoke billowing from crematoriums at the back. And Noah saw the small blue WHO vaccination tents that would later proliferate all over the world like pustules on a dying body.

At the cave, the convoy stopped for Hackman's final orders. The team was large – about fifty men and women, experienced soldiers and Bio agents.

'This area requires careful purging. Our primary target is the Hindu temple here,' Hackman pointed to a building on the map.

'The temple has been carved out of the vertical rock face. It is a contiguous piece of stone the size of Capitol Hill.'

Noah flicked through the file on his handheld. He had heard about Sivanadana before. His father said it was stunning.

'Do not be deceived into reverence,' Hackman cautioned. 'In this part of the world, reverence leads to the suspension of compassion and humanity.'

'Remember why we're here. Remember what happened.'

None of them could forget. Five years ago, Sri Lanka had incubated and released the virus of religious war. World War Righteous had weakened an already compromised world, but it didn't destroy it. Instead, war created the perfect host for the Great Ebola Pandemic – contagion did the rest.

Hackman pulled more detailed maps onto the screen.

'This site is vast. We don't have the firepower to raze it to the ground right now. But,' he paused to make sure everyone was listening, 'I want all statues to be smashed, all frescoes and artwork burned. Anything that reminds these people of their religion.

'There are about a hundred families in the temple compound – refugees and a few priests who led them there.'

Hundreds of people who thought that sanctity equalled salvation, Noah thought.

'They are in the early stages of Ebola – and not contagious yet. However, we have isolated them as per the Containment Protocol. Stay alert. If you encounter any resistance, you have shoot-to-kill orders. When you're done, we'll blow the surrounding rock face. Are there any questions?'

Hackman looked around. Noah willed his face to remain impassive.

'No? Good. This is an historic moment. It is 27 June 2025, and it is our privilege to help execute the Great Purge across the East. The convoy leaves in thirty minutes. Be ready.'

*

The team divided into smaller groups and worked in a grid formation.

'Don't leave anything standing. Destroy it all,' Hackman warned one last time.

The cave entrance was lined by a stone parade of celestial dancers, their arms raised in salute. Noah approached the central temple for Lord Shiva, the Hindu god of destruction.

Ragged men, women and children huddled together in the courtyard, cowering as the soldiers approached them.

Noah pulled his face mask up like the rest of the team. *Ebola is not airborne. I have been vaccinated with the new wonder drug,* he reminded himself. The refugees were not contagious, but they were sick: not just from Ebola but from starvation, from the trauma of war and all the diseases that came with it.

Sunlight drifted onto the wall of the temple. He thought he was looking at a detailed fresco. But as the cool grey stone began to glow, he realised it was not a painting. A stonemason had become a storyteller, carving every scene and subplot of the *Mahabharata* into the wall.

Noah reached up and touched the faces of the family that had been torn apart, doomed to fight each other for a kingdom they could have shared. He didn't know stone could convey emotion: love, anger, envy and so much grief.

'What are you doing?' A soldier emerged from the shadows, an MF-25 automatic weapon strapped around his chest.

'Nothing . . . I was just reading the stone.'

'Reading the stone?'

'The panels tell a story. It's a mythical battle that happened thousands of years ago. See –' He pointed to a section. 'That's Arjuna, the great warrior. He's holding his young son who died alone on the battlefield. And there he is cursing his cousins who killed the boy. They betrayed their code as warriors and killed him through deceit.'

It wasn't a righteous kill, Noah's father used to say.

'What's he doing there?' The soldier pointed to the next panel with the tip of his gun.

'There, Arjuna avenges his son's death. He hunts down the killers.' The stonemason showed Arjuna avenged but still overwhelmed by loss.

'It's big, isn't it?' The other soldier craned his head up to survey the entire series of panels.

It was big and beautifully narrated in stone. The *Mahabharata* was told to Hindu children; it was a thousand stories within a story that taught them how to live.

'This panel here – it's the most important one.' Noah touched the carving of Lord Krishna, the magnificent blue god, now conceived black and shining. The god's hand was raised as he stood on the battlefield, the armies of good and evil gathered around him. Arjuna, his disciple and warrior, was crouched prostrate at his feet, hands folded in prayer. Lord Krishna was speaking to Arjuna, giving him the *Bhagavad Gita*, the song of god, the religion's most prized scripture.

'Hinduism says we are bonded to this cycle of life, death and rebirth. But we yearn to be free of it. Man's true nature is a divine energy. This moment in the war here –' Noah placed his palm on the cool stone again. 'It's when God tells us the way home.'

'How do you know all that shit?' the soldier asked.

'My father told me,' Noah whispered into the stone. His father, a theology professor, had studied that 'shit' for decades, teaching Noah when he was willing to listen. He waited to hear if his father's voice, calm and sure, would whisper back.

'Well then, let's start there. Move away.' The soldier unclipped the safety on his weapon, adjusted the strap around his shoulders and stood with his feet apart. He braced himself and then opened fire. A staccato of metal tore into the stone. It echoed throughout the cave. Noah flinched in spite of himself.

Behind him a withered mass rose from the shadows. He turned and saw the men from the courtyard stagger towards him. Some called out for their gods. The women sat transfixed by what they knew was about to happen. Their eyes followed the men and the men followed the bullets, but they were too late.

The *Bhagavad Gita* fell to the ground in pieces. And then Commander Hackman was next to Noah, shouldering him to attention.

'What are you doing, Williams? Fire, fire, fire.'

Fire.

The ragged men were close enough to him that Noah could see the disbelief in their eyes, and feel the disgust in his own as he did what he was ordered. Soldiers joined him at his side.

He had never heard the sound of metal ripping through layers of shrivelled muscle and brittle bone. It passed through body after body, like a child's fingers in playdough. He heard people scream in agony, the air rattle from their chests, the life rush from their wounds in a fountain of dark blood. When it was over the pieces of their bodies lay twisted, mangled and merged with the pieces of their gods.

Chapter 1

Noah had watched the interrogation for seventeen hours but lost interest after nine.

It was going nowhere. The London office was impatient, forcing him to intervene. He nodded to the three interrogators as they left. One of them, the best in his team, shrugged his shoulders apologetically.

With his right hand, Noah dragged the metal chair over and placed it in front of the naked man. He sat and wiped the sweat from his forehead with the back of his arm. The small room was kept airless at his command.

In his left hand, he held the gleaming orb of a human skull, the kind used in medical school. He tossed it and caught it, casually adjusting its position in his hand.

He excelled at Human Anatomy. It had been his best subject at the academy all those years ago when he was just starting out. That wasn't entirely true. Analytic Tradecraft was his best subject. Virology was his second best. He excelled at Theoretical Killing too but partly because he was so good at Human Anatomy. The latter could be more accurately described as his favourite subject.

He ran a hand through his dark hair, pushing it out of his eyes. He needed a haircut. And sleep. He looked at his watch and then spoke loudly for the benefit of the recording devices in the room: 'Interview continued at 22.34 on 8 December 2040 by Agent Noah Williams. Location: Interrogation Site 45, South Asian Sector.'

He turned to the naked man. 'This is Louis,' he said, introducing Hassan to the skull. 'He and I have been together a long time.'

The man licked his lips, his tongue lingering on the cracked, peeling skin. He reached higher, licking the sweat above his lip.

'It's hot in here, isn't it? How about we talk to Louis for a little while and then I'll see if I can get you a cold beer? A soda if you prefer.' Noah smiled at him and then at the skull whose grimace remained fixed.

Hassan squinted with his one good eye – first at Noah, then at the skull, confused. He raised his head stiffly to the security camera protruding from the ceiling corner. In the room next door, Noah knew the agents watching them on the monitor would be smiling. Things wrapped up pretty quickly when he brought out Louis.

'Don't look at them.' Noah slapped Hassan's face lightly, his tone friendly. 'Look at Louis.' He raised the skull. 'I named him after Louis Pasteur. Do you know who that is?'

Hassan tried to speak but couldn't push words through his parched throat. He nodded his head and coughed.

'That's right, cough it out. Your throat is fine. I never touch the throat. You need it to breathe, eat and most importantly to speak.' Noah leaned in for the next piece of information. 'To be honest, you don't really need it for breathing and eating. We can enable those functions in different ways if necessary. But I find communication is best done face to face, through the throat, the organs of articulation and the poetry of language.'

Hassan began to cry.

'It's okay. Louis and I are not going to hurt you anymore. As you know, Louis is actually French so I should really call him *Louis*. But I think it sounds a little pretentious under the circumstances, don't you?'

Hassan's tears streamed into the cuts on his face.

Noah held Louis up again and Hassan cringed, pulling instinctively against his restraints. He cried out. His body was heavily bruised. His skin was stripped in places. Any movement hurt.

'Louis helps me explain something to you. My boys have roughed you up a little. I know it doesn't seem like a fair fight with you tied to the chair. But we'd only end up hurting you more if we allowed you to fight back. So the boys have had their turn and, to your credit, you've told us very little. Nothing in fact. You are very brave and very strong. Surprisingly strong for a public health official.'

'I'm a doctor,' Hassan whispered.

'Yes, of course. You're a qualified vaccinator, entrusted by the WHO to maintain herd immunity against Ebola. Your parents must be so proud. My mother always wanted me to be a doctor. A medical doctor, that is. She'd be hard pressed to find a medic who knows anatomy the way I do. She thinks I work in pharmaceutical testing for the government.'

'You're a doctor,' Noah repeated. 'So you know that there are two parts to your skull. The cranium creates a vault around your brain and brainstem.' He traced the outline of Louis's cranium with his finger.

'Your brain weighs 1.7 percent of your total weight – not much. And yet it absorbs twenty percent of your oxygen intake. The second part of your skull is your facial skeleton – the bone structures that give shape to your face.

'Your braincase – the cranium – is strong. Nature has made it hard and although it can be cracked by any number of implements, the *process* of cracking is often imprecise and can inadvertently damage your brain. For now, I need your brain as it is – parts of it at least. I need your higher-level thinking, your short- and long-term memory and some of your executive functions.' He rattled off the names, using the fingers of his empty hand, like items on a grocery list.

'There are parts I don't need – for example, your motor cortex or your sensory cortex, although I'm sure you'd like to keep those.' He motioned again to sections of Louis's skull.

'The problem that Louis and I have is this: because you won't tell us what we need to know, we have to hurt you to extract the information. However, we don't want to *damage* you, because then you're no good to us or your wife and three children back in Mumbai.'

The man's head snapped up, one eye widening a little.

'Yes, that's the limbic system activating in your brain. It's primitive but important. It hasn't evolved much over the thousands of years that man has walked the earth because it hasn't needed to. When in danger, it makes us fight or run. Judging by the look in your eye, you'd like to fight me.

'That's good,' Noah said agreeably, leaning his tall frame back in the chair. 'It was a strong reflex from the beginning; strongest in those that survived and propagated the species.

'Interestingly,' he continued, as though they were in a lecture hall instead of an interrogation room, 'while our limbic system didn't change much, our higher-level thinking evolved rapidly, enabling us to create more sophisticated and previously unimaginable ways to fight each other.

'You won't win a fight with me, but *flight* is still an option for you. Of course, there are only so many places a family can run to.'

The man understood. 'I'll talk,' he rasped through his dry lips and broken teeth. One eye was now completely blinded by swelling, the other bloodshot and fearful.

'Excellent, thank you.' Noah placed Louis gently on the cement floor next to his chair and leaned forward, elbows on his knees, hands loosely clasped. He used to teach Body Language at the academy. This posture indicated confidence, physical strength but a willingness to exercise restraint, and emotional interest in the other person's opinions.

'You'll be surprised by how much we know already, so save your strength while I fill you in,' he said kindly. 'We know you switched out the Ebola vaccine and replaced it with your own. Like our vaccine, your substitute is engineered to create Ebola antibodies – except that your antibodies are decoys.

'They don't create immunity in a population set – but whenever the blood serum of those population sets were scanned, the Haema Scanner detected enough of the antibody markers to *think* that the population had been fully vaccinated. You subverted the Global Vaccination Programme, and we missed it every time.'

Hassan nodded slowly, the expression on his face changing.

'Yes,' Noah continued, 'you should be proud. No one's fooled the Haema Scanner before. Your vaccine is more sophisticated than anything we've seen.'

'How did you catch me?' the man whispered.

'We didn't – you were caught by the virus.'

'What?'

'It's ironic, isn't it?' Noah replied. 'The problem with Ebola – I should say the *main* problem with Ebola,' he corrected himself, 'is that it still exists. Despite the most effective vaccination programme ever designed, despite almost one hundred percent herd immunity, it still exists. Its will to live is stronger than even our own. Imagine the limbic system in that virus – that's one tough fight reflex, don't you think?'

Hassan was silent. Noah continued. 'When you switched our vaccine out, and vaccinated your population set with the substitute, you created a gap in the Immunity Shield. You and your friends undermined herd immunity. The virus was watching, waiting quietly for just this moment to attack.'

'I don't understand.' Hassan shifted uncomfortably in his chair.

'Let me be clearer then.' Noah unclasped his hands and ran them through his hair again, wiping away the sweat on the back of his neck. 'We were alerted to your decoy vaccine by an outbreak of Ebola in a set you vaccinated two months ago.'

'No, no . . .' Hassan shook his head. 'It's not possible . . .'

'No one tells Ebola what's possible and what's not. You think we killed its life cycle with the vaccination programme? Ebola is millions of years older than us – we just slowed it down.' Noah pulled out his handheld from his pocket and flicked through various screens until he found what he was looking for.

'Maharashtra 310. Remember that one? A small village on the banks of the Narmada River. It's one of India's cleaner rivers.'

'When?'

'A week ago – the Department for Biological Integrity and the WHO went in quickly and contained it. You might have read about a typhoid scare. We didn't want to start a panic. The surviving population set tested positive for the antibody markers even though forty percent of the village died of Ebola. Further analysis in Bio's lab in London, using a new scope, picked up your decoy.

'Let me assure you, Hassan, we will test every population set you've ever vaccinated. We will find the other gaps in the Immunity Shield – hopefully before it's too late.'

'Too late?' the man asked, dazed.

'Ebola is always evolving and when you give it a host – as you did – you give it an opportunity to improve; to change itself into variants that we are defenceless against. Our vaccine, EBL-47, only protects us against Ebola Strains 1 to 47.

'If Ebola establishes itself in one population and mutates, it can be carried – across communities, countries and continents – like last time. It *will* create another pandemic.

'That's why you shouldn't have done what you did.' Noah sounded like a scolding parent. His throat closed a little. He swallowed hard.

'Tell me about the decoy vaccine. In the past, anti-vaxxers have used placebos. They're a little pedestrian, don't you think?'

'Placebos don't pass the scanner,' the man whispered.

'That's right, eventually someone walks into a hospital, a high security building or an airport and sets off the Haema Scanner. But your decoy is special. It's sophisticated *and* stealthy. The scanners had no idea.

'How did you develop it?'

'We didn't,' Hassan replied. 'We're bacteriologists; that virology expertise was beyond us. Someone else delivered it to us.'

'The source,' Noah replied simply. 'Give me the source.'

'I don't know the source – none of us do. The decoy arrived with our usual pharmaceutical shipments and we just administered it, as agreed.'

'Agreed with whom?'

'We communicated online. We never met or spoke. I swear it on my children.'

Noah exhaled. His Cyber Surveillance team had told him all of this already. He leaned back in his chair, and lifted one foot onto his knee, indicating calm amiability.

'You've worked for the WHO for seven years. You've had postings all across the South Asian Sector and, in the next round of promotions, you were considered likely to receive a lucrative job in the Middle Eastern Sector. You were highly trained and specially vetted for competence, discretion and commitment to the Global Vaccination Programme.

'Your pension, while decent for a public employee, is largely comprised of share options in Abre de Libre – the pharmaceutical company that supplies the cocktail of vaccines and boosters that, until recently, you administered on an almost daily basis.'

'You know everything about me.' Hassan licked the blood and sweat from his lips again.

'I know you're not an anti-vaxxer. You're no conscientious objector. I hate those guys, I really do. I hate their sanctimonious bullshit about personal freedom and the right to choose. I hate their bogus science and the assumption that people are so stupid they'll listen to any alarmist crap. Of course, people are stupid but that's beside the point. The *point* is I hate them and their complete lack of regard for the safety of the herd and future herds.'

Future herds. He pushed through the pain, seeking comfort in the familiar cadence of his rant. 'I hate them so much I can pick them a mile away, so I can tell – you're not one of those rabid, antibiotic-refusing, organic-only fuckers.' He paused. 'So what I want to know is why – why did you do this? Why did you put yourself – and your family – at such risk?'

The man remained silent. Noah's hands clenched.

Why? He always wanted to know why. His ex-wife, Maggie, said it was a big part of his problem. Maybe she said it was a big part of *many* of his problems. But it helped him create order in a world of chaos and grief.

He shook his head and focused on the task at hand.

'I asked you a question,' he repeated softly.

Chapter 2

Hassan Ali dropped his head, tears merging with the sweat on his heaving chest.

Noah couldn't hit him. He had to leave the cranium undamaged and Hassan didn't care about the rest of his body – yet. There were pain thresholds they hadn't explored but Noah was running out of time. Hackman would expect answers tonight.

Hassan was running out of time too.

'I'm not going to hurt you. I won't let anyone touch you again.'

Hassan raised his head slowly, suspiciously. Noah looked over his shoulder and nodded at the camera behind him. The door opened. A colleague dressed in army fatigues entered, bearing a metal briefcase.

'Take Louis, would you?' Noah said. 'I don't like him seeing this part.' He handed the skull to the soldier before the man left the room.

On the side of the briefcase was a small scanner. Noah swiped his security tag against it and the case clicked open. A row of ten small glass vials slept snugly in a bed of grey foam.

'Do you know what these are?' he asked.

Hassan shook his head, blinking his good eye rapidly.

'It's EBL-23: a much earlier – and failed – iteration of the Ebola vaccine.'

'No, no, no . . .' Hassan shook his head vigorously. He pulled against his restraints, rocking his chair.

'Don't do that. Falling over, tied to a chair, hurts a lot more than just falling over.

'You will remember that the successful development of the vaccine EBL-47 is one of our greatest achievements. After four years of the Great Ebola Pandemic and World War R, vaccination saved us from almost certain extinction in 2025. Success sometimes rides on the back of years of failure.' His father used to tell him that when he was a boy, although perhaps he had meant it in a different context.

'Please don't be alarmed. I'm not going to use this on you.' Noah shook his head regretfully. He was comfortable with hurting people. That was an unfortunate but necessary part of the process.

But he hated the look Hassan would give him in a moment – when he explained what he would do with the vaccine in the briefcase.

'Look at me, Hassan.' Noah slapped the man's face again as his eye began to bulge. 'You are going to disappear into a cell or you'll be executed. There won't be a trial. No passionate human rights lawyer is going to storm in here with a habeus corpus writ and a camera crew. It's just me and my colleagues – and you. You and your family, that is.'

Noah held Hassan's jaw in his hands. 'If you talk – your wife and children will simply never know what happened to you. They will wonder about you every day, some days more than others. They will suffer the tortuous uncertainty of a loss not fully realised. At best.'

He tightened his grip on the man. 'At worst – I won't use this vaccine on you.' He picked out one of the small vials. 'I won't even use it on your wife. I'm sure you're ready to sacrifice her for your cause, whatever it is.'

Noah tossed the vial in his hand so its sealed mouth was in his fingertips. 'Your children are innocent. I know they had no part in this. You were prepared for them to spend the rest of their lives without a father, possibly without a mother.

'But were you prepared for me?' He looked at Hassan. 'You see, if necessary, I will use this on your three children, sweet as they are.'

And there was the look he hated.

Noah wasn't weakened by fear the way some agents were. He felt fear, but it was a necessary reflex, primal but vital. He was grateful to his limbic system and he used it to stay alive.

The man tied to the chair looked at him with a different, deeper kind of fear. Hassan's bare feet twitched as urine trickled down his legs and pooled between his crushed toes. He sobbed.

Noah turned away.

The question remained.

'Why, Hassan? What did you think you would achieve by substituting the vaccine? Why did you do it?'

'Because it's wrong,' the man replied. 'What you're doing – it's wrong. I'll tell you everything I know, but, I beg you – leave my children alone. This was me, Assif and Sumith from the clinic. You arrested them already. You have all of us. The children are so young – so young.' He broke down again.

'Tell me everything and I'll see.' Noah knew what it was like to plead with the doctors, to bargain with God. The doctors had apologised and God – God had remained silent.

'The vaccine is poison. You're changing us with it.' Hassan raised his face.

'What do you mean? We're trying to protect you from a resurgence of Ebola.'

'I'm not talking about Ebola,' Hassan interrupted. 'You know what I'm talking about.'

'I don't –'

'You know – you are so lucky you know.' Hassan talked over him now, in a hurry to speak.

'The vaccine makes us forget things – who we are, why we're here, whom we belong to.' He closed his eyes as if praying, except Noah knew this man could not pray. But his words echoed the lessons of his childhood.

'You're insane – the vaccine doesn't make you forget anything,' he lied. 'It protects you from a virus that nearly wiped out all of humanity. It keeps you and your children safe.'

A thought occurred to Noah suddenly. 'Have you vaccinated your own children?'

'Yes,' Hassan opened his eyes and replied sadly. 'I vaccinated them. I didn't know any better. It was only later I realised . . .'

'Realised what?' Noah slapped Hassan's face. Something was wrong. 'What did you realise?' he shouted.

'Be at peace, brother, please don't be angry with me. I'll tell you.' Hassan dabbed his swollen lower lip with his tongue, licking the fresh blood. 'A year ago I started to feel things I'd never felt before.'

'I need more than "feelings" if I'm going to save your children.'

Hassan flinched. 'I don't know how to describe it better than that.' He shook his head. 'It told me what to do; it told me the vaccine is poisoning us.'

'A voice inside you told you that?' Noah repeated.

'Yes, a voice. It told me what to do . . . come closer.' Hassan coughed and lowered his head. 'Come closer.'

Noah leaned in, his face next to the broken man, his body tense and ready in case Hassan tried anything, despite his restraints.

Hassan whispered feverish words into Noah's ear.

*

The air in the back room was thick with the smell of sweat. Men and women looked at Noah, waiting for instructions. He sat down, studying Hassan on the monitor.

'Let's give him time to think.' He needed time too. 'I don't believe this population set is the only target – there must be more in India.'

He was sure that was the endgame; no one went to this much trouble for a single Immunity Shield breach. There were more and they had to find them.

He turned to the soldier next to him. 'Talk to Garner at Bio. Tell her we need to check the herd immunity of all of the population sets this guy has covered over his career.'

'What are we looking for, Chief?' the soldier asked.

Noah tried not to show his impatience; they were all tired. This was the third interrogation in the sleepless week that had followed the detection.

'We are looking for vaccine tampering – *deliberate* breaches of the Immunity Shield.' He spoke slowly and clearly. 'We'll start with the Ebola outbreaks that have occurred since the shield went up. There haven't been many. And I think we need to be prepared for a wider check: across all of the Eastern Alliance – we want to find the breaches before Ebola does.'

'All of the East? But that's . . .'

'Yes, that's half the world. In fact, population wise, Asia, the Middle East and Africa now comprise far more than half the world.

'If we want to ensure the safety of our part of the world, and the stability of their part, then we can't allow any gaps in the Immunity Shield. Global herd immunity must be maintained.'

'Got it.' The soldier stood up and then stopped. 'What did he say, Chief? When he whispered to you – what did he say?'

'Nothing – the mad ramblings of a terrified, tortured man,' Noah said.

'What should I put in the transcript? The surveillance system couldn't hear him. You'll need to . . . give me details, sir.'

'There's nothing to give – he was talking rubbish. Let me see the replay. But keep watching him. Keep recording.'

The soldier clipped the file of the interrogation and brought it over to Noah on a handheld. He pressed play.

'The vaccine makes us forget things – who we are, why we're here, whom we belong to.'

Then Hassan had whispered to him: 'It is an energy. All around us. Inside me. It has names . . .'

Hassan had whispered low and fast, but Noah had heard every word. He knew what each individual word meant. His father had taught him the same names. But in the strange sequence Hassan used, they were incomprehensible.

Like the words, 'I'm sorry, Dr Williams, there's nothing more we can do for her.'

'It is beautiful,' Hassan had said. 'It guided me. It yearns to be felt by others.'

He replayed the words in his mind again and then stared at the man on the monitor.

*

Noah pushed through the metal door. It was heavier against his body this time. Hassan opened his eyes.

'Water?' he pleaded.

'Not yet,' Noah replied. 'Who told you to do this?' He didn't know how to structure the question without conceding the premise of the previous answer.

'I don't understand –'

'Someone created a decoy vaccine for you. You replaced the EBL-47 with your decoy. Why? Which population sets have you breached? Which sets are you going to breach next?' The questions were tumbling out too fast.

Hassan stared at him blankly. Noah motioned for water and a soldier quickly brought him a cold bottle. He cracked the seal and poured the water over Hassan's head. The man cried out and then opened his mouth, his head darting.

'Feel better?' Noah asked without concern. 'Now, again: who and why and which population sets?' He leaned forward and snapped the man's middle finger back in its socket. Hassan screamed and jerked in the chair, almost knocking himself over. Noah held the chair down.

'You have nine more of those. And as I mentioned before – one wife and three children.'

'I swear, I'm telling the truth. There was no one else. It told us what to do – me, Sumith and Assif. The voice – it told us your vaccine was hurting us and that we had to find a way to stop it.'

Noah reached for another finger.

'Sumith and I tried to develop a decoy for months but we couldn't get it right.'

'And what was Assif doing while you were cooking up a storm in your lab?' Noah asked.

'He approached us one day. He sensed "It" too. He said he knew someone who could create a decoy vaccine.'

'We've spoken to Assif and he showed us the chatroom where he found a like-minded traitor. However, his contact has disappeared without a trace. This casts suspicion on the whole story –' Noah paused for a moment. 'Except that I believe you – you don't have the virology expertise to create the markers.' Noah knew enough about virology to identify who knew more.

Hassan exhaled deeply, his head sinking onto his chest.

Noah lifted the man's chin and shook it hard.

'You were willing to compromise herd immunity against Ebola. You have compromised the lives of your children. I just don't understand why.'

Nothing on Earth could have made Noah risk his children. His child. He didn't believe any psychosis was powerful enough to override a parent's instinct to protect. And he certainly didn't believe any voice – any 'It' – was persuasive enough. No matter how beautiful.

'Why?' Hassan repeated, confused.

'Yes, why did you do it?' Noah asked. Hassan hadn't intended to invite Ebola back into the world, but he had risked it – why?

'But I already told you – It wanted me to. It told me this was the right thing to do. It wants to be loved again. It wants to come back to us here.'

Noah reached out and snapped another finger. Hassan screamed, this time his back arching as much as the restraints would allow. He closed his eyes, teeth biting into his torn lip. And then, very clearly, through his tears, he began to pray.

Except he shouldn't have known how.

Chapter 3

The plane door exhaled open. Noah walked down the narrow aisle of the private jet and stood in the doorway. He pulled the collar of his jacket tightly around his neck. He had missed the bitter winds of London; they penetrated every part of him, like a quick bolt of electricity.

London was his base, although he no longer called anywhere home. He had been raised among the brownstones and maple trees of the Upper West Side. Then recruited and trained by Bio in an off-grid facility in Rochester, New York State. On graduation he was sent to London, ostensibly to finish his PhD in virology – in reality to help expand the Department's European operations.

He had met and married Maggie here too. Maybe that was why he always came back.

He hoisted his sports bag over his shoulder. The steward reluctantly passed him the small cooler box he had stored in the plane's refrigerator.

'Thanks,' Noah said.

'No problem. It smells divine.'

'Doesn't it.' He laughed and stepped out into the cold, crossing the short distance to the preliminary meta-scanner. He always felt like he was walking through a crystal tunnel. It detected the guns on his ankle holster and in his bag, although it wasn't looking for them. He exited the meta-scanner into the Sanitising Room.

Unlike him, most travellers had come from within the Western Alliance and therefore didn't need the Sanitising Room. Noah was part of a select group – Bio agents, senior politicians, WHO officials and soldiers – who were approved by Bio to travel to the Eastern Alliance. On their return, they were required to sanitise.

He entered the steel cubicle and stripped. The high-pressure spray covered him in chlorobicide. His skin felt hot but the antiviral chemicals no longer irritated him. The spray was followed by a stream of coarse defoliator and another spray of the sanitiser.

He kept his eyes and mouth shut tightly, using the sterile brush to scrub his body and nails. Three cameras watched him. When it was done, he dressed and waited for the cubicle door to open. He followed the directions to the immigration line, noting the surveillance along the way.

He passed large WHO signs advising travellers in different languages how to maintain hygiene and recognise the symptoms of disease.

The enlarged words were consistent in every country he had been to: Ebola still exists. Vaccination and boosters every three years are our only line of defence.

The signs were accompanied by images of people washing hands, drinking bottled water and wearing face masks. He didn't look at the posters showing the stages of disease progression. He had seen that before. Every fifty metres there were units attached to the walls, dispensing chlorobicide, disposable gloves and pocket face masks. Ebola wasn't airborne but most people were extra careful in high-density areas.

The air around him smelled faintly of gardenias, an added perfume to camouflage the biting smell of the chlorine compound that was pushed through the airport's vents.

He approached the immigration section. The thirty or so lines of the general population snaked for hundreds of metres. People stood, masked and quiet. Occasionally someone coughed and people turned. Parents urgently quelled crying children. Soldiers stood at regular posts, taser batons on their belts, guns across their chests, safety clips unhooked.

Noah approached one of the lines reserved for government officials.

'Dr Williams?'

He turned to see a young soldier holding a small device. The man looked from the screen to Noah's face again, confirming his facial identity.

'Yes?'

'Come with me, sir. You'll still need to clear quarantine but it's much faster – this way please.' The soldier directed him down a narrow corridor to a metal door with a panel for biometric identification. Noah submitted his eye and palm for scanning.

The door opened to a sparse room. He nodded at the soldier standing at the table.

'Good to see you, sir, we've been expecting you.' The soldier motioned to the chair.

'I'll stand, thank you. It was a long flight.'

'The meta-scan indicates that you're not carrying any biohazardous material in or on your person. Your historic Haema Scanner records show that your Ebola antibody levels are sufficient. All markers required for entry into the United Kingdom are present. You don't need an EBL-47 booster.'

'I wouldn't have thought so.' Noah smiled.

'No, but we still have to check your blood. Sorry, sir.'

'I understand.' Noah took off his coat and pulled up his shirt sleeve.

The soldier held the portable scanner above Noah's wrist without touching his skin.

'I hope you clean that after.'

'Only if I make contact, sir, it's non-invasive,' the soldier replied.

'Clean it anyway. It's good practice.'

'Of course, sir, sorry.' A few moments later the scanner beeped. The soldier studied the screen. 'You are clean for all known biological threats. The meta-scan indicates that you have a few things to declare. May I please check your bags?'

'Sure. Two firearms, one skull and one other item. I have papers for everything.' He handed over his documents. The soldier reviewed them carefully and then opened the bag. He looked at the skull, wrapped in Noah's Columbia University basketball jersey, but didn't take it out.

'I've heard about Louis,' he said, trying not to smile.

'Louis is famous.'

'So are you, sir.' The soldier reached for the small box.

Soldiers on his side of the alliance might not admire him so much if they knew exactly what he did and how he did it. Not everyone had the stomach for his work.

'Careful with that. You'll see that I've had its skin and fluids tested back at base in Mumbai. It's as clear as me.'

The soldier opened the box slowly, revealing a mango. Its skin was a perfect sunset of pink, yellow and orange. A small section had been cut and biopsied. Noah had covered this with thin plastic bandages, holding the cut together.

'May I?' the soldier asked.

'Go for it.'

The soldier leaned forward and inhaled. He closed his eyes for a moment. 'It smells divine.'

Noah laughed and reclaimed the fruit and his luggage. He nodded goodbye and walked out the exit and into the cold London air. A driverless black SUV was waiting for him.

*

The Department for Biological Integrity was headquartered in Atlanta, Georgia. Before World War Righteous, it was called the Centers for Disease Control and Prevention. The catastrophes of WWR required a more interventionist approach to disease control. Bio combined military tactics with the tools of scientific innovation and the objectives of public health and security.

Bio's London office was its largest base outside the continental US. The office had a sixty-storey administrative building above ground and twenty-three floors of laboratories underground.

It had been built out of the remains of Waterloo Station. In the chaos that followed the Great Pandemic and WWR, people were so used to the recasting of public buildings into quarantined hospitals, refugee camps, morgues and crematoriums, that no one cared when one of London's largest, most important train stations was transformed into something entirely different.

Noah walked through the preliminary meta-scanner and antechamber that protected the building with reinforced concrete and projectile-proof glass. Two layers of sliding doors opened, allowing him to the lift.

'In the Western Alliance, my voice identifies me as Agent Noah Williams.' The programme assessed his voice for signs of duress.

At the twelfth floor, Patrice was waiting for him.

'Hello Patrice, you look beautiful as always.' He kissed her on both cheeks. He wasn't lying. She was always groomed impeccably. She'd been with Hackman from the very start of his career but no one knew how old she was, except, of course, Hackman.

'You look terrible. The pilot says you didn't sleep. And you need a haircut.'

'You sound like my wife.' He smiled.

She patted his unshaven face. 'Ex-wife. You should listen to her. She still loves you.'

He passed the box to her. She looked up in disbelief when she opened it, and then brought the fruit to her nose.

'I think *I* love you!' She laughed and kissed him again. 'How did you know?'

'You mentioned it once.'

'Do you miss anything?'

'Salmon,' he answered. 'Real, just-pulled-out-of-a-clean-river salmon. If I try hard, I can almost remember the taste – creamy yet meaty. Sweet, but a little salty.'

'Stop. You're making me hungry. He's expecting you. Go straight through. I'll pull him out of his meeting.'

'No hurry, I've got time.'

'I saw the communications. I don't think so. I'll get him.' She put the mango in its box and hurried back to her desk.

Noah entered the office. It was clinically organised and devoid of anything that might give a sense of the man, except for a photograph of Hackman shaking the president's hand on the day of his appointment. Behind them the star-spangled banner framed the pair in patriotic fervour.

The walls were covered with military cartography and charts tracking the implementation of the Five Virus Eradication Policy. The viruses were priority-coded by colour. The Ebola virus, coloured red, was number one.

There was a Sixth Virus but its map wasn't pinned to the director's white walls. The information in front of Noah was low-level security clearance only – it could be mined from the internet by a lesser security agency or the growing subculture of hackers who kept trying to penetrate the Information Shield's firewall from both sides.

Noah picked up the photograph on the desk.

'Patrice insisted on that one.' A voice spoke from behind him. 'She bought me that tie for a Kris Kringle. Apparently turquoise warms the blue of my eyes.'

Noah turned around. 'She's right. Remarkably, your face looks warmer.'

'If Patrice was your assistant, you'd do as you were told too.' Hackman snatched the photograph from him.

'New brooch from Patrice too?' His eyes focused on Hackman's lapel. A small silver tree was fixed next to the American flag.

'This is a pin, not a brooch. It's from an old friend – the tree of liberty.' Hackman touched the pin.

'The one that must be refreshed with the blood of patriots and tyrants?' Noah raised his eyebrows.

'The very same. My friend is partial to Jefferson. I'm an Abe Lincoln man myself – ideology over practicality. How was the flight?'

'Fine. Thanks for sending your charter. You didn't need to but I enjoyed the in-flight bar and turn-down service.'

'No problem. I wanted you back fast and it was either that or make you ride caddy with one of the stealth jets. The pilot said you didn't sleep. You were supposed to rest.'

'The pilot should have kept his eyes on the radar. I was fine. I closed my eyes for a while and the single malt helped some.'

'Okay, so let's talk.'

Noah exhaled deeply and sat at the large table. 'I assume you've seen the recordings?'

'Yes, all three interrogations. And I've read the transcripts. It's the last one I'm most interested in – Hassan Ali.'

'Thirty-five years old,' Noah recited the profile. 'WHO-employed vaccinator, respected bacteriologist with no suspicious financial activity over the last ten years.'

'A zealot then?' Hackman sat back in his leather chair and flicked through the file.

'Yes, of indeterminate ideology.'

'Well, not entirely indeterminate,' Hackman replied. 'What did he say to you – the audio didn't catch that part.'

'Nothing – rubbish. It wasn't worth putting in the report.'

'I'll decide that,' Hackman said, without recrimination. 'He talked about an energy, didn't he?'

Noah looked up sharply. 'How do you know that?'

'Because it isn't the first time I've heard it. What were his exact words?'

'He said . . . It was a force, an energy inside him and all around him – guiding him. He said it wants to come back . . .'

Hackman didn't look surprised. 'It sounds like the Sixth Virus, don't you think?'

Chapter 4

Noah was surprised by Hackman's words. The Sixth Virus had been eradicated from the Eastern Alliance at the end of the war. 'Hassan's ramblings are nonsense.' Noah replied. 'Someone has put him up to it – probably the contact who provided the decoy vaccine. If we can find him, then we can find out if this is an isolated incident.'

'No sign of the chatroom contact yet though.'

'He's a ghost. If he's smart enough to develop this vaccine, then he's smart enough to cover his tracks and only come out when he wants to. Cyber Surveillance is building a false profile of a rebel vaccinator. They'll plant him in chatrooms and start to make a little noise – disillusionment with the Global Vaccination Programme, fear of big pharma etc. And then we wait for the ghost to find us. We only get one chance at this – if he senses a trap we'll lose him for good.'

'Good idea – yours?'

'It's a team effort.'

Hackman shook his head. 'You'll never get the top job with that attitude.'

'I don't want the top job.'

'How could you not want all this?' Hackman fanned his face with his tie.

Noah laughed. 'I'm putting Garner in charge of CS.'

'Is she ready for active duty yet?' Hackman asked, interested but not concerned.

'Almost. We'll see. We need to assume that the ghost is either an accomplished virologist himself, or he's using one. But substituting a defective – or ineffective – vaccine might not be the only way he'll try to undermine herd immunity.'

'You're assuming that the purpose of the attack is to breach the Immunity Shield?' Hackman challenged.

'No – the purpose of these breaches is unclear to me.'

'Okay then,' Hackman replied. 'While your false profile is waiting in various vaxxer and anti-vaxxer chatrooms, what will you do?'

Noah sighed. He was so tired but sleep eluded him. He doubted it would help anyway. 'I think I should probe Hassan further.'

'I thought you might say that,' Hackman replied. He put the file down and connected his fingers like the arc of a cathedral roof across his chest. 'Would you really have used the EBL-23 on his children – after everything that's happened . . .'

'You know the answer. That's why you sent me.'

Hackman spoke, almost sadly. 'He won't tell you more, regardless of whether you fuck with the minds of his children, or not. If anything, he will recant and say whatever you want, in order to protect them.'

Noah felt a muscle twitch in his jaw. He clenched his teeth, almost biting the inside of his lip. He forced himself to relax.

'What do you want me to do with him, then? And the others from the lab?'

'The usual. I want it clean.'

Noah nodded.

'I'm going to tell you something now – it's classified. Your clearance has been upgraded.'

'I'd really rather not hear it.' Noah tried to sound flippant.

'There have been three other breaches,' Hackman said.

Breaches.

'In Bangladesh, Pakistan and Assam. In all cases, the vaccinators we interrogated cited two common factors: an energy or an "It" that made them do it, and a ghost that supplied the decoy vaccine. We think it's the same ghost.'

'And the same It – you believe the "why", don't you?' Noah shook his head in disgust.

'I do, and I'm not the only one. People above me have looked at the recordings and they believe these people are telling the truth, at least in their own minds. They believe they are being guided to do this by a higher power. Watch the other recordings. The vaxxers all talk about an energy that's enlightening them about the vaccine we're using in the East.'

'An omniscient energy with exceptional technical expertise?' Noah asked. 'Why didn't it tell them how to create a proper Ebola vaccine then, without the other active ingredient? They would maintain herd immunity against Ebola in the East, the same as us. And, like us, they would be free from the Faith Inhibitor.'

The Faith Inhibitor. FI-85. Sometimes Noah still couldn't believe what they had done. What his father would have thought of it. The Faith Inhibitor targeted and damaged the part of the human brain that generated faith. People stopped *feeling* faith. They stopped yearning for and seeking a loving, vengeful and powerful God. A Memory Inhibitor was also added to the vaccine so that people no longer remembered the ancient, lost ideas.

Religion. The Sixth Virus. The virus of the East. As an agent of the Western Alliance, Noah had been there during the Great Purge when the West made sure that all reminders of religion were excoriated from the East. From cities, temples and even its people.

Sometimes Noah thought it was ironic that he lived in the Western Alliance where people could still feel faith, and yet, these days, he felt nothing.

Hackman swung himself out of his chair and stood up. 'First rule of Sunday School: God helps those who help themselves. Right now, the ghost or whoever's supplying this decoy, doesn't have the strain he needs to create an Ebola vaccine. No one does except us. Which is why *we* produce the vaccine for both the West and the East.'

'We don't *produce* it,' Noah corrected. 'Your drug lord buddies at Abre de Libre Pharmaceuticals produce it.'

'Play nice,' Hackman replied.

'You don't pay me to be nice.'

'I suppose that's right.' Hackman nodded. 'Right now, all this ghost can do is study the existing vaccine that we supply, and create a decoy without the Faith Inhibitors.'

Noah shook his head in confusion. He stood up. 'How does the ghost *know* about the Faith Inhibitor? Who told him?'

Hackman looked at him for a moment and then replied. 'If you believe Hassan – God told him.'

Chapter 5

Noah left Hackman's office with the access codes to a high-level data server. His boss's final words to him were: 'This is a long one. Before you start, I want you to get some sleep. At the very least go out tonight, get drunk, find some beautiful, bookish woman with red-brown hair, and fuck her brains out. When was the last time you did that? You look like you need it.'

He took the elevator down to the lobby and walked out. The car was still waiting for him. He knocked on the window.

'I'll walk, thank you,' he said to the car's driver-unit.

'You sure, sir?' The unit replied with the standard Texan accent of all recent models.

'Positive. I need some fresh air.' He waved his face mask at the car.

The driver-unit laughed.

He walked along the Thames back towards New Waterloo station, heading east, following the old stone wall that hugged the river. The Thames gleamed blue against the bright morning sky.

There was a time, during the Great Pandemic, when families dropped their dead into the waterways. The mortuaries, hospitals and funeral homes couldn't keep up with the body count. Neither could the school halls and stadiums. People disposed of their loved ones in their own way. The river had never carried Ebola, but the decomposing bodies brought colonies of other diseases.

The Thames was unrecognisably clean now, pumped with several levels of cleansers: chlorine compounds, antibacterial and antiviral agents, antibiotics and anti-protozoa medications. After WWR, Bio's Sanitation Division took control of the waterways. The Thames, like all of Britain's rivers, was full of mutagens. If you could afford to eat fish, it had been raised in tanks the size of football fields, on industrial farms.

Noah sat on a bench under the shadow of London Bridge, its recently rebuilt steel towers rising sharply into the sky.

Sometimes he imagined that Sera was with him. He sat and talked to her. They fed the pigeons together and laughed as the birds fought over the scraps.

'Don't tell Mummy I gave away her sandwich,' he whispers.

'I promise. Daddy, do you think the pigeons will give it to their babies?' she asks.

'Of course,' he replies. 'Everyone loves to feed their babies. You eat some too, sweetheart,' he says, tearing her a strip.

Sometimes he just sat there and cried.

He checked his watch: 1.23 pm. He looked up and smiled. Maggie was always early. He stood up and reached out for her automatically. She turned her face so he could kiss her cheek.

'You've cut your hair. It looks great. You look great.' He put his hands in his pockets. Her hair was boyish, her features made sharper by it.

'You look exhausted. When did you get back?' she asked.

'This morning. Thanks for coming to see me.'

'You don't have to thank me. How are you?'

'Okay. You?' He motioned to the bench. She sat reluctantly. He took a seat with her but not too close.

'Okay.' She paused, looking out at the bridge. 'Why this bench, Noah? There are benches closer to Bio, or closer to my office – why do we always meet at this one?'

'This one . . . London Bridge reminds me of the price of safety.'

She laughed at him. A harsh, empty laugh. 'It reminds most people of the nursery rhyme.'

'How's work going? I heard you're back at Repop.' Maggie was a scientist at the Department of Repopulation.

'It's fine.'

'Come on, Maggie – I haven't seen you in four months. I just . . . I just want to know how you are.'

'You want to know *now*? *After* we divorced?'

'Maggie –'

'Work's great, Noah. It keeps my mind off things. We're reviewing a new product – it's a fertility scanner. It tracks the movement of the egg from the ovary to the uterus and identifies the precise date and time for conception. It's portable and slimline too. You can fit it in your handbag. You know, in case you need to conceive on the go.'

'Does it come with a payment plan and a free set of steak knives if I order now?'

She smiled. 'Just six months of free fertility booster supplements. Repop is very interested in it – I think the manufacturer will pass the approvals process.'

'Do you ever think about –'

'No, I don't.' She answered quickly. 'Noah, I came here to . . .' She opened her handbag, 'To return this to you.' It was his wedding ring. 'You have to stop giving it to me.'

He looked at the ring but didn't take it. 'I've been assigned again. I want you to keep it for me until I get back.'

'We're not married anymore.'

'I know, it's just that – you know what it is.'

Before he went on a job, he had to take off his ring and place it on her side-table. He had to kiss her goodbye and say, 'Don't lose that, I'll need it when I get back.'

'It's a sweet ritual, Noah, but it's not us anymore.'

'I have to do it, Maggie . . . to be sure I'll return.'

'God damn you,' she whispered and shook her head. 'You have no right to make me responsible for that. We are not a part of each other anymore.' There were tears in her eyes.

He looked out over the river. *You will always be a part of me.* Say it, he cursed himself. *You will always be a part of me. You and Sera.*

'Please, Maggie – just one more time. The last time.' He closed her hand around the ring.

'It's never the last time with you.' She tried to pull away but he held onto her.

'If you don't take it, I'll have to break into your apartment and leave it on your new side-table.'

She laughed in spite of herself and pulled back harder. 'That's illegal and creepy.'

'That's me,' he smiled. She was so beautiful. He wanted to touch her.

She put the ring in her bag. 'Be safe, Noah.' She kissed him on the cheek and stood up before he could do more. She walked away, facing straight ahead. He could tell she was crying.

He looked at the bridge again.

London Bridge is falling down, falling down, he hummed.

In 2022, London Bridge had fallen down, just like the nursery rhyme. When the Great Ebola Pandemic had reached London, the government shut the city off from the rest of the country in the hope the virus would burn itself out. London's beautiful bridges, which spread like the fingers of a hand, were broken by four jets and ten missiles. The result: 29,734 casualties and

18,956 fatalities. People desperately trying to escape across the bridges before the cordon was dropped.

They didn't have a chance. They screamed and ran. They crushed each other. They jumped into the grey water with their children.

He had watched it from the safety of New York. The television flashed scenes from a movie. He sat in his kitchen, his father reaching for his hand. Tears in both their eyes. He had seen the people go under.

He had prayed for their heads to reappear. He saw the bridges snap and fall on top of them.

The virus didn't burn itself out. It found a way – Ebola always found a way – and it was carried across the country and beyond.

'The truth is, Maggie,' he said to the empty bench, 'I like to sit here because it reminds me that life jogs on. I watch people. They go past me, their minds and memories never stopping at the bridge or the sound of the parents screaming or the children crying.

'I like that people can run past this bridge and feel nothing. I am intrigued by it.

'I resent it too.'

He stood up and stretched in the midday sun, his body still stiff from the plane trip. People were emerging from office blocks in their running gear. He headed towards the nearest tube entrance, pulling his face mask from his pocket and then shoving it away, as he descended into the tube's mouth.

*

He dropped his bag by the front door of his apartment. It wasn't good to be back, but it was familiar. He ignored the flashes on his answering machine. They were either from his mother or his drycleaner. He turned on the television and flicked through the public health channels, until he found the cooking channel Maggie liked. He left it on and walked away.

After a quick shower, he took out a Deca-Vit syringe from the fridge and checked its expiry date – it was three weeks past.

'Danger is my middle name,' he said, cracking open the seal. The daily cocktail of vitamins was supposed to be taken with food but he didn't feel like a shake.

He flicked through the mail indifferently and then threw the pile on his desk. It splayed out like a fan, knocking a photo frame off the edge.

'Shit.' He bent down and picked it up, resisting the sudden temptation to hold its cold, glass façade to his chest. It was a photograph of Maggie, him and the baby at the hospital. Their first family photo.

He remembered holding his daughter when she emerged into the world, her eyes squinting in the light, her face puckered and angry. She was so ugly and so beautiful. He held her, terrified he would hurt her with his hands roughened by years of hurting others. Carefully, he touched the curve of her head, inside which would come to rest all the feelings, hopes and memories that life would give his child.

Life had been selfish.

He would have given her all the rest of his days if he could have. These empty, endless days he spent extracting information, watching people, catching them. Killing them.

He whispered the name they had chosen. Seraphina. Sera. Like the angel.

'There are forty-four small plates of bone,' he said to his exhausted wife. Ex-wife. Maggie smiled at the quirk she used to love.

'Really? Do tell, because now is really the time.' She closed her eyes against the hospital pillow.

'They will harden and fuse eventually, but for now they're held together by the connective tissue. See?' He leaned closer to her with their baby and she opened her eyes.

'At the top, here.' He motioned to the anterior fontanelle. 'This space can remain soft and open for her first eighteen months. Look closely, you can count her heart rate.'

He stroked her sticky tufts of dark hair and found the strong pulse in the gap between the bones. He felt her life beat in that place.

Noah put the photograph down. Face down.

Chapter 6

Noah held onto the wall of the lift as it descended into the earth.

A digitised female voice announced each subterranean level of the Bio Building as the lift dropped. Noah felt like he was plunging deeper into water that was pressing on his body and fogging his hearing. The lift door opened at Subterranean 16 and his inner ear equalised – the main body of the building was pressure controlled.

He entered the prep room for a laboratory. A protective suit hung on a locker, bearing his name on a post-it note. He liked these new suits. They fitted well, like a reinforced outer skin.

At the entrance to the lab he punched in a passcode and the seal of the door opened reluctantly, lips pulled apart mid-kiss. He felt the cool air of the lab through the suit.

The room was equipped with microscopes, computers and refrigerator units with security panels. At one end, Dr Jack Neeson peered into a microscope as tall as Noah, with a series of lenses stacked above it, like the perspex bellows of a church organ. Neeson was dressed only in trousers, a collared shirt and a white lab coat. Without lifting his face from the eyepiece, he issued commands.

'Objective lens 1000XR, please.'

A mechanical arm that Noah hadn't noticed before unfurled itself from the ceiling. With precise fine motor skills, it exchanged the lenses in the microscope. The spider-fingers of the hand pincered the condenser lens and adjusted the angle and light of the illuminator, anticipating the scientist's physical orientation.

'It's incredible, isn't it? It's a hybrid of the LightCycler and the nano-microscope. Has both functions with spectacular resolution. Even the electron microscope is integrated into it. Everything I see is recorded by her computer,' the man said, finally raising his head. 'And she's completely un-hackable: she has her own server and firewall. She's not even networked to Bio.'

The mechanical arm swung forward to wipe the sweat from his brow. 'Roberta, say hello to Noah.'

'Hello Noah,' a female voice said.

'Her voice box is in a hard drive behind the arm,' Neeson pointed vaguely. 'But I've connected it to the lab speakers so it sounds like she's everywhere.'

'She has a lovely voice,' Noah said.

'Thank you,' replied both Neeson and the computer. 'Admit it,' Neeson continued, 'she's alarmingly sexy.'

Noah laughed. 'That's because you've always found smart sexy, and yes I am alarmed.'

'I have an IQ of 192,' Roberta confirmed.

'I feel overdressed, Neese.' Noah indicated the other man's lack of protective suit.

'You're suited up for legal reasons and the cameras. I find the colour makes me look pale.'

'You never leave the lab – you are pale.'

Neeson ignored him. 'I'm just admiring your new vaccine.' He took off his plastic gloves and reached forward.

Noah smiled and shook the older man's hand. Neeson clasped his arm for a moment longer.

'Did you read those journal articles I sent you?' he asked.

'They're on a list –'

'With all the other articles I sent you?' Neeson shook his head.

'Tell me about the vaccine,' Noah asked.

'It's beautiful, perfectly formed, deceptive and able to emulate Nature and Nature's expectations. I think I'm in love.'

'You know I find it creepy when you talk about micro-organisms like that.'

'I've named her Martha Rose, after my mother. I've been saving her name for something special.'

Noah laughed again. 'Thanks for your preliminary report. It helped with the interrogation. The vaxxer – Hassan Ali – said he didn't develop the vaccine himself.'

'He didn't – we're looking at the work of an exceptional virologist. The decoy produced the right markers enabling it to fool the scanners. But it did it without producing functional antibodies or without damaging the faith centre.

'The scanners in the West look for Ebola antibody markers in human blood serum. The scanners in the East are programmed to look for two types of markers: the Ebola antibody markers *and* the Faith Inhibitor markers.'

'Programmed by Abre de Libre?' Noah asked. 'Or Bio?'

'Good question. The scanner settings are regulated by the Department for Biological Integrity – we are a governmental organisation after all and the immunity status of the population is a public health matter . . .'

'But?' Noah prompted.

'But Abre de Libre calibrates and controls the actual machines,' Neeson replied reluctantly.

'They control the scanners *and* the vaccine production?'

Neeson nodded. 'It's a good thing they're on our side.'

'I suspect it's a good thing we're on their side.'

'Ah, Noah, so much cynicism in one so young.'

'I'm not that young anymore,' Noah replied.

'Let Roberta look at your brain, she can identify the debilitation of age and abuse.'

Without waiting for a response he opened the drawer next to him, pulled out a skull cap and swivelled it on one hand like pizza dough.

'Roberta has a built-in neuro-navigation system. Using infrared, CT and MRI technology, she can construct a 3D image and accurately localise each part of your brain, better than ever before.'

'Just relax, Dr Williams,' Roberta soothed. Neeson fitted the cap over Noah's head.

'Don't mess up my hair,' Noah replied as the robotic arm connected electrodes to the cap, inserting their wires into her hard drive. 'Watch the screen, Doctor,' she commanded gently.

Both men looked up at the screen. 'There we go,' Neeson said. 'It's beautiful – God is an artist.'

Noah shook his head.

'Stay still. That –' he reached up and pulled the image out of the screen, holding it in his hands, 'is your frontal lobe – your faith engine as it were. The emotional aspects of religious experience are in the temporal lobe here –' he pointed again, 'and here in the medial frontal gyrus.

'The Faith Inhibitor, or FI-85, targets the frontal lobe and interacts with it to stop the generation of faith. Yours,' he brought the image of Noah's brain closer to his eyes and peered over his glasses, 'is in perfect working order despite your refusal to use it.' He clapped his hands together, extinguishing the image.

'Thanks for that. So what's making you so hard about this decoy vaccine?' Noah pried off the skull cap and ran his hands through his hair.

Neeson laughed. He wheeled his chair back from the microscope towards his computer.

'Watch the screen,' he instructed. 'The first image is our vaccine.'

Noah recognised the structure of the vaccine that was administered in the Western Alliance. It was a pure vaccine, the crowning glory of Abre de Libre's pharmaceutical range. The vaccine only contained the viral vector EBL-47, engineered to create immunity against Ebola.

'This next one will also be familiar. Roberta, show Dr Williams what we were looking at, would you?'

'Of course, Doctor.' Roberta's voice startled him.

Another image came up on the screen. The torso of the vaccine was the same but it had an additional strand of cells that tilted the structure's symmetry. It was EBL-47-E.ALL, the vaccine that was administered to the Eastern Alliance after the war, as part of the Armistice Accord – although the citizens of the east were unaware their vaccine was any different.

'And now, one last vaccine,' Neeson spoke again.

The third image looked identical to the second image. Noah looked at Neeson and shrugged.

'Exactly,' Neeson replied, shaking his head. 'This is the vaccine from your fellow in India.' He reached up with a pointer and drew a circle around the extra strand of cells. The Faith Inhibitor.

'It always looks like a broken limb to me.' Noah moved closer to the screen.

'It's more of a grafted limb,' Neeson replied. 'The Faith Inhibitor strand is attached to the EBL-47 molecule, in the vaccine. The inhibitor needs this section here,' he pulled the image out with one hand and pointed to the EBL-47 with his other, 'to piggyback into the bloodstream.'

'Piggyback?' Noah challenged. 'It's more of a Trojan Horse.'

'I prefer to think of it as an enhancement. Trojan Horse has such negative connotations.'

'Depends on whether you're Greek or Trojan.'

'Given the current geopolitical division of the world, we are the Greeks. But in the end everyone felt sorry for the Trojans.'

'They brought the bloodshed on themselves.' Noah shrugged.

'You should write foreign policy.'

'I only execute it.'

Neeson laughed, turned and threw the image back onto the screen. 'In the new vaccine, the one Hassan Ali and others are using, this section here –' Neeson pointed again to the additional cells that usually constituted the Faith Inhibitor, 'is a decoy.'

'I thought you said the entire vaccine is a decoy.' Noah looked at Neeson who couldn't take his eyes from the screen.

'It is. The entire vaccine is pointless, a kind of complex placebo. It's extremely difficult to create it – you would need to know your virology, be fluent in genetic modification, and possess a laboratory almost as sophisticated as this one. This wasn't cooked up by some bored PhD student or even her disgruntled university head of virology. No – whoever's behind it had skill and patience. And an ideology.'

'A passionate anti-vaxxer?' Noah suggested sceptically.

'Maybe,' Neeson mused. 'I'm the scientist, not the spy. Although I've always thought you'd enjoy life more if you did more science than spying.'

'I might live longer. This isn't the work of an anti-vaxxer. At best, they protest and launch court battles against us, the WHO and the pharmaceutical companies they think are driving their armchair conspiracies. At worst, they bomb vaccination clinics and assassinate vaxxers.' Noah looked at his old friend, noticing for the first time how his hands shook a little. How Neeson compensated for the tremor by plunging his hands into the deep pockets of his lab coat. How he always diverted conversations back to the screen and the images in front of them. Neeson had been his mentor and guide through the complex world of virology for almost two decades. Neeson wasn't that young anymore either.

'This –' Noah pointed at the images on the screen. 'This doesn't fit the profile of an anti-vaxxer.'

'Then what? A bioterrorist perhaps – someone trying to breach the Immunity Shield so that when another outbreak of Ebola occurs more people die?'

Noah shook his head. 'When I told Hassan that there was an Ebola outbreak in his population set – that *he* had put people at risk – he looked terrified, like he had no idea that would happen.

'Don't look at me like that, Neese – of course I lied to him. I needed to know what he was planning to do next. I lied to him and then I broke his fingers – and then I left him and his colleagues to our Wet Team.'

Neeson shrugged. 'Hackman told me about the rest of the interrogation – the bit that was for your ears only: an energy that wants to be remembered; wants to be loved. God's plan, perhaps?'

Noah couldn't get Hassan's words out of his mind either. 'God doesn't have a plan.'

'I thought you said God doesn't exist.'

'He doesn't, at least not to me anymore. He doesn't exist, ergo he doesn't have a plan. Don't tell me you buy the divine dog shit this guy was peddling? He was delirious with pain; you can't rely on the credibility of suspects under torture.'

'So says the professional torturer?'

'Yes – when the professional scientist starts believing a suspected bioterrorist is being guided by God.'

'We are all guided by God, Noah – even you, if you would just let yourself listen to Him.'

'Does God have a plan for you too?' Noah laughed bitterly.

'He does. I didn't realise it until recently.'

'Let me guess – he helps you deliver the Faith Inhibitor through the Global Vaccination Programme? Eradicating faith and therefore religion in the Eastern Alliance was his will? God helped you put himself out of a job in fifty percent of the world.'

'Seventy-two percent by population,' Neeson corrected him. 'They are reproducing much faster than us.'

'They had a head start,' Noah replied. 'The East lost more than half its population during the Great Pandemic but still comprised sixty-four percent of the world at the end of the outbreak.'

'So Hackman likes to remind me. He's terribly insecure about that. Anyway, enough about God's plan for me. When you find this ghost, I want his vaccine – keep that in mind when you're doing Hackman's will.'

'You already have his vaccine.' Noah motioned to the image on the screen.

'I want all of it – the research, the failures and past iterations, the future ones. It's the process of synthesis as much as the outcome. *How* God created man is as important as man himself.'

'Have a look.' Neeson moved away from the microscope.

'I don't know what I'm looking for,' Noah hesitated.

'That's because you never read the journal articles I send you. You've been around these organisms enough to recognise their resilience. Now I want you to admire their artistry. Take a look,' Neeson urged again.

Noah positioned himself at the eyepiece and focused the lens.

Neeson instructed the bionic arm: 'Roberta, maximum magnification please – slowly, he may be young but he doesn't have my eyes.'

'You have beautiful eyes, Doctor,' Roberta replied.

'Thank you,' both men responded and laughed.

Noah heard whirring and felt the arm brush against him as it adjusted the lens, the strength and angle of the light.

Neeson continued. 'There are only three microscopes in the world – here, Atlanta and New York – that can show you what you are about to see. Just relax your eyes.

'Focus on the signature please, Roberta.'

Noah heard the whirring again as the arm made adjustments, sliding the viewfinder and plate. A familiar design came into sight.

'All people – not just artists, but bombmakers, geneticists and virologists – we all have a signature. We cannot help but leave our mark. It's in our nature – even God leaves His mark on all things He creates. Call it hubris, vanity or simply a need to be known. A desire to be understood. That infinitesimally small structural tag you see there – it's present in all of the decoy vaccines we found. It is deliberate.'

It is beautiful, Noah thought. It was a circle inside a square. Inside the circle was a geometric symphony of shapes; a complex series of connected and overlapping triangles that created a mesmerising pattern of stars – stars within stars within stars.

A universe.

'How many virologists could create this?' Noah didn't lift his head from the scope.

'In the East? Only four or five I know of,' Neeson replied.

'You?'

'Of course. The signature makes me wonder . . . was it just for him, or was he trying to tell us something?'

Noah looked up at the enlarged image of the signature on the screen. There was no beginning to the pattern and no end. No inception and no completion. There was only continuous energy.

'He's trying to tell us something,' he replied.

Chapter 7

Noah sat in Neeson's lab, alone. He was still looking at the image of the structural tag.

It was the artist's signature. The scientist's way of telling them who he was. His father had explained the pattern's meaning to him many years ago. Before the war. Before his death. Before Sera.

He opened another search box and typed the word 'mandala' from Sanskrit, a symbol that signified the universe. A tool that was supposed to create a sacred space and guide man towards his inner-self.

He added more terms to the mainframe's search algorithm: 'Theology, Hinduism, Buddhism, Islam'. It narrowed the search too quickly but he was prepared to take the risk. He was starting to understand the ghost and he sensed commitment to a cause. An underlying urgency and a plan.

*

That evening he spoke to his newly assembled team in a data analysis room on Subterranean 13 of the Bio Building. They were surrounded by the enormous screens that were used to track the behaviour and movement of diseases, people, governments and armies.

'You've read the case files and watched the interrogations. You know what we're looking for.

'Your security clearance has been temporarily bumped up, but please remember that all of your keystrokes will be monitored by Internal Affairs so do not use your new status to access irrelevant but interesting information, betray your country or download top secret pornography.'

Some of the younger analysts laughed nervously. Like all agents and military personnel who had permission to gather intel on or enter the Eastern Alliance, they were the guardians of the Sixth Virus Eradication Policy. The vaccine had worked in the East, but Bio was vigilant and prepared for the possibility that one day that might change. The analysts were as integral to its success as the Bio scientists that supervised the Global Vaccination Programme. All of them had been chosen by Noah for their proficiency in analytic tradecraft. He'd trained all of them.

'Excuse me, sir.' Crawford put his hand up. He had never lost his Ivy League prettiness and slightly smug wit, even after a decade in the service.

'Yes, Crawford?'

'You've asked us to start with the breaches in India, Pakistan, Assam and Bangladesh. I was just wondering about the other countries in the South Asian Sector. Should we broaden our search for potential breaches in Sri Lanka and Nepal too? We could use the profiles of the current breaches to guide us.'

'Excellent idea.' Noah nodded. 'Their historic vaccination records are being run and crosschecked by the mainframe. Nepal has been quiet for years; I think there was a bad case of total regicide towards the end of the war, but aside from that, nothing.'

'Is there ever a *good* case of total regicide?' Garner asked, her voice deadpan.

Noah laughed. 'We shouldn't overlook them just because they're politically quiet and officially enthusiastic vaccinators. The same for Sri Lanka. If anything, the fact that we haven't detected a breach in those countries makes them suspicious. If I was the ghost, I would target zones away from my own country to protect my location.'

'Unless that's what you wanted Bio to think you were doing,' Garner replied. 'So what do we know about him, sir?'

He admired her focus. She was as proficient in the field as she was in the analysis room, but after a few bad missions she'd asked to be rotated out of active duty. He understood.

'We know he makes contact with the WHO vaxxers through the internet. He's clearly good enough to sit in the tall grass of a number of chatrooms and then get the hell out of there when his work is done. We're trying to trace him back from the forum Hassan Ali and his buddies used. He's covered his tracks well, so either he's hyper-tech literate or he has friends who are. I'm guessing the latter.'

'What about the other sectors in the Eastern Alliance? From a chatroom he could contact the Middle East, Africa and the rest of Asia – there are a bunch of countries that would make good targets.' Garner was looking at the map on the second screen. 'We haven't even talked about Afghanistan.'

Noah followed Garner's gaze to the map. It showed a world divided into two separate alliances, each one divided into sectors. Along the borders between the two sides, there were Security Militarised Zones and armies that prevented the movement of people, and the Information Shield, which prevented the movement of knowledge from one side to the other.

'We are looking at the other sectors. Hackman has briefed other teams for that. My team – *this* team is looking at South Asia.

The problem is that a ground search will take too long and it'll raise alarm. We want to find the ghost quickly and quietly.

'He could be based anywhere in the Eastern Alliance but I think he's inside South Asia and, so far, he's limited his activities to that sector.'

'How can you tell?' Crawford asked. When Noah didn't answer, Crawford repeated the question. 'Based on what, sir?'

Noah didn't know why he was certain the ghost was in the South Asian Sector — there was just something about him. He didn't even have anything to base *that* assumption on — he just knew the ghost was a man.

'He hasn't contacted any other sector, yet. If he had, we'd know about it. The Middle East would have gone mad. We wouldn't need to find the breach. The breach would find us. No, he's starting close to home. He's developing and testing the decoy vaccine until he gets it right. He's moving carefully. I know we're behind him but if we read him right, we can catch him.'

He could just tell.

'Cyber Surveillance is setting up a dummy vaccinator as bait in various chatrooms, but, Garner –'

'Yes, sir?' she looked up from the file.

'I want you to supervise them – you've a good eye for that work.'

'Yes, sir.'

'In your packs are the more detailed search matrices. Look at the breaches and the people involved in them.' He began pacing as he rattled off questions.

'Who are these vaxxers? Who do they work with? Look at the population sets they gave the decoy to – were they chosen for a reason? What do they have in common?'

Crawford raised his hand again but Noah ignored him.

'The mainframe has run this algorithm already – the results of its search and cross-references are in your file. Look at those results and then keep looking – you can do better than the mainframe.'

He heard some of the analysts laugh confidently. He put his hands up to quieten them.

'Yes, yes – you're all geniuses, I know. I want you to look at each of these vaxxers and tell me why they did it; then tell me where the other breaches are – current and future.'

'What about you, sir?' Crawford asked, without insubordination. They were all curious to know what Noah's gut was telling him.

'I'm hunting a ghost,' he replied. 'Starting with the virologists in the South Asian Sector who could have developed a vaccine this sophisticated. It requires skill and facilities – there aren't many who have it. Dr Neeson has identified four virologists in the Eastern Alliance.' Scientists Neeson knew and respected.

'Will you review these virologists against the existing breaches and perpetrators in the same way?' Garner asked. 'Look at who they've trained or worked with?'

'I will. The mainframe is analysing that right now. If we're lucky, we'll get a match. But like you said, if one of these guys is the ghost, he's more likely to target population sets and vaccinators who have no relationship with him. Nothing that could trace them back to him.'

'Beyond the shared aspiration of undermining public health and political stability,' noted Crawford.

'Yes, but that's not something you put on a CV,' said Garner.

'Fridge magnet maybe?' Crawford suggested.

Noah didn't turn back to the group. His eyes focused on the biggest screen at the front of the room. He touched it and opened a folder. The four virologists appeared above them. Noah looked at the images as he spoke.

'You're actually not as charming as you think you are, Crawford. And you'll never make it with Garner. Your obsession with personal hygiene is off-putting. Plus, she likes men who are at least as physically strong as her.

'You're bored with being everyone's superior, aren't you, Garner?' He asked, still facing the screen.

'Thank you, sir,' Garner said, her tone steady.

He didn't respond. He was staring at the virologists, memorising the detail of their faces. Traitors never looked like traitors.

*

Noah typed in the code to the R&R cubicle and pushed the door open with one hand, his laptop in the other. Patrice had insisted he take a break but he didn't have time to return home.

'Please don't tuck me in,' he said.

'You wish, darling.' She placed the files on the small desk reluctantly and shook her head as he unrolled his laptop.

'I'll sleep, I promise – I just want to look at one more thing.'

Once she had left, he began the biometric identification process. Then he requested the high-level data portal and punched in the passcodes Hackman had given him.

Icons filled his screen, arranging themselves in alphabetical order. A search box opened in the middle, awaiting his command.

His fingers hovered over the keyboard. He was supposed to type 'ISB – Critical'. Usually, Immunity Shield breaches were organised by year of occurrence. They occurred so rarely.

He started typing: 'ISB . . .'

And then he deleted the letters.

Instead, he typed: 'Surveillance'.

The surveillance sub-portal opened, giving him another search box. He typed: 'Cit: SMW02/18/2034_SNC03081974'.

Hundreds of folders appeared on the screen. He stared at them for several moments. His heart hammered in his chest. Each folder represented a date field – days, months and years of a person's life – captured on the tens of thousands of cameras and microcameras embedded around every Western Alliance country.

He clenched and unclenched his hands, and began searching. Two years ago. He pulled up the month and then found the day they took Sera to the London Zoo for the first time. Ninth May 2038. She was only four.

The 3D recording was projected from his screen onto his keyboard; the holographic image blurred and then steadied itself into focus in front of him. He tried to touch it, his fingers falling through the mirage.

He watched his daughter pull at his hand, insistent and excited. She marched straight past the penguin-feeding. She only wanted to see the 'baby dogs'. Little girls and puppies; it was a timeless connection. He stopped her and said, 'Look, Sera, look – penguins.' The caretaker, dressed in a full protective suit, was throwing synthetic fish protein pellets at the animals, who jostled each other, necks craned as they caught the pellets in their mouths. The mothers swallowed and then regurgitated the food into the mouths of their hungry babies.

She laughed at that. 'Let's try it, Daddy.' She threw a sultana at him. He missed and she tried again. He caught it.

'Now give it to me,' she commanded. She opened her mouth. He laughed and swallowed it himself.

'Sorry, all gone,' he teased, shrugging his shoulders. She picked up the small box and was about to throw it at him when Maggie caught her hand.

'You're not a penguin, sweetie.' She laughed, pressing a kiss to her daughter's sticky palm. Maggie and Sera had dimples in the same places.

'You try, Mummy.' Sera extracted more sultanas from the box and threw them at Maggie. Noah watched himself intercept the flying fruit.

'Hey! Naughty Daddy!'

Noah turned around and pulled Maggie close to him. He kissed her. He remembered how much he loved kissing her.

She pulled back, her face flushed with surprise, and swallowed a sultana. He took the box from Sera, threw another into his mouth and winked at her.

They walked to the puppy exhibit. The Department of Animal Health, Husbandry and Sanitation had approved a three-month interactive display. Families that could afford the ticket had to apply and, even then, there were thousands of disappointed little girls and boys across the country. Hackman had given him the tickets.

Sera entered the tent, with her parents on either side. They were dressed in protective suits and light face masks. The caretaker was holding a squirming mass of black and white hair.

'He's called a border collie,' Noah whispered. 'They used to work on farms, chasing sheep and cows, telling the other animals what to do. They're bossy and clever – like you.'

She laughed at that, the chime of it muffled by her mask. The caretaker placed the dog on her lap. Her eyes widened in amazement. He thought she'd be afraid. Puppies in books and dreams were different from the real thing. She put her arms around the animal and held it close, nuzzling her face against the top of its head. The caretaker tried to separate her from the puppy.

'She's fine,' Noah stopped him. Sera stroked the dog's soft coat with her gloved hand.

'Here, give his belly a rub,' Noah said. 'He'll love that.'

She tried it and the dog whimpered happily against her, positioning himself for a full-belly rub. 'How did you know, Daddy?'

'It's just something I remember from a long time ago.' He looked from his daughter to his wife and saw the tears in her eyes. She pulled her mask down.

'What's wrong, Mummy?' Sera asked.

He saw himself lean in towards Maggie and obscure the camera's line of sight for a moment. He remembered he had pulled his mask down too and held her face to his own. He whispered in her ear and kissed her lightly. She had smiled at him.

'Move back, move back,' he whispered, watching his family.

He moved. He saw them again and exhaled.

'Nothing, sweetheart. I'm fine,' Maggie replied.

'Then why are you crying?' Sera wiped Maggie's tears. 'Would you like the puppy?' She tried to offer the dog to her mother.

'No, thank you. You hold him. I'm not sad, I'm just very happy.' Maggie bent down and buried her face in the puppy's mane.

'Me too, Mummy.' And then Sera said her favourite phrase at the time. She'd heard it on a television show. She looked up from the dog and said, 'Thank you, Daddy, this is the best day of my life.'

Noah pressed stop and closed the folder. A month earlier, Sera had started getting headaches. Their family doctor thought it was her eyesight or perhaps the sanitisers in the food. Too much television, not enough water, not enough sleep, not enough Vitamin D. Perhaps the preservatives in the vaccines; there were so many of them, Maggie always said. Maybe the anti-vaxxers were right.

Eventually, they were referred to a specialist.

Noah closed the portals and turned off the laptop. He went to the bed and lay down, his gun by his side. He closed his eyes and slept.

*

After four days of analysis by the team and the mainframe, they were no closer to finding the nexus between the vaxxers who had committed the breaches. Noah stretched back in his chair and then put his arms down, rotating his shoulders. The analysts were starting to look defeated.

They had narrowed Neeson's four suspected virologists down to two: Dr Amir Khan from the Department of Immunology, Colombo General Hospital, Sri Lanka; and Dr Muthu Sagadewa, Head of the Infectious Diseases Department, Benazir Bhutto Memorial Hospital, Pakistan.

The data could not eliminate either man.

Noah opened a subfolder on the screen at the front of the room, and pulled out their surveillance photos. In the Western Alliance, Bio could tap into the network of millions of existing cameras, in addition to the ones it had installed itself.

It was harder to access information about people in the Eastern Alliance. The Information Shield stopped the flow of information between the two sides. The firewall erected in 2025 was policed every minute of every day by Bio's Cyber Intelligence and Protection Division. Its key priority was to ensure that information about the Sixth Virus Eradication Policy was never revealed to citizens on either side of the shield.

The firewall was so effective that Bio technicians needed to be in-country, standing on Eastern Alliance soil, to access the camera and computer networks there. The surveillance of Noah's suspects was therefore quite limited.

He pulled the photographs of the first suspect up on the screen and clicked through them slowly. Some of the analysts sat up straighter in their seats.

'Dr Amir Khan's life is not very interesting. He is sixty-three years old, and had a wife who was also a well-credentialed immunologist. She died during the Great Purge. Here he is giving training seminars to vaccinators and being honoured for his service to disease eradication. Here he is swimming.'

'Yes, swimming,' he repeated.

According to the surveillance, Dr Khan swam at a quiet Colombo beach every morning. In the action shots, he emerged from the surf, his grey chest hair clinging to his body, his raised arms revealing sagging flesh and the lines of his rib cage.

Khan had lived in the same modest house for the last thirty years. He drove a twenty-year-old Peugeot to work but often caught a tuk-tuk, rather than use the car and driver his status afforded him. He spoke at conferences but didn't participate in the junkets the way other scientists did. He seemed genuinely dedicated to disease eradication.

Noah shook his head and closed the folder. He opened the next one.

'Dr Muthu Sagadewa, a child prodigy. He seems the stronger suspect. He has three fellowships from various prestigious Eastern Alliance university hospitals. He used to work for Abre de Libre.

'Despite an impressive salary for helping ADL develop its commercially successful immunity-building vitamin range, Dr Sagadewa left the company to return to public health work. He also attended training seminars in the four cities where the known breaches occurred.'

Noah looked at the photographs of Dr Sagadewa on the big screen. In one, he was playing tennis at an ADL staff party. In another he was about to launch into a pool, his muscular body poised on a diving board. He was audaciously athletic.

Noah stopped for a moment. He moved the photographs over to the right side of the screen and pulled back Dr Khan's folder. He clicked on the photographs icon and the photos flew onto the screen, arranging themselves in chronological order.

He touched one image, expanding it with his fingers. He reached for another photograph, taken several months later and enlarged it too; and then another.

'What are you looking for?' It was Hackman behind him. 'Patrice says you've barely left the data room. I thought I'd check on you. What are you looking for?' he repeated.

'Attrition,' Noah replied.

'Attrition?'

'Yes, the attrition of illness – look at this. Over the last two years, Dr Khan has aged ten years or more. Worse than aged – his skin is flaccid, his eyes are dry and red. He's lost at least thirty-five pounds, and from this stoop here I'd say he's lost significant core strength or bone density. He's sick.

'The tree of liberty, Hackman – the tree of liberty . . .' Noah smiled for the first time in days.

'The tree of liberty?' Hackman touched the pin on his lapel, confused.

'Yes, it "must be refreshed from time to time with the blood of patriots and tyrants". Remember?'

'Garner,' he looked past Hackman at his colleague. She was already typing fast.

'I'm checking their Haema Scans right now.' Noah took a deep breath and ordered his thoughts. 'Check if they're sick – the scanners only sound the alarm when there are fluctuations in antibody levels or the presence of a virus. But they screen and record everything about a subject's blood.'

'Dr Khan's Haema Scans – the results are up, sir,' Garner said.

'There . . .' Noah read the numbers on the screen. 'The good doctor's blood shows a heightened level of carcinopetra antigens. What about the vaxxers?' he asked impatiently.

'Coming,' Garner replied, unfazed.

Noah flicked through the photographs faster, creating a motion picture that showed the rapid decline of the human body.

'You're right, sir,' Garner said, triumphant and awed. 'There are twelve vaxxers involved across the four breaches. All of their scans show the same elevated levels of CPA. I think they're all seriously ill. I'd have to check with medical to be sure.'

Noah turned to Hackman. 'We've been looking for the wrong common thread. They haven't connected through virology; virology is just the common tool they have at their disposal.'

'How do you know?' Hackman asked.

'Those antigen levels –' He had read scan results with those levels before. 'They're all dying.'

Chapter 8

Noah stood at the front of the data room. Most of the seats were empty.

'The rest of the team should all be en route to the South Asian Sector by now,' he told Garner and Crawford. 'They're working the four breach sites as WHO personnel, implementing the Global Vaccination Programme.'

'And us?' Crawford asked.

'We're going to play a hunch,' Noah said. 'The common thread between all of the vaccinators and our prime suspect, Dr Khan, is that they are dying of cancer. We can't access their full medical records from here, we need to be in the Eastern Alliance to do that. Garner, what else have you found?'

'Nothing, sir – which is highly unusual. We haven't picked up any levels of chemo toxins or radiation in their historic Haema Scans. None of them are undergoing treatment.'

'The vaccinators found the ghost through virology chatrooms,' Crawford added, 'but it was their disease that must have opened the door to the higher level of mutual trust.'

'I agree. We need to know more. We're going to Colombo.'

'We're tracking the ghost?' Crawford smiled.

Garner tried hard not to show it, but she looked concerned.

'That's the plan. Crawford, your security clearance is still good?'

'Yes sir, no recent demotions.'

'It's only a matter of time,' Garner replied.

Noah turned back to the photograph of Khan. Under the dark wells of the man's eyes, the skin was raised in bagging pouches. Like sacks of tears, small reservoirs of grief. Amir Khan had sad eyes.

'I've sent you all the intel we have on him. Study it. We're going as employees of the WHO.'

Crawford sighed loudly but Noah ignored him.

'Study your legends. It's important you know your back story flawlessly. We're doing more than just making routine checks on vaccine protocols and delivering public health education.'

'Could we do stakeholder consultation, please, sir?' Crawford interrupted. 'You know how much I love that. I could take my weapon *and* my clipboard.'

Noah didn't laugh. 'This is a long game – we need a reason to build a relationship with Khan. We can't just zero in on him, he'll suspect us immediately.'

'We're usually in and out of the Eastern Alliance in a few weeks, as long as the WHO cover allows,' Garner said.

'This time, we are going in because five cases of Ebola will be identified. The Immunity Shield breach will trigger a lockdown of all zones within Sri Lanka. We'll go in with a large WHO team to contain the outbreak. We can stay on to investigate the breach and trace contact. That could take months.'

'How are you going to fake five cases of Ebola?' Crawford asked. 'There hasn't been a reported incident in Sri Lanka since the GVP was implemented. Not even you and Hackman could create a small Ebola outbreak. You could infect a group with an old store of bubonic plague or something that prima facie presents as Ebola —'

'Lassa or Marburg Fever,' Garner interrupted.

'What?' Crawford turned to her.

'Lassa or Marburg prima facie present as Ebola — not the bubonic plague. It's completely different — they both cause necrosis but one's a bacterial infection and the other's a virus, with different symptoms.'

'God, I can only imagine your flirting.' Crawford turned back to Noah. 'You could try using a lower-level contaminant but the scanners won't be fooled by a disease just because it's similarly symptomatic.'

Noah didn't like this part of the plan, but it was the only way around the problem his team had identified.

He took a deep breath and explained what had to be done. Neither of them replied. He continued before he could read the judgement in their faces; the judgement he too was struggling with.

'We leave in three days. Study your legends and, Crawford, make some time with Neeson to brush up on any immunology concepts you should be fluent in. You are WHO employees after all.'

He didn't ask if there were any questions.

*

Noah sat down and rested his elbows on his knees, his head in his hands. Hackman's office was cold but he felt the sweat slide down the inside of his shirt. He stood up restlessly and surveyed the maps on Hackman's wall, his mind not absorbing the colour-coded regions.

He moved to the window, overlooking an almost aerial view of the post-war developments. From amongst the reinforced concrete tower blocks, Noah could still see flashes of medieval granite, marble and sandstone. The gothic spires of the Royal Courts of Justice refused to be cowed down, piercing through the newly ordered landscape.

'They took it well?' Hackman asked.

'Of course, they're professionals.' He looked back. His agents always took these things too well.

'Sri Lanka has changed since you were last there,' Hackman said.

'I should think so.'

'Don't be like that, Noah. If I didn't know better, I'd say you were avoiding the place.'

Noah returned to the seat at Hackman's desk.

'I go where I'm sent, Hack.' He picked up a glass paperweight from a stack of documents. It was shaped like a miniature iceberg, jagged and dangerously sharp in places. He set it down again.

'Sure. You put your hand up for hellholes like Afghanistan and Iran but not Sri Lanka. You'll like the country now. Aside from the usual post-war poverty and increasing incidence of Rapture addiction.'

'I assume you won't be waging a war on drugs over there?'

'No – not when the drug they're taking gives them a deep sense of happiness and connection to each other.'

'You mean the kind of happiness and connection they might also get from faith in a benevolent but most likely non-existent, or at the very least sadistic, God?'

Noah was glad his father hadn't seen him lose his faith, although perhaps if his father was alive he might still have had it. He would never know. The bitterness in his voice couldn't be disguised by the humour in his words. Hackman didn't notice. 'Rapture is a cheap substitute and it won't lead to slaughter – unlike faith.'

'Faith never led to slaughter. Religion did,' Noah corrected. 'Or rather, mankind's use of religion as a weapon of mass and minor destruction did.'

'Jesus, you're a pain in the arse. Faith leads to organised religion – mankind can't help but get organised.'

'Sure – but why are they craving a quasi-religious high? The frontal lobe damage should have taken care of that.'

'It's not a *quasi-religious* high, Noah. It's just a high. Neeson looked into that; he loves a good scientific conundrum.'

'And what did he come up with?'

'That the simplest observable explanation is often the best.'

'His own version of Occam's Razor?' Noah asked. 'Neeson really wants a scientific principle named after himself.'

'Yes.' Hackman tried not to laugh. 'World War Righteous and Ebola hit the East harder than it did the West. People seek solace – it's what they do. If they want to get high, they're welcome to it, for now.'

'As long as they don't get organised?'

'Exactly.' Hackman pushed a bundle of documents across the table. 'Patrice printed these for you – she said it's better for your eyes. She doesn't care about my eyes.'

He leaned back in his chair. 'Sri Lanka's reconstruction was well-funded by the World Bank and the Western Alliance. We needed stability in the region.'

'Stability?' Noah echoed.

'It's more important than democracy.'

'Thank you, professor.' Noah opened the file and began sifting through documents, country reports.

'More people die in new unstable democracies than tyrannical stable regimes,' Hackman continued. 'Everyone agreed that stability was best created by investment in the region. Sri Lanka may have started the war but they also lost it – they needed help.'

'They had been penalised enough?'

'Something like that.'

'And what went wrong?' Noah asked.

'Nothing. You're always so pessimistic.'

Noah pulled out photographs of the Sri Lankan president. 'I'm guessing that somewhere between the rousing rhetoric at global development conferences in DC, the complex loan and aid agreements that followed them, and the actual implementation of funding, something got lost?'

Hackman picked up a photograph of the president leaning against a gold-plated Maserati. In the background, the rest of his impressive car collection gleamed no less brilliantly in the tropical sun.

'He's enjoying his reign, isn't he?'

'The country is stable, Noah. It was the first country to achieve complete national vaccination within three months of the Sixth Virus Eradication Policy – and it has *maintained* complete national immunity. They take their three-yearly boosters like clockwork. That's all I need to know to sleep well at night.' Hackman threw the photograph back on the pile.

'How many undercovers do you have in play?'

'We have three in Colombo and another three elsewhere in the country. It's allocated by Bio on the basis of population and risk level. Sri Lanka has been low risk since the war. We had a lot more undercovers during the war.'

'We needed a lot more UCs there *before* the war,' Noah said.

'Hindsight is a wonderful thing. If it wasn't Sri Lanka, it would have been Pakistan or somewhere else. It was always going to happen.'

'What was – war, religious slaughter or slaughter generally?' Noah asked.

'All of it. Including the beginning of the war in Sri Lanka, I suppose. Their Buddhist clergy were more militaristic than monastic. They organised pro-Buddhist demonstrations which always ended in anti-Muslim riots.

'The Sri Lankan government let the monks frenzy up the masses like a well-trained rabid dog. Set them loose on the local Muslims and the rest is history.'

'You can't train a rabid dog, Hack.'

'Exactly. Post-war, the country has been desperately contrite and very eager to please.'

'Then why don't we just ask them to turn over Dr Khan and his hard drives? Better yet, forget permission – how about rendition and research theft?' Noah asked.

'You'll see when you get there – President Rajasuriya doesn't play ball like that.'

'Will you tell him I'm coming?'

'Yes – respect for sovereign leadership, sharing of biosecurity intel and all that.'

'Since when?'

Hackman ignored him. 'You're going to need all the help you can get. The undercovers are well-connected and well-placed. There's one I trust for this job. She's one of ours who stayed on after the war.'

'She liked the tropical beaches and spicy food?'

'Something like that. She can get in and out of the hospital ward. We'll give her Neeson's modified Ebola Strain 48.6. Most people around the targets will be immune if they've taken their boosters on time. The targets will be scanned shortly after contamination. The virus will be detected and you'll be called in immediately.'

Noah wondered what kind of agent – what kind of person – could deliberately infect five people with Ebola. Bio had identified high-risk patients who were awaiting vaccination. They had no immunity. They didn't stand a chance.

Noah kept his eyes resolutely on Hackman's face, away from the window and the beautiful spires.

'The one thing I still don't understand is how you're going to get the virus into the country? No one stores it except Bio. If I try to carry it in, the scanners at the Sri Lankan airport will pick it up immediately. I wouldn't get through *our* airports without detection.'

'But if *I* carry it in, I don't get scanned the same way you do,' Hackman said.

Noah studied Hackman's face carefully to see if he was joking. Hackman was impassive. Noah felt his pulse quicken.

'Of course you do – we all get meta-scanned the same way. The protocol ensures that no one, no matter how high their clearance level, can carry the virus across countries.'

'That protocol applies to most people, not all.' Hackman stood up. 'It was changed to allow a handful of exceptions. Let's leave it at that.'

Noah stood up too and knocked the table, jolting the glass iceberg from its sea of papers.

'Let's not leave it at that. In 2023, it wasn't a bioterrorist or a naïve aid worker who brought Ebola into the homeland. It was the US ambassador, returning from Istanbul, where he'd been fucking his driver's sister.'

'I know my history, thank you. I was there.'

'Were you? Were you there when my father died from Ebola, vomiting and shitting blood?' he choked. He could still recall the smell of his house, his father's body.

'Not even the president can travel without a full meta-scan.' Noah was losing control of his voice. 'The protocol is there to protect us!'

'Focus on the mission. I will take care of the outbreak; small and contained, such as it will be. You take care of the clean-up and investigation. Understood?'

'Understood,' Noah managed to reign in the emotions on his face and look Hackman in the eye, but inside he knew he had to get out.

He couldn't keep doing this. Hackman had got him into Bio. Noah would have to get himself out. After this mission.

Chapter 9

Sahara stood in the security room on the first floor gallery, her eyes flicking between monitors until she saw the person she was looking for.

'There you are,' she whispered. The security guards ignored her, as she'd paid them to do.

Hackman looked unusually casual: top button undone, tie loosened and jacket folded over his arm. He kept his eyes straight ahead, uninterested in the other passengers. They stood in long queues, papers in one hand, children sometimes in the other, nervously waiting to be herded through the scanners.

Sahara followed Hackman across the monitors as he headed for the priority government line. Again he presented his passport, but not his wrist or the small suitcase he carried. He shook his head at the immigration official calmly.

The man scanned Hackman's passport and when his profile came up on the computer, he ushered him through, apologising awkwardly.

'You cheating bastard,' Sahara hissed under her breath. The

guards looked at her and then remembered their instructions, turning their heads away.

What was in the suitcase? she wondered.

The security team that had chaperoned Hackman from London dispersed into the crowd. Another local team converged to take over his protection detail. They maintained a well-trained distance. Hackman found a table at an airport café and sat down without making eye contact with any of them.

'Tea, sir?' The waitress activated the news-tablet while balancing a tray with a steaming pot.

'Why not? When in Sri Lanka . . .' He smiled at her. Sahara remembered that smile.

'I'll have two teas; I'm expecting a friend.' The sweat sat on his skin and beaded at his hairline. He undid another button and pulled his shirt away from his body. He opened the screen on the news-tablet and paged through.

Sahara wondered why he bothered; it was just a rehash of the Western Alliance news, except Bio removed any references to religion or god for the Eastern Alliance bulletins. She checked the other monitors and noted the formation of the security team one more time before leaving the room.

She crossed the concourse and sat down. Hackman didn't look up immediately. He closed the news-tablet, pushed the tea across the table and said, 'You've absorbed the local sense of timing.'

'I've absorbed a lot of the local characteristics. It's been better for my health.' She added two spoonfuls of sugar to her tea and sipped it. Her blouse sleeve slipped back, revealing the scars and burns that decorated her arm, like carvings on a sinewy totem pole.

'You look like a local,' Hackman remarked, referring to her embroidered shirt, cotton trousers and slippers.

'I've always looked like a local, that was why you wanted me here in the first place.' She had pulled her hair back in a bun, but some of it curled, damp, at the nape of her neck.

'You didn't have to stay though, you'd earned your right to come home.'

'Earned it? I suppose you could look at it that way.' She laughed bitterly. 'I prefer to stay here. Call it inertia, another local characteristic.'

'Back at Bio they call it self-imposed exile,' Hackman replied.

'I don't expect people to understand. I like it here. Life is simpler. Redacted,' she pointed to the news-tablet, 'like the news from the West. Repurposed to be suitably benign. It's what I needed after . . . everything.'

She hadn't died in World War Righteous but she often wished she had. She deserved it.

'You were a soldier, following orders. You shouldn't blame yourself.' She had heard this speech before. She'd even given it herself to junior agents. She could tell he was about to launch into its opening verse.

'*You* should blame yourself more,' she cut him off. 'What do you need? You don't usually call when you're in town.'

'No, I like to leave you alone.'

'I've earned it,' she mocked.

'Yes, you have. But I need you to do one more thing.'

'It's never just one more thing, let's not pretend. What do you need?' She looked at the suitcase on the ground.

'There is a contaminant inside it. Classification R, Bio Hazard Grade 1. Do you think you can access a particular ward at Colombo General Hospital?'

'I can access most places,' she replied. There was only one contaminant with Classification R.

'You will need to bypass the meta-scanners.'

'I know what I need to do to get in with a contaminant – what do I need to do when I get there?' she asked, irritated.

Who. She meant *who*.

'You need to infect five targets with it.' He slid the suitcase under the table towards her. 'Details inside.'

'Pre-vaccination?' Her voice was steady.

'Yes, pre-vaccination. Is there a problem?' He picked up his tea and blew softly on its surface before draining the cup.

'No, there's no problem.' She looked down.

'That's why we wanted you here in the first place.' He stood up, threw a few notes for the waitress on the table and left, heading towards Departures. Sahara sat back and finished her tea.

*

Colombo General Hospital was crumbling. It was once a proud and prestigious teaching hospital, gleaming white on Perera Mawatha Road, surrounded by lush gardens and a tall wrought-iron fence that made it look more like a summer palace than a hospital.

But now it sat quietly covered in dust. It had served its people well during World War R and the pogrom in Colombo that precipitated it. Twenty years ago its white stucco had been splattered in blood when armed mobs invaded its wards, pulled people from their sick beds with their IVs trailing, and beheaded them on the front lawn. Colombo General was a building that wanted to forget.

Sahara parked in the side alley and waited. At ten o'clock the janitors filled the last of the massive bins and locked them to prevent people from rifling through for drugs. Not that hospitals stocked Rapture but they did have the chemicals used to synthesise the powerful mood-lifter.

Three men wheeled the bins around the building to the side alley where the garbage van would collect them in the morning. At eleven o'clock there was a changeover of staff from the evening shift to the night shift. Nothing else happened until five o'clock the next day.

She turned off her handheld. She had memorised the floor plan. The maternity ward was on the sixth floor. She kicked off her shoes and put them in her small backpack. She couldn't walk through any of the doors on the ground floor carrying a contaminant. The meta-scanners would detect the substance immediately. She needed to enter the building either from the roof, the sewer or a window. She had seen secret agents crawling through sewers in movies. They seemed laughably immune to the nauseating fumes that emanated from the last sewer she'd been in. The fifth-floor window was the best option.

She was relieved it was only five floors up. In her youth she could have free-climbed much higher but she was forty-five years old and her age and injuries were catching up.

She checked her equipment one last time. Gun and silencer, ankle weapon, night vision goggles, rope, hooks, gloves, knife for a fast kill and a garrotte for a soundless one. She pulled her gloves on and opened Hackman's suitcase, using the passcode that had been assigned to her two decades ago.

The suitcase was small but heavy. Its insides were a micro-refrigerator with its own portable power source. Two hours left on the battery, then the suitcase would return to room temperature. In Colombo, at this time of the year, that was thirty-eight degrees.

She loaded the weapon. There was only one syringe and a twenty-five millilitre vial with the contaminant. Obviously hygiene wasn't a priority for Hackman. Sahara put the needle back in its sheath and then placed the syringe into the small insulated box that fitted into her chest pocket.

With her night vision goggles, she surveyed the alley once more and left the vehicle, her bare feet hitting the ground quietly. The bin smelled foul, even through reinforced steel. Its location beneath a tall sash window was what she had been scoping all week. She climbed onto the bin, pleased that her assessment had been right.

She stretched her arms and legs again and walked back to the edge of the bin. It was a short run up, but it was all she needed.

She ran and then sprang up. Her gloved hands grasped the ledge and she swung her torso right, her foot reaching for and locking into a small but sufficient groove in the wall.

She didn't stop to stabilise herself, instead pushing hard from the groove and launching higher into the window frame. Her left hand hit and collapsed uselessly against the window pane but her right hand caught the narrow horizontal gap where the upper pane of glass met the lower pane. She held on with one hand; the force from her jump left the rest of her body dangling by four fingers as her feet searched for the ledge beneath her. She found it and curled into the window frame, resting for a moment.

And then she was up again. At the top, right-hand side of the window was the base of a rusted chimney. The west wing of the first floor had once housed a small waste disposal furnace. All of the furnaces had been relocated to the basement years ago, but this pipe remained.

She placed one foot onto the metal clip that bolted the disused pipe firmly to the brickwork. She tested it, shifting a portion of her weight once, twice, three times, from the ledge to the girder. It held.

And then she was on the pipe, hand over hand, toes finding each clip or using the grooves in the bricks, to propel herself up. She slipped once, dangling by her fingertips from the last clip, her hands in agony as they carried her body weight.

She forced herself to breathe slowly, in through the nose, out through the mouth, and then extended her left leg until she reached the window ledge. She transferred her weight from her hands to her left foot, and rested, suspended awkwardly, three floors above the bin. She slowed her pace, continued, and didn't slip again.

THE BARRIER

At the fifth floor, she stopped. Holding onto the pipe she swung her body like a pendulum and let go, landing on the ledge, hands reaching for the exact point between window panes she had found, four floors below. It was enough to hold onto.

She pulled her knife from its leg sheath and wedged it into the gap, shimmying the lock between the two panes. She opened the window and slid inside, crouching next to the hospital bed and the comatose patient who lay on it. The fifth floor was the palliative care ward.

She tied one end of her rappelling rope to the bed and tugged it slowly. The patient would anchor her escape route. She hid the coil of rope under the bed and lowered the window without closing it.

From her backpack she pulled out a doctor's white coat which fit easily over the lightweight bodysuit she was wearing. She slipped on her shoes and removed her leather gloves, swapping them for an identity card and disposable gloves. She put the stethoscope in her front pocket and hid the backpack behind the curtain. She was ready. The rest of the job wasn't complicated.

She located the elevator and took it to the sixth floor. At the nurses' station she casually grabbed a clipboard and kept walking down the corridor, past the maternity ward towards the neo-natal ICU. If anyone asked, she was the new paediatric consultant. She was covering for Dr Fonseka who had called in sick that afternoon. Fonseka had a vicious case of gastroenteritis after Sahara had contaminated her lunch. Her legend was robust and involved details she'd used before. She was almost disappointed when no one stopped her.

She paused at the door to the ICU, her hand resting on her chest and feeling the small box one last time before she entered the room. It was dark and dimly lit in the corners by heat lamps. Short flashes of light came from the machines that monitored the fragile lives of the babies who took refuge there. She could hear the rise and fall of the pumps that breathed for some of them. As her eyes adjusted, she could see the outline of seven humidicribs, the plastic shells in which the children slept, sterile and protected.

She shook her head in irritation. IV lines emerged from only four cribs. Those would be the easiest ones. She could inject the virus straight into an IV line or bag. She should do those ones first.

She pulled out the syringe. It held twenty-five millilitres, but its needle was much shorter. Hackman was a precise man with an excellent eye for detail. Two centimetres of needle was all that was needed.

She stood next to the first baby, needle poised. She held the IV line in one gloved hand and with the other, injected three millilitres into its plastic vein. She pumped the IV bag twice with a well-trained hand. It pushed the virus through more efficiently. She did this three more times to the other babies with IVs.

Hackman wanted five 'Patients Zero' to create confusion when they tried to trace contact, and to ensure a sizeable outbreak that could still be contained within the hospital. She looked around the room. One baby whimpered.

She picked up the child's chart: 'Baby Karthik, four weeks old, born four weeks premature. Strong vitals and now able to feed by bottle. Immunisation due 12/23/2040.'

His first immunisation was due tomorrow. If she infected him, he would be scanned soon and wouldn't suffer long. She reached her gloved hand through the hole in the crib and picked up the small chicken-wing of the baby's thigh. She felt the small, floppy muscle that hung from the bone.

The baby responded to her touch and opened his eyes. His body was covered in feathery hair. She stroked his chest in a circular motion. It was a surprisingly successful gesture. The baby's arms and legs curled around her hand, locking it against his chest. She could feel the fast drumbeat of his heart, beneath the frame of his rib cage. She could have crushed it with one hand, sparing him what was to come.

Four Patients Zero or five – did it really matter? The child would probably get the virus anyway from fluid transfer between nurses and doctors. But he would stand a chance of living through it, however miraculous.

The baby's mouth opened, searching for milk. She extracted her hand and picked up the milk bottle on the side of the crib. She checked it was still fresh and then threaded it through the hole. She held it at the baby's mouth, letting him gulp erratically. She adjusted the angle of the bottle, remembering something her sister had said. Apparently trapped wind caused great discomfort to infants.

She placed the bottle on the side, next to his head and stroked his chest again; it seemed to soothe him.

'Don't worry, baby, it's all going to be fine,' she murmured.

Hackman wanted five patients. She picked up the needle and quickly inserted it into the little thigh, whispering 'There, there,' when he cried out in pain. She injected three millilitres, closed the syringe and put it back in her pocket. She left the room and the hospital, the same way she came in.

Chapter 10

Noah hadn't been back to Sri Lanka since his first mission, when all he saw were refugee camps, disease and death.

Hackman was right – Sri Lanka was beautiful. The drive from the military airport followed a coastal road. The beach was luminous; white sand lapped by sparkling waters. Palm trees fringed the roads. They stood tall but their heads were bowed gracefully, deferring to the majesty of the ocean in front of them.

The landscape was interrupted by billboards, familiar sentries emblazoned with stern health warnings. Sometimes there was a billboard of the president, his hands raised victoriously over his people.

As the road moved further inland, they passed small farms, fields of okra and snake beans; plantations of papaya and avocado trees. They saw roadside vendors: men, women and children hawking mangoes, purple onions and small rambutans like red, spiky sea urchins.

'Sri Lanka has everything, sir,' their driver Vijay chatted happily. 'The three essentials –' He pointed his fingers in the air, punctuating his list. 'History, culture and nature.' He put both hands back on the wheel, honking the horn viciously with one and swerving the car around a clattering truck with the other.

'Oh, Jesus,' Crawford whispered, bracing himself against his seat.

Noah shook his head at the slip-up.

'Sorry, Chief.'

Every fifty kilometres they passed military posts that checked their WHO papers but didn't scan their blood. There were cameras at each one, watching them.

On the outskirts of Colombo, Vijay stopped at a roadblock and a larger military checkpoint. The cars in the queue were all older model sedans, faded shells on either side of the polished onyx of their SUV.

The cameras were more sophisticated this time, with facial recognition capability.

'There are no cars coming out of Colombo,' Garner whispered, looking around her.

'The city should be in lockdown. People are allowed back into Colombo, but not out. The threat level was lowered one notch yesterday,' Noah said.

The driver, Noah and the team got out of the car as a group of heavily armed soldiers approached them.

'Don't worry-worry, sir, I'll take care of everything,' Vijay reassured them. He had been assigned to them by Bio but Noah didn't know anything about his background. Vijay peeled his sweat-soaked shirt from his body and pulled a large handkerchief from his pocket, wiping his forehead and hands before tucking it away.

He raised an appeasing hand to the soldiers and walked towards them slowly, speaking in Sinhalese, the local language. One of the soldiers pulled the rifle off his shoulder and shook it at Vijay. Another soldier stepped forward with a Haema Scanner, motioning to Noah and the team.

Vijay raised his hands higher in the air, his back to the team, the wet V between his shoulderblades widening with each movement. He stopped walking, but shook his head at the scanner, speaking rapidly.

'Just relax, guys.' Noah sensed Garner stiffen and reach for her weapon. 'Just relax. Weapons down.'

They had been scanned at the military airport's security department which was staffed by Bio. Once inside the Eastern Alliance, they were given a Scanner Waiver and their blood wasn't supposed to be tested by a Haema Scanner again. Their blood serum would have revealed that they had complete Ebola immunity, but no markers for the Faith Inhibitor.

Beyond the roadblock Noah could see the station that would have housed a unit of soldiers, an interrogation room and several cells. Between him, Garner and Crawford, they had six side-arms and twenty-four clips. There was another cache of weapons at the WHO office in Colombo and the hotel they were staying at. No good to him right now though. He didn't know if Vijay was armed.

'Chief, if they try to scan us –' Crawford whispered.

'I know, Crawford. Let Vijay take care of it.' He didn't take his eyes from the station. They were inside, watching, waiting to see if he would panic. They didn't know him.

The soldier barked another order and Vijay handed over their papers. He continued to talk to the soldiers as though he was holding court at a cocktail party. Occasionally he leaned in conspiratorially to one and whispered something that made the soldier laugh in spite of himself.

The soldiers looked at Noah and the team closely and then checked their paperwork again. They were allowed to travel into Colombo by Executive Order and with the protection and authority of the WHO. Finally, without checking their blood or their bags, the soldiers nodded and waved them through the roadblock.

'I told you, sir.' Vijay merrily started the car. 'I can take care of everything. Tell me if you want to see the rest of the country – it is a paradise. You want safari, I can organise it. You want pretty clothes for your wife, sir, I can organise it.' His voice sang through a familiar song. 'You want women, I can organise it. You want superb cuisine, I can organise it.' He stroked his pot belly.

'Both hands on the wheel, Vijay. Just get us through the next five roadblocks.' Noah laughed.

'Eight, sir, there are eight roadblocks today – there is protest in the city. I will take you around but military detours are not very well-planned. One of many reasons we lost the war.' Vijay smiled, revealing surprisingly straight, clean teeth. His employer obviously provided dental.

Eventually the fields turned to suburbs covered in a thick film of dirt and pollution. Tall apartment blocks rose like anthills out of the cemented earth. They were interspersed with clusters of shacks and tents, small shanties propped up against each other.

'Who lives there?' Crawford asked.

'Mostly refugees from the war – people who haven't been resettled yet. Government buildings are slow to grow.'

They saw people wandering the streets, their clothes torn and stained. Some dragged children behind them. Others crowded around bins, foraging.

'Some are soldiers – they came back from WWR but it is better they died.' Vijay shook his head.

'And the drug addicts? Is this where they live?' Garner asked.

'A few – but it isn't just the poor who take Rapture. Rich, poor – anyone, everyone. My son's schoolteacher died last year from overdose. His supplier was the music teacher – everyone wants to feel Rapture.'

'Any thoughts on why, Vijay?' Noah asked. The drug had been named after Christ's second coming and his gathering of the true believers. Someone had a sense of humour.

'Why, sir? Because people are sad and they want to be happy.' Vijay manoeuvred the car deftly through the traffic, turning sharply and frequently, driving down badly pitched roads and narrow alleys. He honked more than he signalled or braked.

'We must wait here,' he said finally, turning off the engine.

'Here? We've got seven more blocks to go,' Crawford complained from the back seat.

'Yes, here. Sorry, sir,' Vijay replied. 'Protest on Gotabhaya Avenue, heading towards Senanayake Plaza.'

'Are all your streets named after your tyrants – I mean leaders?' Crawford asked.

'Yes, sir,' Vijay replied. 'We wait.'

'For what?'

'For protest to pass or soldiers to come. Then we go across avenue, around plaza, to hotel. Simple.'

'How long do we have to wait?'

Vijay looked at his watch. 'Twenty minutes,' he answered confidently.

'Twenty minutes?' Crawford repeated. He held his bottle of water against the back of his neck.

'I want to see what's going on,' Noah said. 'We're going to walk up along the traffic jam towards the avenue. If you start to move, Vijay, just pick us up – three white people, you can't miss us.'

'Soldiers can't miss you either, sir,' Vijay replied. 'My job is to keep you safe, take you to hotel. Soldiers will know you are here, sir.'

Noah was already out of the car looking around: at the faded posters of the president, the washing hanging out on apartment balconies catching the sun and the dust – and the cameras. He leaned through the open window and patted Vijay on the shoulder. 'We'll see you at the top of the street.'

He pushed through the cars and crowds with Garner and Crawford, following the low hum coming from the avenue. They threaded their way towards the frontline of the protest and then stopped abruptly.

A river of women flowed slowly down the wide street. They wore plain white saris and no makeup or jewellery. Even the children, the little girls, were dressed in white. The traditional garb of widowhood and mourning jarred against their young faces. They each carried a large photograph, held tenderly against their chests. At the bottom of each photograph was a date.

Noah didn't need to speak the language to know why these women were here. They weren't protesting, they were pleading. They wanted to know where their loved ones were. If they were living, they wanted them back. If they were dead, they wanted them back.

There was some comfort in holding your dead. Some. Not much.

'What is this?' Crawford whispered.

'A funeral march,' Garner answered. 'Of sorts. Before WWR, Sri Lanka's claim to fame was the highest number of disappearances per capita in the world. Almost entirely state-perpetrated.'

'And now?' Crawford asked, his voice unusually sombre.

'And now, thanks to the Information Shield, we have no idea about the numbers. My guess is they're rising,' Noah replied.

'Where do you hide so many people on such a small island?' Garner asked.

'There are always places, if you try hard enough,' Noah replied. If you dig deep enough, he remembered.

'The dates are when their people disappeared.' He read some of the numbers – 2035, 2031, 2029, 2022 – and tried not to look at their faces.

There must have been thousands of them, the white stretched in both directions further than he could see. The women didn't speak but hummed softly, creating a vibration, strong and steady.

And then another colour appeared. The familiar green and brown of army fatigues. The shiny black of army batons. The crowds along the side of the street pulled back as they heard the thunder of boots running towards them. The river of white froze still and silent.

'Christ,' Noah whispered. 'Run – run, run, run!' he shouted at the women. 'Run!' he shouted at the little girls who clutched the photographs of their fathers and brothers to their tiny bodies.

'Jesus fucking Christ,' he yelled again. 'Run!' The crowds pushed against him, a tide pulling him away from Garner and Crawford. He pushed back towards the women who now sat on the ground. Why weren't they running? The mothers covered their children with their bodies but they still didn't move. Silent outrage was the only protest left to them.

He watched in horror as the soldiers raised their batons high, in a swirl and flourish he knew well. They beat their batons hard into the river of white, creating an arrhythmic vibration of their own. The colours changed: army green on white, cold black on white and finally blood red on white. The women didn't scream. The children cried out – a wail but no words. Even they didn't scream. They cowered, waiting for it to start, and then cowered and cried more deeply into each other, waiting for it to stop.

A child sat curled into a ball. She raised her head from her knees. She had dark hair and dimples. He squinted and stared again. It wasn't her. Of course it wasn't her. He looked again and she was gone, lost in the tumble of people.

He remembered another massacre in Sri Lanka. His first one in an ancient temple. And then, even though he knew better, he was moving.

He waded through the panicked bystanders running away from the soldiers. He reached the first soldier and caught the baton as the man raised it again. He twisted the stick out of his gloved hand

and smacked him across the head with it, sending a follow-up blow to his stomach and then pushing him out of the way.

He stabbed the baton into the back of another soldier, once with its tip and then beat him twice more across his spine with its edge. A third soldier lunged at him, baton in one hand, the other reaching for the gun in his shoulder holster. Noah stepped into the blow to miss it, the soldier's baton overreaching and swiping the air behind him. Face to face with the soldier, he grabbed the hand on the gun and twisted it back. He swivelled, pulling the man tight behind him and over his shoulder onto the ground. He stamped hard on the man's chest, and then ducked as another soldier lunged at him.

More fleeing bystanders surged against the soldiers, sweeping Noah up in their current. He was pushed into a doorway, gasping for breath. He hadn't drawn his weapon yet. He felt a hand tug on his shirt. Instinctively he reached for it, ready to break it and strike back.

It was Vijay.

'Come, sir,' the driver insisted, ignoring Noah's stranglehold around his wrist. 'Come. I have the others. We go now – traffic has moved.' He let Vijay pull him away towards the waiting car.

*

'What the fuck was that about, sir – if you don't mind me asking?' Crawford hollered from the back seat. Vijay inched the car through the opening carved by the soldiers. He locked their doors and picked up speed.

'Chief?'

'I heard you. I forgot how much I hate Sri Lanka. I don't know. I'm sorry.' He didn't know what had come over him.

'No need to apologise, sir. Next time we'll help.' Garner's hand was still clenched around her weapon.

Chapter 11

They checked in to their hotel to the muttered complaints of Crawford. It was a small house, converted into a simple pensione. The manager was used to Western Alliance delegations and rewarded well for his discretion.

After a thorough sweep of their rooms for devices and a quick shower, they were ready for the meeting.

'Remember, only the president and his brother know we're Bio. For the purposes of this meeting and all other contact, we are a WHO delegation. I won't get Khan to trust me any other way.'

'Understood, sir,' Crawford replied. 'My clipboard is armed but not dangerous. I still think we should have gone with the big pharma cover story – their people get unlimited expense accounts and the Cinnamon Grand instead of this dump.'

'This *dump* is where the WHO usually stays. A team from a previous mission has wired a security system into the hotel boundary. Cameras and perimeter alarms. You can tap into that – it's not the Cinnamon Grand but it'll be safe.' He looked into Garner's eyes as he lied. He owed her that.

Noah and the team made their way to Government House where they sat in the air-conditioned boardroom, waiting. An hour later, the door finally opened and people filed in: President Rajasuriya; his younger brother General Rajasuriya, the Chief Minister for Defence; his brother-in-law, the Minister for Health; and their various undersecretaries.

The Rajasuriya brothers initially bore little resemblance to each other. The general was tall and broad-shouldered. Despite his age, he still did combat training every day. He was a clever, violent pragmatist for whom war was just an effective strategy. He didn't enjoy it, but he had never shied away from it.

On closer inspection, Noah realised the president had facial features in common with his brother, but they had blurred, through excess. He carried too much weight around the belly, which he tried to hide underneath a long white cotton shirt and a gold-trimmed silk sarong. Around his neck he wore a magenta scarf, woven in the region of Sri Lanka where he was born. It was supposed to represent his humble origins.

The last man to enter the room was Dr Khan, who seemed to have come straight from his laboratory. His grey curls fell into his eyes. He kept pushing them back impatiently and adjusting the glasses that slipped down his nose every time he moved. He looked older than the last surveillance photographs. Thinner too, his lab coat flapping around him. He tucked his shirt into his trousers as the others assembled.

'I'm sorry to trouble you so late,' Noah began. 'We need to start work early tomorrow.'

'Nonsense, we must apologise. This is obviously a matter of urgency. I'm sorry we kept you waiting.' The president held on to Noah's hand, his voice devoid of contrition.

'General Rajasuriya,' President Rajasuriya addressed his brother formally. 'Perhaps you'd like to talk us through what you've done to contain the outbreak. I'm sure our WHO colleagues here have read our daily briefings, but an overview would be helpful.'

'Thank you, Mr President,' Noah nodded.

'Yes, thank you, Mr President.' The general cleared his throat and straightened his heavy uniform as he spoke.

'Eight dead: five babies and three grandparents who hadn't done their boosters on time. We believe that the babies are our Patients Zero. Fortunately, because of their vulnerable condition they were isolated from people other than their families and hospital staff.'

Noah looked up from his notes. 'The perimeter, sir? I see that you've implemented a Lockdown Protocol Level 1. You achieved that within thirty-three minutes of the first detection.'

'Of course, Dr Williams,' the general replied. 'We locked down the hospital four minutes after detection and the country in thirty-three minutes. Only WHO personnel are currently allowed to enter Sri Lanka and no one is allowed to leave. The national border is easier to patrol than the city border, but you would have noticed the heightened military presence on the roads.'

'Yes, we saw that. And the victims?'

'The victims were quarantined in a special ward and their bodies cremated at an off-site facility.'

The government had many off-site facilities.

'Thank you, General. What have you told the public about the lockdown?' Noah asked.

'We said we've had an outbreak of cholera – it worries people but it doesn't create widespread panic.'

'After Ebola, cholera seems like a bad case of the runs,' Noah replied.

'That's right. We can't afford to have people storming the city boundaries until we are one hundred percent positive we've traced all contact. We've assumed a radius of at least three levels. So we've extracted the parents, their families and the families of the hospital employees. They've been cleared by the scanners but we are still watching them.'

'They don't have the virus.' Khan finally spoke, squinting directly at Noah. He rubbed his left temple and then self-consciously dropped his hand.

'How can you be so sure, Dr Khan?' Noah asked.

'Amir, call me Amir.' He took his glasses off and wiped them with a handkerchief from his pocket. He put them back on and his eyes relaxed. 'Much better. You're a handsome man for a scientist.'

Noah laughed.

'He gets that a lot,' Crawford said.

'Thank you, Amir. Again, how can you be so sure the contact radius isn't infected?'

'Because the scanners never lie, Noah, you know that.' He looked at him closely. 'And the virus is too deadly. It killed all its hosts before it had a chance to spread. There is always a trade-off between virulence and infectivity. You know that too.'

'So you're saying we were lucky?' Noah asked.

'There's nothing *lucky* about haemorrhagic fever, although I suppose it was merciful that it was so virulent. It was over quickly. We barely had time to administer supportive care and in the end opted for intensive palliative care.'

Noah knew about futile supportive care and intensive palliative care.

'What I'm saying, Noah, is that we were able to avoid a larger outbreak, partly because General Rajasuriya is outstanding at his job, and partly because the virus is outstanding at *its* job.'

'Ebola doesn't have a job, Dr Khan,' Noah replied sharply.

'Of course it does, all disease does. The virus was so successful it was self-devouring; a little like us really.'

'Ebola and us – similar, sir?' Noah repeated.

'We have more in common with the virus than we care to admit.' Khan rubbed his temple again.

Noah didn't know how to respond.

'Thank you, Dr Khan – I think,' replied General Rajasuriya. 'The real question is, of course, how did those babies get infected in the first place? The autopsy revealed that they contracted it at the same time as each other. Transfer had to have taken place through the medical staff – fluid contact. Fortunately it's not airborne.' He looked at Khan for confirmation.

The old man nodded. 'Correct, but it still spreads easily. This Ebola strain was infectious *before* the symptoms appeared.'

'Like the strains that moved into North Africa during the Great Pandemic . . .' Noah said.

'That's right – when the West African Ebola and a local bat flu combined in 2021 the new virus was far superior to the original because it became infectious *before* its symptoms appeared and before patients could be isolated. It was incredible . . .'

'Like your hospital outbreak,' Noah pulled Khan back to the present.

'Yes, yes – staff only realised what we were dealing with at 9.30 am when the oldest baby in the ICU ward, Karthik, had his pre-immunisation scan. By that time it had spread but the babies were still completely asymptomatic.

'Four hours later, all babies presented with a fever at the same time, followed by vomiting. We couldn't save them, although we tried a number of aggressive treatments. It was also too late to contain the virus. The babies had already come into fluid contact with their parents, grandparents and medical staff.'

President Rajasuriya cleared his throat and spoke, his accent and diction almost identical to his brother's. 'Our military, led by the general, locked the hospital, city and country down, as soon as we knew. The information cascade worked efficiently, even though we haven't used it since . . . since it was established fifteen years ago.'

'No, but we do drills every month. One can't be over-prepared for an outbreak,' the general responded.

'True, and you were highly prepared, General. The WHO commends your efforts at successfully containing this outbreak and minimising the loss of life.'

'Thank you, Dr Williams. We appreciate the WHO's continued support and ongoing public education efforts.'

'Of course.' Khan looked directly at Noah, all traces of his squint and headache gone. 'That still doesn't answer the question that was posed at the beginning before we all started congratulating ourselves. How did the outbreak begin in one of the most sterile wards in the hospital; in one of the most hygienic places in the country?'

'You are quite right, Dr – Amir. Have you any thoughts on the initial contamination?' Noah asked.

'No.' Khan shook his head. 'There's a lot of scientific literature about the cyclical nature of Ebola. According to the prevailing guesswork, Ebola may mutate and emerge from time to time in a life cycle that we can't understand or predict yet. Hence we are urged to dutifully and pre-emptively vaccinate our children and take our boosters. I'm not convinced about that theory but here we are, with an outbreak of Ebola. It mystifies me, which doesn't happen often. I took a sample of the live virus –'

'You did what?' Noah interrupted. All eyes in the room suddenly turned to Khan.

'I'm sure what the doctor means is . . .' the general tried to assist Khan.

'Don't worry, General. I haven't violated national and international law. I am well aware of the WHO framework on the handling of a suspected or actual Ebola virus,' Khan replied. *Too quickly, too calmly*, Noah thought.

'I harvested a sample of the live virus and transfected tissue culture with it. It consumed and killed the culture faster than I could study it, despite my best efforts.' He sighed.

'It closely resembled Ebola Strain 47 but it operated differently. It had improved itself. The virus was fulfilling its genetic potential.'

'You seem impressed,' Noah said.

'I'm a virologist.'

'Yes, you are – an exceptional one. You must have a theory. Surely the most likely suspect is one of the nurses who was on duty and had access to all four children.'

'Indeed, Dr Williams,' the general replied. 'We are exploring that line of investigation at the moment.'

'Five children . . .' Khan mumbled.

'Sir?' Noah said.

'Five children were infected and five children – babies – died.' Khan spoke louder. 'Of course we considered that the babies weren't the Patients Zero. We traced all hospital staff and family members who had been in contact with the children since birth. The staff were predictably and reassuringly clean – as health professionals they undergo regular Haema Scans and take the booster at shorter intervals than others. The family members – the grandparents – all presented with the virus at an earlier stage of incubation. That is to say, they were infected later.'

'I know what you mean,' Noah said.

'Of course, you are a virologist too. And yet we all struggle to explain how such a virus came to exist in Colombo General Hospital. We struggle to identify *how*, but I think for the families of the dead, the real question will be *why*. Why were their children – and not someone else's – chosen to die?'

'There is no *why*, Dr Khan. It was utterly random,' Noah replied. These things happen, his mother said when his father died. It is God's will, she said, when his daughter died.

God's fucking will.

'I'm sorry to hear you say that, Noah. You are a man of science and for us men – and women – of science,' Khan nodded politely at Garner, 'there is always a why. Or there is always a search for the why, in here.' Khan clenched his hand into a fist. It hovered in front of his chest and then relaxed and tapped the side of his head. His left temple where Noah suspected his headache had been.

'Thank you, Dr Khan,' President Rajasuriya intervened. 'Perhaps you can discuss the philosophical underpinnings of science with Dr Williams later. He's here to supervise the lockdown and ensure that we have traced contact properly.'

'Hardly, Mr President. I think you and the general have that all in hand. If Dr Khan doesn't mind, I'd like to join his team and help investigate where this virus might have come from in the first place. Now that the immediate threat of contamination has been removed, our priority is to locate the genesis of the virus and ensure it doesn't happen again – here or anywhere else.'

'I'm sure I speak for Dr Khan and all of us when I say that we are very happy to have you here and welcome the WHO's expertise. Dr Khan?' The president looked at Khan.

'Agreed. Excellent, Noah. My laboratory is your laboratory, as we say.' Khan smiled. 'We can start first thing in the morning. I get to the lab by 7 am after a quick swim.'

'Thank you, Doctor, I'll see you then.'

The meeting ended with more handshakes and formalities. It was only much later, in the middle of the night after Noah had tried to sleep and failed, that he replayed the meeting in his mind several times. He realised that Khan had addressed him comfortably by his first name; as though he was waiting for him.

*

The next morning Noah gave the others their instructions. 'Garner, I want you at base for now – analysing anything Crawford and I find. Put together the narrative behind our suspect – what is he doing and why?' Garner nodded, her relief just discernible.

'Crawford, I want you to inspect Ground Zero at the hospital with the WHO team. Make sure you're comfortable the Sri Lankans can't work out how the virus got in.'

'Will do, Chief.'

'Let's take the opportunity to look around while we're here. I want to know how good their intel and surveillance is.'

'You saw the cameras, right, when we were driving in?' Garner asked.

'I did – they were located in a standard grid and 270-degree angle arrangement in public places. And those are just the ones we could see. Which reminds me – our rooms need to be swept every time we enter and every time we wake up.'

'Every time we wake up? That's a little paranoid, isn't it?' Crawford asked.

'He's a spy,' Garner replied.

'It's called not underestimating the enemy,' Noah said.

'I thought Sri Lanka was an ally?' Crawford said.

'They're an ally, not a friend.'

'Do we have any friends?'

'No – only allies and enemies, all of whom are suspects.'

'Do you have any friends?' Crawford asked.

'No, just a mother and you guys.' He laughed. 'Get your protection equipment ready just in case there are samples you need to look at.'

'Got it,' Crawford replied.

'And what are you going to do, sir?' Garner asked.

Noah tapped the case given to him by Bio's Technical Surveillance Division – his new contact lenses. They fit perfectly.

'I'm going to Khan's laboratory.'

Chapter 12

The Department of Immunology at Colombo General Hospital was surprisingly modern compared to the rest of the building, like a shiny new prosthetic limb on an ailing and ageing body. A young lab technician greeted Noah with a swipe card for him. It was already personalised with his biodata.

'Dr Khan says you are to be given full access. The rest of your team will have the usual access that's given to WHO personnel. I hope that's acceptable?' The man led him through various sealed doors.

'That is acceptable, thank you,' Noah replied.

'You can thank Dr Khan. Here we are.' The man cleared three levels of security at the door.

Khan's laboratory was not what Noah was expecting. It was large and filled with microscopes, secure refrigerators and other pieces of equipment. Scientists were engrossed in their work, only a few raising their eyes for a moment to acknowledge him before returning to their scopes.

'This way, Dr Williams. This is the main laboratory. Dr Khan's personal laboratory is here.'

Noah followed the man through the lab towards another door, where he stopped and pressed on an intercom panel.

'We're here, sir.' He waited for the door to open and ushered Noah through alone.

'Dr Khan,' Noah extended his hand. 'Thank you for having me.'

'Welcome, welcome Noah. Thank you for joining me.' Khan rushed forward to shake his hand. 'Come, this is where I do most of my work. Through there is the isolation lab for live viruses.' He pointed to a room on the right.

'As you know, we are only permitted to study and store Bio Hazard Grade 6 and below, as per the Five Virus Eradication Policy.'

Noah stopped at the sight of a large, familiar machine.

'Aah yes, that is my integrated microscope – the Artificially Intelligent Laboratory Assistant, or AILA. Look at her robotic extensions. She has two kinds of scopes so I can switch between approaches. She's exquisite, isn't she?' Khan stepped back to admire the microscope. 'I call her Devi. She is all-powerful and all-seeing.'

Noah looked at Khan, shocked. Devi was the Hindu Supreme Mother Goddess.

'Of course you won't know Sri Devi – she was a Bollywood superstar.' He laughed. 'Devi – prepare the Ebola outbreak photographs, please. Screen on,' Khan instructed.

Noah watched in amazement as a robotic hand whirred around the room.

'She's tidying up first,' Khan whispered proudly.

Garner's voice spoke in his earpiece: 'This is the AILA Reina. Just bringing up its development history now, sir.' She paused, obviously scrolling through information as she accessed it. 'Okay. It's not as advanced as Dr Neeson's. This is an older test model. It was taken offline because its nanoscope resolution wasn't good enough for –'

'Got it,' Noah spoke out loud, cutting her off.

'Of course, sir, sorry. Like Dr Neeson's, it's not networked. If Khan's using the AILA to make the decoy vaccine I'm not sure I can hack into it – at all.'

Noah nodded. Garner could see everything through his contact lenses.

'Where did you get Devi from, Dr Khan?'

'Please, you must call me Amir. We are colleagues, explorers with microscopes. This beauty,' he stroked the side of the machine, 'was a gift from one of our corporate investors. The accuracy of her finger movements is based on thousands of hours of research and the robotic emulations of bombmakers.'

'Bombmakers?'

'Yes, those fellows have exceptional fine motor precision. They never make a mistake.'

'Until they do and they blow themselves up.'

'Quite the pessimist, aren't you?'

Noah laughed. 'It's beautiful. So is your lab, Dr – Amir. I'm impressed.'

'No, you are surprised. What were you expecting? That we would be sterilising our equipment with a Bunsen burner instead of an autoclave?' He laughed. 'I'm very happy to disappoint your expectations and perhaps create new ones about the kind of science we do here in Colombo. Our laboratory is state-of-the-art.'

Khan led him around the room. 'We take disease prevention seriously – and our obligation to protect the global herd. In Sri Lanka we still carry the burden of guilt for our role in the war – we take our share of responsibility for what happened.'

'That was in the past,' Noah replied.

'Perhaps, but it's important to remember the past and to learn from it. Now all of this –' Khan waved his arms at the laboratory around him '– this is the future, surely? Where science is the new philosophy and scientists the new philosophers. Let me show you what you came for.

'Come, come – bring your own chair. These images are from Devi's electron microscope.'

Noah looked up at the screen on the wall. He recognised the image immediately. It was Ebola Strain 48.6, the virus that Neeson had engineered for the hospital outbreak.

'I've never seen it before,' Khan said. 'It's almost identical to Ebola 47. People who were fully vaccinated with EBL-47 were immune to it. But one codon within a protein has changed, here, Noah, an intelligent design . . .' He pointed to a section. 'It's hyper-functional – an outstanding killer.'

As a weapon, it was risky but effective. Neeson had said the hosts would not survive and neither would the virus – this strain would burn itself out quickly, assuming that the hospital's lockdown procedures were efficient. Hackman knew about the drills. He'd won this round.

'Baby Karthik was the one who sounded the alarm,' Khan continued.

'What was his full name?' Noah asked. It was important to remember the names of his dead. 'The patient files only refer to him as Baby Karthik.'

'His full name is Karthik Raghavan. After the war, babies and children in Sri Lankan hospitals are only ever identified by their first name and a barcode on their ankles,' Khan replied.

'Why is that?' Noah turned away from the screen, towards the old man.

'During World War R . . .' Khan chose his words carefully. The lab was watched, but it was more than that. He was picking through words and images. 'Some factions were given a . . . legitimacy by the state – an official mandate to hurt . . .' He looked hard at Noah, as if deciding whether he could trust him with a more accurate word: 'To massacre people who were not like them. Others, those that were different, had no such legitimacy. Only the desperation of self-defence. Neither side was less vicious ...' His voice and mind drifted inward to the memory of an old violence.

'The babies, Doctor –' Noah prompted.

'Ah yes, the babies. I'm sorry.' Khan took his glasses off and pressed his thumb into the space between his eye and his brow bone.

He has a migraine again, Noah thought. Persistent. Mild squint forming in the left eye. The familiar inventory of symptoms hurt him somewhere in the base of his chest. He waited for Khan to speak.

'You see, during World War R, mobs came to the hospitals. They took the patient charts and walked the hallways.' He put his glasses back on. They were smudged but he didn't seem to notice.

'They went from ward to ward with the charts and attacked patients, based on their surnames. No matter how sick they were. They dragged them from operating tables. And ripped them from their mother's arms, from their cribs and their incubators. They took them down to the front lawn – there is a memorial there now but the grass doesn't seem to grow, no matter how hard they try. They took all the patients there. The lucky ones were beheaded ...'

'The others?' Noah whispered. He had to ask.

'They covered them in petrol and set fire to them.'

Khan shook his head but the image stayed with them both.

'What does a name tell you? It's our actions that tell us who we are – and babies, well – they've not had a chance to ... do anything.'

'But you don't label children by their surnames anymore?' Noah prompted. Even though the violence had ended and the vaccine in the East would stop it from ever beginning again.

'No – it's a tradition, I suppose. A way of remembering our past ... we use their first name and the barcode. We don't want children to be classified by their last name. They are simply children.'

Simply children.

Khan stood up abruptly. 'Come, let me introduce you to my monkeys.' He led Noah to an antechamber. 'I presume you brought your own PPE?'

Noah nodded.

Once Khan and Noah were suited up in their personal protective equipment, Khan opened another door to the isolation room. They were assaulted by a chorus of angry cries and the smell of faeces from a row of monkeys in cages.

'Chh, cch –' Khan whispered to them. 'They've been very nervous lately. They're not stupid.'

'You injected them with the virus sample?' Noah asked.

'I did. I tried it on the tissue cultures first but, as I mentioned, the virus invaded the cells and destroyed them too quickly. I barely had time to observe its progress, let alone play with it.' He poked a finger through a cage and tickled under a monkey's chin. The animal calmed down and lay back, giving Khan his tummy. He laughed softly.

'Aisha, my wife, hated experimenting on them. She treated them like her children. She used to cry when they died, which in our line of work, is unfortunately quite often.'

'What happened when you injected the virus into them?' Noah asked.

Khan kept walking past the other cages, some empty, some not. He stopped at the back of the room, at a large glass tank, much like the humidicribs used for premature babies.

'This is what happened.' Inside the tank, a monkey lay curled into the foetal position, its chest rising and falling in rapid, shallow breaths. Black blood pooled around its eyes, nose and mouth.

'This is the last one. It's almost over, little one.' Khan reached into the tank with his gloved hands and stroked the animal. It shuddered and then relaxed.

'They all died within thirty-six hours of displaying the same symptoms as the human victims. They looked like they had a really bad flu for eight hours before they presented with the signs of rapid multi-system failure. I've recorded everything – including the Haema Scans. Devi is mobile, so she worked with me here and we took bloods every hour, sometimes every twenty minutes.'

'Why?' Noah asked.

'Why did I take bloods?' Khan asked, confused.

'Why did you infect the monkeys with the virus? The WHO Protocol requires you to contain and destroy it, not perpetuate it. What are you doing with their blood?' There were any number of things Khan could do with a live sample of Ebola 48.6.

'I'm studying it – the virus adapts rapidly within the host, adjusting to its strengths and finding better ways to kill it. But the patients all produced antibodies before they were overwhelmed by it. If we can understand the virus and the body's immune response, we can create a vaccine of course,' Khan replied.

'I need another end-stage blood sample. The last antibodies are the best. Put your hands here, Noah. Hold his shoulders down – be ready, he might fight me.' He moved over so Noah could position his hands on the dying animal.

He braced himself just in time – the monkey thrashed with its last energy, screaming and coughing blood, curling its lips back and baring yellow teeth. Khan plunged the syringe into its atrophied thigh and filled it with thick blood.

The monkey snapped its powerful jaws at Noah. He felt its teeth graze his glove, a putrid liquid spray towards him. Khan pushed him out of the way and dropped the syringe.

Noah checked his gloves and protection equipment, his heart racing. It was all intact. He exhaled and looked at Khan.

'You're bleeding!' Noah grabbed the older man's arm and held it tightly. 'You're bleeding,' he repeated. Khan's glove was torn. Blood seeped through.

'We need to quarantine you.' He didn't let go.

'We don't need to do anything.'

'The WHO Protocol –'

Khan interrupted him. 'I know what the protocol says.' He pulled himself free and picked up the portable Haema Scanner. 'Scan me,' he held the machine out to Noah. 'Scan me. Check my blood and then decide.'

'You've been bitten by an animal infected with Ebola – I don't need to scan you. I need to quarantine you before you become infectious.'

'Scan me, Noah,' Khan repeated calmly, pulling back his protective clothing.

Noah held the scanner above his wrist. The reading was normal. He checked its setting and scanned Khan again. It was clear. He did it a third time – it showed the blood work of a man with the right antibody markers and no Ebola contamination.

'I'm fine, Noah. The scanners never lie.'

*

Khan sealed the plastic body bag around the monkey, took his gloves off and made a phone call.

'I need a clean-up team. Bio Hazard Grade 1 – now, thank you.' He put the phone down.

'You should be dying.' Noah shook his head.

'We're all dying. Life kills us from the day we are born, and yet we are still so surprised by death. So unready. I'm fine, Noah. I'm merely using one organism to explore and improve the behaviour of another organism. I'm trialling a vaccine for this new strain – the blood serum from the monkeys helps me tailor it.'

'You're trialling it on yourself?' Noah whispered.

'I'm prepared to back myself, yes. It's a promising vaccine. I'll show it to you soon, if you like.' Khan stopped, framing his words carefully again. 'This body, like cancer, is just a group of cells.'

'Cancer is much more than that.'

'No, son – it isn't. It is a particular group of cells that do not listen to the body's imperatives anymore. They are renegades who cannot be controlled by the body's signals that tell it how to grow and when to die.'

'You make it sound so benign – so unintentional.'

'And you make it sound so malicious. Each day your cells divide nearly 300 billion times. And seventy billion cells will die as they are programmed to do. Cancer cells can evade programmed cell death even though cell death is designed to target such mutations.'

'I'm not sure what you're trying to say,' Noah replied. He was staring at Khan, still incredulous the man seemed unaffected by the monkey bite.

Khan pulled the mask over his head and threw it in the bin. He sat down on a stool and fiddled with the dials on his benchtop centrifuge.

'Cells divide all the time – I don't think it's unreasonable to expect that sometimes, occasionally, these cells will replicate in a different way – they will mutate. Perhaps they mutate for a reason.'

'Now I'm sure you're a mad scientist.' Noah shook his head, surprised at his own vehemence. He was here to investigate this man, not debate him. 'Cancer has a reason? And Ebola – does that have a reason too? It's an act of aberration.'

'Or an act of Nature that has a purpose – a motive,' Khan replied.

The scientist had tried to keep the virus alive – did the virus have a purpose and a motivation, or did Khan?

'Please don't tell me you think the virus is sentient?'

'It wants to thrive – just like us, Noah. I think it longs to live.'

'It longs for nothing – like all organisms it simply follows a genetic imperative to survive. Part of its survival modus is that it kills in order to survive.' *Just like us. Just like me.*

'Do you think that is every cell's core imperative? Simply to survive? I think there is more to every cell than that. The virus, cancer and us – we want more than that.'

'What more is there than survival?'

'There is meaning.'

'There is *nothing* beyond birth, survival and death. Some cells survive longer than others. Some cells adapt in order to survive. Some survive at the expense of others. That's the only distinction between any of us and that is our only purpose.' Noah stopped. He was breathless.

'I'm sorry you feel that way.'

He brushed off the old man. 'What do you propose we do – learn to live with the virus peacefully? We can't even do that with our own species. You're a virologist – your job is to destroy viruses.'

'No,' Khan shook his head. 'My job is to study them and learn from them. They have so much to teach us about ourselves. My wife, she told me that. She wasn't afraid of the cells in her body that were aberrations – despite what people said . . . or did. She embraced the disease that killed her in the end.'

Khan had said too much and yet he seemed relieved to have shared his thoughts.

'She was unusual then,' Noah said, suddenly sad. 'And very lucky.'

'Yes, she was. Shall we call it a day, Noah? You seem tired. Tomorrow we study and learn again.' Khan instructed Devi to turn off the equipment and the lights.

Chapter 13

Noah inhaled the sharp salty air rolling in from the ocean. He curled his toes in the sand, feeling the grit of broken shells prick his skin like dull pins. The sand was warm despite the early hour.

'Thank you for joining me.' Khan stretched his body up towards the sky.

Noah copied Khan's movements, even though he knew the sequence. The only people on the beach were fishermen. Vijay was parked on the side of the road, smoking his breakfast cigarette and watching them.

There was a green sedan, four cars away. Noah had seen it several times before. The surveillance team following him should have rotated cars. It wasn't good practice to use the same team every day either. He had recognised them immediately – they were the porters outside the airport.

The fishermen had already cast their nets out in the deeper water and were pulling their small wooden boats back in to shore. They wrapped their sarongs high around their waists, stopping occasionally to retie them when they slipped into the water and ballooned like colourful puffer fish. They called loudly to Khan, laughing. He waved back, held up two fingers and then ten.

'What are they saying?'

'They want to know how much fish I want for dinner. I said tomorrow I want two cuttlefish and ten king prawns. I want you to try our fruits from the ocean – we don't need tanks.'

'That's very kind of you but you don't have to entertain me, Amir. I usually eat with my team after we've completed our daily report.'

'You shouldn't eat late, it's bad for your digestion.' Khan raised his arms again, arching his back, his palms folded. He then dropped and stretched his torso along the sand, pushing himself up like a cobra.

'That's what my mother tells me.'

'Your mother is right. My wife used to say the same thing.' Khan sat down, legs crossed. He looked out across the horizon. 'She used to love it here. I've been thinking about her a lot lately, I don't know why.'

'How did she die?' Noah asked. It wasn't relevant to his investigation but he was intrigued. Khan had said his wife embraced the disease – the aberration – that killed her. He could never have done that.

'It was . . . an illness, many years ago.'

Noah sat next to him. 'I'm so sorry.'

'Thank you. It's bearable now, the grief. Still heavy but bearable. It is part of my daily routine, like this exercise. She was sick for a little while before she died. We were never able to have children. She would have been a good mother.'

'You would have been a good father too, I think.' Noah surprised himself.

'Thank you. I wasn't there with her at the end. I wonder about her last moments – was she afraid? Did she think about me, or her life, or whether she had remembered to soak the dhal for dinner.' He laughed sadly. 'I wonder if she was angry at me for leaving her.'

'You shouldn't blame yourself. I –' Noah hesitated. 'I've been with people when they died. I held my father's hand.' *And my daughter's*, he thought.

Khan turned to him. He looked so much older than his years. Grief did that to people. He stood up. 'We should begin our day. The virus waits for no man. I need to do a quick swim out there.' He pointed to the lifebuoy bobbing in the distance, just shy of the churning waters of the break.

'I'll meet you at the lab. Please begin your search for the genesis.'

As soon as Khan was in the water, Noah headed for his car. The green sedan started its engine. They should have waited for him to leave.

'Vijay, let's get to the lab.' He had his work clothes in a bag on the back seat. He pulled out his phone.

'Garner? Are you awake?'

'I've been awake for two hours, sir. Watching your location right now.'

'Of course you are, sorry. Can you access Dr Khan's wife's full medical records? Her COD wasn't in our files. He said she was sick . . .'

'Sure, we can get to level 4 in the Eastern Alliance mainframe. If we try the three levels above that, we'll set off a massive alarm. Crawford thinks he can work out how to enter quietly. He always overreaches.'

'It's a fine quality in some professions.'

'But not all.'

'Okay. Until you're absolutely sure, leave those levels alone.'

'Yes, sir, we know.'

'Sorry.' Garner and Crawford were the only people he ever apologised to. And his wife.

'We're in. Haema Scans for Aisha Khan are being sent to your handheld.'

'Thanks. Give me the headlines.' Noah changed his clothes as he spoke.

'Aisha Khan died on 12 August 2025 – cause of death . . . says viral infection. Let me pull up her medical records. Just checking. No – nothing. At the time of her death she was in good health.'

'What does the postmortem say?'

'There wasn't one. That's unusual. No details on internment of body. Organ donation . . . none that I can see from the records.'

'That doesn't sound like Khan. He's lying.'

'I'll keep looking. Sending you what I have now, the usual encryption. What's he lying about – the wife's sickness or her death?'

'Both, I think – I don't know,' Noah replied slowly.

Garner hesitated but spoke her mind. 'That's not like you, sir. I'll keep looking,' she repeated.

'Thank you. Good work, Garner – you too, Crawford, I assume you're on the line.'

'Always, Chief,' Crawford replied.

Noah put the phone down and picked up his handheld.

*

From her car, Sahara watched the men on the beach. She was twelve cars away from the president's surveillance team. In the morning haze, Khan and Noah looked like father and son, one teaching the other an ancient sequence of movements that saluted the sun god. She watched them, remembering the movements her grandmother had taught her a lifetime ago, when she had felt reverence for divinity; reverence for life.

Reverence, hope, faith – she wasn't sure what she had left. She could only list the lives she'd ruined.

Penance. She still had that.

Khan returned to the water's edge and waded in smoothly, not shuddering as the cold waves enveloped him.

Noah returned to his car. She wanted him to smile. He was handsome although from the surveillance photos he rarely smiled. He turned towards her, unseeing. She felt her body tingle. An old hunger. She ignored the muscle memory.

He got into his car. The surveillance vehicle pulled out too early. Amateurs.

The sun hit the ocean's surface like a thousand stars, carried by the waves towards the shore. She checked that she was a safe distance from the surveillance team on Khan. She was always a safe distance. She stripped off her dress to her swimmers underneath and headed out to the break.

Redemption – perhaps she still had that too.

*

The main lab was empty. It was only 6.15 am. Noah had more than half an hour before Khan arrived. He entered the doctor's personal lab and went straight to the computer that interfaced with Devi. He activated his lenses for Garner.

'Place the handheld on Khan's biometric ID panel. That's it – fingerprint copy complete.' Garner guided him through his earpiece. 'Now place it next to the computer, sir. Closer – just leave it there and it will copy the files. It won't work with Devi, but anything else is fine.'

Later, he would back up his handheld to Garner's hard drive and process the stolen information.

'Good morning, Devi,' he said, 'How are you today?'

'I am well, thank you for asking, sir. How are you?' the voice replied in a synthetically smooth tone, imitating his polite inflection. There was no way he could access the information she contained without her realising it.

'I am well. Dr Khan said I could make an early start today. I hope you don't mind me being here without him.' Noah had already noted the surveillance cameras.

'Not at all, sir. Dr Khan has asked me to show you the time-lapsed film of the children. He looked after the babies himself when they quarantined the maternity ward.'

'Which child does he want me to watch?' Noah's throat suddenly felt tight.

'Baby Karthik – the first one. Please take a seat, sir.'

Devi pulled a chair closer but he didn't sit. The lights dimmed and the recording started on the large screen. Her hand breezed past him to pluck the image out, giving him the 3D replay.

Baby Karthik lay in a clear crib. It was sealed, but tubes curled through its vents like shiny red veins. The child's small chest was covered in adhesive pads that connected wires to the machine next to him. Its low hum reminded Noah of the chorus of geckoes he heard at night outside his hotel. Geckoes were bad luck in Sri Lanka. Or was it good luck? He could never remember. Bad luck at weddings and good luck on other days, like today.

The vitals monitor showed an irregular line, the peaks and troughs of tachycardia.

Noah touched the screen to expand the monitor.

'All good, sir, I can see the numbers,' Garner replied in his ear. 'The oxygenation level and blood pressure is too low, the heart rate and temperature is too high.'

'Was,' he whispered to himself. *Was* too high.

He made himself look at the baby – Karthik Raghavan. He recognised the blue roses under the translucent skin, blood seeping from a myriad of internal wounds. If he turned the child over, his back would be a deep purple from the blood that gravity had pooled underneath.

He heard the cries and screams quickly fade to whimpers as the child's lungs withered, and his vocal cords corroded.

He saw seizure after horrific seizure and he wished the child would die.

Khan entered regularly, dressed in full protective gear. He checked vitals and wiped the blood from the baby's eyes, nose, mouth and ears. He intubated Baby Karthik, masterfully inserting a narrow tube into an even finer, collapsing trachea.

He changed the baby's nappy when bloodstained faeces spurted out. He tried one antiviral after another. He administered it through the child's IV, the veins, his rectum – any way he could. He spread ointments on the sores that flowered all over the small body, the ulcerated skin and muscle that fell away from the barely living carcass.

And he drew blood sample after blood sample – and studied it. He moved quickly between the baby, Devi, the three computers in the room and its equipment.

'Replay that please, Devi,' Noah commanded.

'Certainly, sir.' Noah leaned towards the image. Khan was checking the samples repeatedly. He was looking for something.

'Again please,' Noah asked. 'Enlarge, slow down and replay.'

He watched Khan. 'What is he doing?' he whispered to himself.

Devi answered him. 'He's studying the Ebola virus, sir – and the antibodies produced by the patient when his body tried to fight it.'

'Why?'

'To engineer more antibodies – with help from my database of over four million samples.'

'You make it sound so easy, Devi.'

'Chief, I'm recording this but I'm not sure I can extrapolate his process from it. Is this the vaccine we're looking for?'

'I don't know.' Hassan Ali's vaccine was a decoy. It didn't create immunity against Ebola. Khan's had made him immune to Ebola 48.6, the variant used in the hospital outbreak.

'Maybe ...' he whispered. But where did Khan store the vaccine and the research Neeson wanted?

A door opened behind him. 'Good morning, Noah.' It was Khan. 'Thank you for watching that – I wanted you to understand why our work together is important.'

'You kept trying to save him – even when you knew it was hopeless ...'

'You would have done the same. It is human nature to hope.'

Noah couldn't meet Khan's gaze. He was afraid Khan would see through to the core of him; see that the child was dead because of him. They all were. He turned back to the image. Khan soothed and sang to the baby, who stopped mewling when he heard the doctor's voice. Sometimes, Noah thought he heard the old man cry.

Noah was good at controlling his emotions. Too good, Maggie told him when she left. He closed his eyes and shuddered.

'Noah, let's begin. Time is short for all of us.'

'Shorter for some more than others.'

'Yes – I know what you mean.' There was a rueful resignation in Khan's voice. And something else Noah couldn't place. But he was sure Khan wasn't talking about Baby Karthik.

Chapter 14

Noah turned the car into the driveway and stopped at the heavy steel gates of the Presidential Palace. He stepped out into the light at the guardhouse. The soldiers searched him and the vehicle but found nothing.

A soldier waved him on. 'Follow the driveway, sir. The president isn't expecting anyone else tonight.'

The man signalled to the guardhouse to open the gates. All of the soldiers stood alert, their weapons poised, until Noah had driven through and the gate had closed behind him.

The driveway snaked across a manicured estate that contrasted starkly with the tired urban decay he had passed outside.

At the northern corner a floodlight traced a lazy pattern over the lawn. Noah noted the silhouettes of two soldiers in the tower, one to manoeuvre the barrel of the light and the other to pick off intruders.

He parked his car as directed. A servant greeted him, smiling but silent. The man led him through the gilded front door and into a sparkling, empty dining room.

Noah looked up at the crystal chandeliers that dripped from the ceiling and the massive oil canvasses that decked the walls. His eyes searched the room for surveillance equipment. An old habit.

He turned at the sound of the opening door.

'Noah – good evening. Thank you for joining me.' President Rajasuriya clasped both of his large hands around Noah's, shaking it warmly and pulling him close. Noah recognised the faint smell of ammonia. Rajasuriya was eighty-two years old but his hair was a deep black that leeched onto his hairline.

A coterie of servants silently entered the room with refreshments.

The president's face darkened. 'No, no! I said we would take dinner in my private library.' He sighed and clapped his hands at the servants, ushering them out. 'I thought we could talk more freely. Your father loved books, yes?'

Before Noah could reply, the president led him out of the reception room and up an ornate spiral staircase. At first Noah thought it had mirrors embedded in it, reflecting the colours of the room, but he soon realised it was a rainbow of gemstones.

'Yes, the staircase is something, isn't it? I had the jewels brought from the temple at Kadiragama when we destroyed it. According to the legend, the god Murugan presented these beauties to the maiden Valli. As if you would need persuasion to marry a god. Perhaps women are different – perhaps they prefer jewels to power?'

The servants had gone ahead; the staircase was empty but it was a risky conversation.

'Aah, Noah, you should see your face. You must learn to relax. I've read your file – yes, we have files on you too. You're always so intense. It's not good for your health. Don't worry about the servants. Heightened confidentiality is part of their contractual arrangement.'

'I'm not sure I follow you, Mr President.'

'How refreshing – something you don't know. To join my service, the servants agree to forgo their powers of speech.' He smiled widely, revealing black gums.

'How exactly does one do that?'

The president opened the door to a large library. Shelves of books swept grandly from the floor to the ceiling.

'Quite easily. They are administered with a combination of the old vaccines, the toxic ones, EBL-22 and EBL-23 – are you familiar with them?' He motioned to a pair of leather armchairs. There was a small table in between them with their drinks waiting.

'Yes, I am.' Noah remembered Hassan Ali's children.

'Of course you are, your people tested it on our soldiers during the war. A convenient lapse in your commitment to the Geneva Conventions. Our slums are full of your experiments – men and women whose minds you broke and voices you stole with all the vaccines that failed before you developed EBL-47.' Rajasuriya didn't wait for him to respond.

'We experimented on our prisoners too. If you get the toxicity level of the old vaccines right, you can achieve muteness *and* inhibit the limbic system.'

'That's not possible,' Noah said. 'The limbic system is primal – nothing short of a stroke, a crushing head injury or a lobotomy can inhibit the brain's fight-or-flight mechanism.'

'You should know by now, anything is possible with the right science.' The president corrected himself. 'Almost anything.

'In time, people come to enjoy working for me. They prefer the vaccine to the ongoing use of other interrogation techniques. They come to love me as I love all my citizens, even those who have sinned against me.' The president smiled hungrily at a young woman who brought in a tray of food. She couldn't hide her prettiness behind the plain white uniform and demure bun.

'Of course, I love some more than others.' He touched the woman's exposed forearm gently. Noah saw the tendons in her arm tense. He heard her exhale slightly as she raised her eyes to the president, expressionless. She nodded and set the tray down on the table.

Some of her limbic system was still working. Noah pulled his eyes away from her face. He studied the food on the table, momentarily unable to look at the president.

'Fish patties? These are a local favourite.' The president slid the plate closer to himself and took a patty, watching the woman shut the door behind her.

'She's pretty, isn't she? If you wish, you can have her.'

'Thank you, sir, I'm fine,' Noah replied.

'I understand your wife left you almost six months ago and you have not taken a woman, man or child since. That's unhealthy and unnatural. Let me help you.'

'Really, thank you, Mr President. I'm here for work –'

'Yes, *work*. Tell me why you're here?' The president asked amicably, picking up another piece.

'You know why I'm here. We're investigating the Ebola outbreak that killed eight Sri Lankans and potentially jeopardised the health of your country.'

'No, Noah, that is why the WHO is here.'

The president paused to dip his fish patty into the mint chutney. 'But you and your small Bio team are here for something else and I want to know what it is.'

Noah didn't falter. 'Bio takes an Ebola outbreak seriously. We always shadow the WHO team when an outbreak occurs. Sri Lanka is very important to Bio – and Hackman. You haven't had a reported case since WWR. We want to make sure your containment protocols are working – and find out where it started.' Noah reached for the food.

'The origin of the outbreak was in the neo-natal ICU,' the president replied. 'We've reviewed the surveillance footage, the meta-scanner and Haema Scanner records at all of the entrances and exits to the hospital. The only thing out of order was that Dr Fonseka, a long-standing doctor on the ward, was sick on the night of the outbreak.'

Three servants walked in bearing steaming hot dishes: goat curry, crab curry and fried okra.

'Have you questioned her?' Noah asked. He cursed himself silently – he should have thought about her, even if Hackman hadn't.

'Extensively. She claims she doesn't know anything. Her postmortem revealed that she did indeed have gastroenteritis.' The president waved his hand, shooing an unseen mosquito.

Noah felt his chest tighten. The collateral kills had started to matter. His list of names was growing.

The president continued to eat. 'Perhaps we lack your interrogation finesse?'

Noah wanted to put his dinner knife into the president's carotid artery. No, a single sharp blow to his throat, and then a quick turn of his neck. He would hide the body behind the re-upholstered colonial divan, ask to use the bathroom, and run across the lawn, avoiding the floodlight. He had memorised the pattern of its sweep. Three minutes to get to the gate, nine seconds to take out the soldiers before they'd even stood up from their card game.

'Won't her family notice she's gone missing? It would raise suspicion and create –'

'People disappear in Sri Lanka,' the president shrugged his shoulders, putting more food onto his plate. 'It is as much a part of our life cycle as the monsoon and the harvest. Perhaps her family could stage another march? You know I punished those women with the EBL-22 and 23 too although they still insist on marching.' The president laughed. 'I let that incident go, Noah – I put it down to your recent tragedy. But I urge you not to involve yourself in my business again.'

Noah stared at the curries congealing on his plate.

'You should eat while it's hot,' the president prompted. 'Tell me this, why are you so keen to get close to Khan? Do you think he did it?'

'Did what?' Noah tried to eat some of his dinner.

'Infected those babies with Ebola, of course.'

Noah shook his head. He moved the food around on his plate. 'I'm sure Khan is clean. He's a natural healer; a seeker of remedies through science.'

'What other remedies are there?' the president asked.

'Exactly – science, technology and pragmatic politics. These are the remedies of our time,' Noah replied.

'Unlike war and religion, the remedies of our past. Hackman says you're his best agent.'

'That doesn't sound like Hackman.'

'You don't give either of us enough credit, Noah. You *are* his best agent – you know it and I know it. Please don't offend me by suggesting otherwise. What I don't know is why he thought an ageing, albeit accomplished, virologist was important enough for you to watch him.'

'Ageing but accomplished – you could be describing me.' Noah laughed.

'You are hardly old – according to your file you're forty.'

'In my line of work that's very old. We usually die a lot younger.'

'And yet you still live – because you are excellent at your job.'

'This is my last job. I'm retiring while I still can. All that danger pay is only worth something if you live to spend it. I wanted an easy job and Hackman did me a favour. Perhaps he felt sorry for me – if you've read my file then you'll know why.'

'Yes, I was sorry to hear about that, Noah. We all love our children. Do you know what caused her illness?'

'Apparently there aren't always reasons.'

'No, of course not. How insensitive of me. I am deeply sorry.'

'Thank you, Mr President, that's kind of you,' Noah replied automatically.

'If you've ruled Khan out – as you say – then why do you still spend time with him? Is he working on something that interests you?'

'No,' Noah lied. Hackman's instructions about the ghost – and Khan's trial vaccine – were clear.

'He's an interesting man,' Noah continued. 'Virology produces some eccentric personalities – all that time spent alone in a lab, talking to viruses.'

'So you're still here because you like him?' the president mused.

Noah shrugged. 'I'm not one for liking or disliking people – I'll go when the job's done.'

'Quite. Would you like us to question him?'

'No,' Noah replied, too quickly. He paused casually. 'I'd prefer to keep watching him in his natural habitat.'

'The lab is impressive, isn't it?' The president smiled proudly. 'Just as good as Bio's, no?'

'Almost,' Noah qualified. 'The Head of Immunology there is an old friend. He'll be very interested when I tell him about Khan's toys. I wondered about the tech-level – how could you . . .' his voice trailed off.

'How could we afford it?' the president finished for him, laughing. 'The Western Alliance and the WHO don't fund us as well as they fund Bio. But we find other ways.'

'What other ways? Humour me – I'm your guest.' Noah took a fish patty he didn't want.

'Aid money, of course.'

'Aid is for reconstruction,' Noah replied. Reconstruction projects required Western Alliance approvals, and there was no way the Western Alliance would have approved that laboratory.

'You fund us enough to survive – but not enough to flourish as the Western Alliance has. That's how you like us: poor but stable. I haven't forgotten my national self-flagellations.'

The president soaked his hands in the fingerbowl. 'We feed from many teats, Noah – not just on the scraps the West deigns to throw us when you come here to remind us how WWR was *our* fault.'

'Do you dispute that history, Mr President?'

'I do not – my only correction is that in 2020, when the war started, we *all* hated the Muslims. The difference between your anti-Islamic sentiments and ours was that you weren't willing to own yours. You were so busy claiming "Islam is a religion of peace, some of my best friends are Muslims; it isn't Islam – it's extremism" – it makes me sick.

'You wanted to blow them all to hell too – ISIS, Al-Qaeda, Boko Haram, the whole lot of them. But you're crippled by international law and debilitating political correctness that insists you should respect all faiths.'

Rajasuriya paused to inspect his hands and nails. 'You see, Noah, we knew we hated them. They were savages. We knew we wanted to kill them so we simply began the process – and you let us do it for a while, not just because you needed us as an ally in South Asia but because, well – how shall I say this? We were only doing what everyone else in the world secretly wanted to do.

'We were so close to finishing the job but then the Middle East stepped in. You can't beat oil money, it's endless. The Muslims reacted *so* predictably. Suicide bombing after suicide bombing in the East *and* West. You were forced to intervene and finish it.

'Under the terms of the Armistice Accord, the people and the religions of the East were found guilty – and we were punished. But you take every opportunity to remind us of our sins; it's something we carry like a heavy, wooden cross on our backs.'

'Are you suggesting you resent the ongoing price of peace?' Noah wondered if he was investigating the wrong man.

'On the contrary, I embrace the price of that peace and pay it willingly. Religion in the East *is* a virus and it should be eradicated, not just prohibited. The law isn't strong enough – the West was right to turn to science. The Armistice Accord was a blessing.'

'And unlike other leaders in the Eastern Alliance, you weren't given the Faith Inhibitor, Mr President.'

'I was given a *waiver* – the same waiver that every citizen of the Western Alliance was given without realising it.

'The Information Shield is as important as the vaccine,' Rajasuriya continued. 'Can you imagine what would have happened in the Middle East if those head-banging, bomb-wearing camel-fuckers found out that *this* was the West's solution to war?'

'Even our happy-clappy Christians in the West would never stand for it,' Noah said, 'despite their closet anti-Semitic tendencies.'

'Exactly. The full conditions of the Armistice were never disclosed to people on either side for good reason. The shield has other benefits for me too,' the President said. 'It allows me to deal with my country as I see fit. I don't have to listen to the sanctimonious hypocrisy of the West anymore.

'I don't resent the price of peace, Noah. I resent you – you and your presence here in my country.'

'I thought you liked me.'

The president ignored him. 'This is a sovereign nation and I am its master. How we choose to execute our obligations under the Armistice Accord is our business, not yours.' He leaned back and smiled, wiping the sweat from his upper lip with his red scarf.

'Not entirely, sir,' Noah replied. 'Bio exists in part to ensure that the obligations of all countries under that accord are complied with. We invigilate –' he was about to add *and enforce*.

'Then invigilate. Instead you look at me like I am a monster. Why? Because I dispose of people who disobey me, because I keep slaves, because I admit that I hate Muslims?

'Your government does all of that and more. Different methodologies and different marketing.

'I can see what you think of me, and I don't care. However, I am aware of what you do for a living and how you do it – and I am galled by the hypocrisy of your revulsion.' He raised his chin belligerently.

The president's neck was exposed. Noah saw the artery. He sensed it throbbing in time with the man's baser rhythm. He saw the dinner knife sparkling silver on the table between them. One swift move. Don't retract the knife. Arterial spray is messy. Puncture, drag, hide the body, still warm.

No. Break the neck. Catch the slump forward. Break, drag, hide the body, still warm. A clean kill, quiet escape, fast execution at the gate – and then out into the dark street, the hot night air, already fragrant with star jasmine.

He smiled. 'Dinner was delicious, thank you. What's for dessert, Mr President?'

Chapter 15

Noah pulled his car out of the presidential driveway and waved to the soldiers at the gate. He turned left towards the beach and stopped at the lights. He had no gun and no knife. He cursed. He raised his left hand to his neck, just in case. Wire was painful. He considered reversing hard into the telephone pole he had just passed. Vijay wouldn't be happy. He looked into the rear-view mirror as he spoke:

'Whoever you are, I suggest you put three bullets in my back now while the car's stationary. It's safer for you. Maybe one to the head – my driver is very particular about his upholstery. Or you could just climb over and come sit with me.'

He heard a woman laugh. It was a nice laugh, surprised and friendly. Unafraid. Perhaps she was like him – perhaps her heart rate hadn't quickened at all when she realised she was made.

He moved to the right so she could slide into the passenger's seat. She smelled like sandalwood.

The lights changed and he kept driving. The surveillance vehicle was three cars behind. At most, they would see another silhouette through the darkened windows of Vijay's SUV.

He looked at her properly, and his heart rate did change. 'What did you think of half-time at the Super Bowl this year?'

She rolled her eyes but repeated the required verification phrase. 'It was fine but Bruno Mars's drum solo in 2014 was much better.'

She didn't wait for his response. 'To be honest, I think Bruno Mars was fine too, but 1994 was my favourite year. I remember watching it on a Top of the Pops retrospective. I'm not that old. The line-up was Clint Black, Tanya Tucker, Travis Tritt and the Judds. It was spectacular.'

'I wouldn't have picked you for a country music fan,' he replied, although wary. A beautiful killer was still a killer.

*

Sahara could tell Noah was on guard. She would have been the same. Trust required more than verification phrases. Anything could be extracted under the right kind of torture.

'It's the pain in the melodies coupled with the redemptive hopefulness of the chorus lines. Lose the tail. Would you like me to drive?' she asked.

'No, thank you.'

'It wasn't a question. I outrank you.' At the junction, she reached across and gripped his door handle.

'My turn.' She pulled herself over, giving him just enough space to move into her seat.

'Don't you think we should get to know each other first?' He strapped the passenger seatbelt on.

As they approached the next red light she accelerated and ran through it. He looked behind at the cars that braked in the middle of the intersection. One car went around the mess, chasing them.

'You'll need more than speed.'

'No problem.' She pulled the vehicle to the right, onto the wrong side of the road. Lights flooded into the car, blinding them for a moment. Outside they heard the familiar screech of brakes being pushed beyond their limit; the screams of frightened people; the roar of metal on metal as cars collided.

She crossed three lanes of oncoming traffic and then braked hard again, skidding the car into a tight U-turn using the emergency lane to help her. They were centimetres away from the balustrade.

'What are you doing?'

'Mingling.' She sped back into the flow of traffic, and then cut left at a slip lane that took them into narrow back streets. People crowded around small campfires. The light danced in the ocean breeze, casting long shadows on the crumbling buildings behind them. Ownership of land was delineated by hedges of rubbish and fences of cardboard sheets.

Finally, she finally parked the car, under a broken streetlight.

'Where are we?' he asked. Sahara could tell he was identifying escape routes, but also troubled by the slum surrounding them. She hadn't seen Colombo through a stranger's eyes for many years.

'A Rapture commune. The army and police don't like coming here – unless they're buying the drug. Sometimes they're selling.'

'What's the plan now?' he asked.

'We talk fast, there are still cameras everywhere. They'll find us eventually. Hackman told me you were coming.'

'Are you the other car watching me?' he asked.

'Yes, I was being discreet. Sahara.' She held out a hand politely.

'Noah,' he replied, 'but then I suppose you knew that. Hackman didn't tell me anything about you.'

'There's not much to tell.' She looked in the rear-view mirror. 'How was dinner?'

'As you'd expect.'

'I'd expect it to be repugnant. Rajasuriya is a survivor – and somehow, with him, that means there's always a body count left behind. He has a lot to say for himself, doesn't he? Although, I've never met a quiet despot.'

She saw the corner of his mouth twitch. 'Me neither. He said he actually *wanted* the accord.'

'That's right. The other governments of the East were duped – they agreed to the Global Vaccination Programme but didn't know about the Faith Inhibitor. Rajasuriya knew what was happening – I don't know how. But he agreed to fast and complete national vaccination.'

'And, in return for compliance, he and his family didn't have to take the vaccine?'

Sahara liked the way his dark hair fell forward onto his forehead. It almost touched his eyebrows. He pushed it back again. Perhaps he cut it himself, she thought.

'His brother, the general, insisted on taking it – something to do with the military brotherhood and loyalty to his soldiers. I can understand and admire that. Even assassins have standards.'

'Is that why you're here in Sri Lanka? You assassinate people at Hackman's request?'

'No. I like to think of myself more as a cultural attaché. I speak English, Sinhalese and Tamil. I'm fluent in the religious and cultural practices of the Buddhists, Hindus, Muslims and Catholics here – I'm ambi-religious. I can move seamlessly between the communities. That's why I was assigned here.'

She thought about the babies she'd infected. She'd moved seamlessly in and out of their ward. In and out of their lives.

'Those communities – or at least those religious communities – haven't existed for fifteen years. The languages and some of the cultural practices might remain but your ability to fit into different groups is redundant,' Noah suggested, not rudely.

'I was sent here a long time ago – it was my first assignment and I never left.'

'Why?'

'I don't know – I like the weather. I was born in London – the rain there got me down.'

'I hear this place was genocidal – that doesn't get you down?'

'No, just the rain.'

He smiled finally. There was a reluctant warmth in it. She was right. It was a good smile.

'So were you here when . . .?' he asked.

'Yes, during The Great Pandemic, while Ebola was taking root around the world, I was here.'

'For cultural reasons?'

'Exactly.' She smiled. 'This country is Patient Zero, as it were – it started World War R.'

'I can imagine,' Noah said.

'No, actually, you can't. Despite what you've seen and what you've done for Bio, you cannot imagine the bloodbath that happened here.' Sahara fell silent. She worked hard on keeping those memories buried deep. She knew that when she allowed one through, others – each more horrific than the last – would follow.

Forty-three thousand Muslims had died in the first week of World War Righteous. The rate had slackened eventually. Even bigots have to rest. Over a hundred thousand by the end of the month. It was such a big number.

Stop it, she said to herself. *Stop it.*

They both sat quietly for a while.

Sahara finally spoke. 'Do you think Khan is the ghost?'

'I'm not sure – he's using the AILA – this robot thing – to develop his own vaccine. I don't know if it's the one we're looking for, but I'm sure Bio will want to take a look at it. He's doing something.'

'I've killed men for less, so have you,' she said.

'Yes,' he replied simply.

'Then why not him?'

'Maybe I'm sick of killing; maybe this time I want to stop and be sure.'

'And then kill him?'

'I suppose so.'

She was intrigued by his hesitancy. It wasn't what she expected from a Bio agent. And she was annoyed by her intrigue. It wasn't what she expected from herself.

'It's a little late for a righteous kill, isn't it?' she asked. When he said nothing, she kept talking. 'It's the sad eyes, isn't it?'

'What?' he said.

'You can't kill him because of his sad eyes.'

'Maybe,' he replied.

'You don't talk much.'

'I'm surprised you talk so much.' He checked his side mirror.

'You're the first company I've had in a while. Except Hackman, but that doesn't count because I don't like talking to him.'

'No one does. We all expect him to shake our hands and then break our necks.'

'Do you think that story's true?' she asked.

'I'm sure of it,' he replied. He paused for a moment and then changed the subject. 'The president talked about receiving unrestricted aid. All Western Alliance aid is tied to specific reconstruction priorities – namely public health, disease control and sanitation. Every dollar is accounted for in some way – it either goes to a project or it goes to the president's personal slush fund.'

'His "In Case of Emergency Exile Fund".'

'Exactly. The lab – Khan's lab – is ultra high-tech. It gives him the same capabilities as Bio, but the funding couldn't have come from the West.'

'Perhaps a company?' Sahara suggested.

'Western companies still have to go through the Western Alliance approvals process in order to trade with an Eastern Alliance Government. You can't just show up in Colombo bearing high-tech and potentially dangerous gifts for the locals.'

'So you want to know who supplied the equipment?' she asked.

'Yes – who supplied the equipment, who paid for it and who approved it,' Noah replied. 'If we can follow the money trail we can see who controls the lab.'

Sahara looked at him closely. He had sad eyes too. And a deep scar on his brow bone. 'I'll look into it. If you need anything before we next meet, then just speak aloud in your room. I'll hear you.'

'Because you are omniscient?' Noah raised his eyebrows.

'No,' she laughed. 'Because I've bugged your room.'

'That's impossible. We jam any signals every time we enter the room. We sweep it six times a day just in case.'

'And you do an excellent job. Garner is very thorough. Crawford too – don't underestimate him just because he jokes around. It's how he manages his fear.'

'How could you possibly avoid detection?' he asked, irritated.

'I have better surveillance devices. Keep this with you. Hackman's orders.' She handed him a small disc. 'Insert it behind the battery in your handheld. It lets me record whatever you're hearing.'

'We have our own gear for that.'

'I know – but if you use *my* gear then I can hear in real time, instead of stealing the recordings from your portable server later. Garner and Crawford do actually sleep you know – although not together.'

'Not for want of Crawford trying,' Noah remarked.

'Remember the disc – this war will be won by science, technology and pragmatic politics.'

'Are we at war?'

'We are always at war, it's in our nature; in our DNA.' She leaned over. Noah's left hand reached for a side-arm that wasn't there. His right hand lifted defensively but she gripped his wrist and pushed it back against his chest, before it came close to her. She was faster than him.

'Good night Noah, I'll see you soon.' She gave him a quick kiss on the cheek, surprising them both before she jumped out of the car.

*

Sahara ran the entire way back to her apartment. Once inside, she poured a glass of water from the jug of tap water she had boiled and cooled that morning. It wasn't necessary – Japanese sanitation had taken care of all that – but it was an old habit.

She reached underneath the sink to the back, where, wrapped in plastic and taped to the wall, was an encrypted satellite phone. She charged its battery regularly but never used it. As instructed, she sat with it on her kitchen table every Tuesday, 10.00 GMT for five minutes, staring at it.

And then one day – after seven years of silence – Hackman had called.

He asked to meet her at the Colombo airport and, after the outbreak, she'd been instructed to check in with him daily.

She sat at the table and opened the file he had given her with the small suitcase. She had memorised Noah's biography. His mission history interested her. They had overlapped once – here in Sri Lanka. There was the résumé of kills, not unlike her own. And a résumé of pain and loss. Even deeper than her own. There was a man at the end of his career, possibly his life. She understood that place. She inhabited it herself. It felt good not to be alone there anymore. She was surprised at how good.

She dialled the numbers. 'I've made contact.'

'What do you think?' Hackman replied.

'He's handsome in that deadened way that some agents have.'

'What do you think?' he asked again, ignoring her.

'He'll be fine. I can see why you chose him. He'll build a rapport with Khan and connect with the old man's grief. Will he be able to do the needful when the time comes?'

'No doubt. I've seen him with other subjects who've lost more than Khan – he's implacable. He just pulls out that weird cadaver sidekick and gets the job done.'

'Maybe so, but you've sent him here for a different job. You need to give him time – both of them need time to trust each other.'

'Did you hear about the protest?' Hackman asked. 'He hasn't done that in a while.'

'Maybe everything is finally catching up with him. Are you worried?'

'No, but he might need more help this time.'

'I suspect this time will be his last time.' She flicked through his file.

'That's what they said about you in 2025 – and here we are.'

It was Sahara's turn to ignore him. 'How was Rajasuriya after the protest?'

'Pissed.'

'Good. The security footage was impressive. He was outnumbered but oh so valiant. He has a weakness. I'm going to enjoy working with him.' She smiled.

'Everyone has a weakness. Watch out for him. I want him back.'

'Sure . . . he wants to know about the lab. What would you like me to do?'

'Just get him whatever he needs,' Hackman replied. 'I'll speak to you tomorrow.' The phone went silent.

Chapter 16

It was 6.23 pm in London. The sky was clouded over, casting grey moonlight through Hackman's study window. He made another call to Sri Lanka on the satellite phone.

'I read your report. This new vaccine he's working on – are you sure it gave him immunity against Ebola 48.6?'

'I'm positive. I saw transmission happen and I scanned his blood myself – repeatedly. It was clear,' Noah answered.

'Neeson made that variant especially for this job – he's feeling usurped as the greatest virologist in his own mind. He wants a sample.'

'Sure – would he like fries with that?'

Hackman laughed. 'I hear you met Sahara. She's a good agent, you can trust her.'

'If you say so. She mentioned she's watching us.'

'Everybody's watching you. You'll thank me later for her.' Hackman scrolled through Noah's report on his computer screen one last time and then closed the document. 'For now, get closer to Khan. You know what to do. I'm sorry to ask you to use that.'

'No, you're not,' Noah replied.

'Okay, I'm not – I use everything.' They'd known each other too long.

'He's protecting something that is more important to him than his own life. He is a zealot, even if we don't know what his doctrine is. A zealot with a potential weapon. He will suspect you, even if he appears to like you. He will feel for your loss – and in turn you will feel for his loss. He will use this empathy against you, Noah. He will use it to throw you off the trail; to make you reluctant to pursue him; to make it impossible for you to kill him if required.'

'I've never had a problem before.'

'I know. Let him feel like he's had to work hard to reach you,' Hackman continued.

'Don't let him get into your head,' Hackman repeated. 'You get into his first.'

'Got it,' Noah replied.

*

Noah looked around his hotel room and briefly considered asking Crawford to sweep it again. There was no point if Sahara was telling the truth. Her technology was better than his. He should have raised that with Hackman.

He sat down at the desk and turned the lamp on, directing its amber light onto the back of his handheld. He pulled out the contents of his trouser pocket, separating the disc from the chaff of other coins.

Garner wouldn't be happy with him, he thought as he opened the handheld and removed the battery. But none of them would disobey Hackman.

According to department legend, over a decade ago, when Hackman was a senior and rapidly rising agent, he was placed in charge of the South Asian Sector – six of the hottest Eastern

Alliance countries: India, Pakistan, Sri Lanka, Bangladesh, Nepal and Assam — the largest region ever assigned to an individual.

Within two years, minor and then larger Immunity Shield breaches were detected in South Asia. An investigation detected that the breaches were linked to Hackman's personal security system.

It turned out that Hackman's younger brother, who worked for the Bio-Weapons Development Division, had experienced something that was understandable to everyone, except Hackman: a crisis of conscience.

Apparently Hackman had asked for permission to arrest his brother himself. They met at the gym where they had learnt to box as children and where they still trained together three times a week. Most agents used the department gym with its biodata monitors and situational stress simulators, but not the Hackman brothers. They boxed. And after a session, no more aggressive than any of the thousands of others they'd had together, they sat in the locker room, side by side.

Hackman told his younger brother what he had learned from several months of surveillance — that his brother had infiltrated Hackman's computer and found out about the department's Sixth Virus Eradication Policy, and he had passed documents onto one person at the Christian Coalition who had passed it on to two more people there.

Hackman didn't tell his brother that these three would be arrested shortly, taken to a secure location and interrogated to find out if they had released the information more widely. Then they would be executed. It would be a fast, clean operation.

The younger brother listened, and according to the classified recording of the event, he wept. He didn't apologise. He knew his brother better than that.

Noah remembered the transcript too clearly. He had never read a confession statement like it before or ever again.

Hackman's brother had said, 'I can rationalise using the virus as a weapon – if we don't, someone else will,' the younger man said, his voice shaking. 'I have nightmares – I see the faces of people who've died because of my work. I'm okay about that; I'm prepared to lose sleep so others can live.' He paused and the transcript noted that he had struggled to control his tears before continuing.

'But you – using the vaccine to control how others live; how they believe, or don't believe. People lining up with their children – thinking we are saving their lives.

'What you've taken away from *them* . . . No matter how much we fear them or hate them or blame them for the war, what you've done to them . . . It's wrong, Mikey,' he whispered. 'God help you. God help them, it's wrong.'

Hackman put his arms around his brother and kissed him on the cheek. He held his face to his chest and wiped his tears.

What happened next was a cautionary tale for Noah and anyone who dared to betray Hackman.

He looked up once at the small camera that had been inserted into the fire alarm across from them. Then he closed his eyes and with one sharp movement he snapped his little brother's neck.

A few years later, Hackman was promoted. He became the youngest director of Bio.

Noah replaced the battery over the surveillance disc and snapped the cover of the handheld back into place.

*

Hackman put the satellite phone away in its secure suitcase.

The door burst open, startling him. Three children ran in, laughing. They were in their pyjamas and smelled like Dove soap.

'Sorry, darling.' His wife wiped her hands on the tea towel slung over her shoulder. 'I hope they didn't disturb anything important.'

'No, but I have one more call to make – and then I'll join you for the movie. What have you chosen?'

'*The Goonies*!' screamed the youngest, pushing his way onto Hackman's lap.

'How do you even know about *The Goonies*? That must be forty years old.' He stood up and carried the child with him, tipping him upside down as though shaking him for change.

'Daddy, Daddy,' the boy laughed.

'I'm studying the classics,' a lanky teenager replied. 'It's fifty-five years old – like you.'

'Daddy's not old – he's mature, like a fine wine,' his wife defended him.

'Daddy doesn't drink,' the upside-down child squealed.

'Quite right, it dulls the senses. Unlike *The Goonies*, which always makes me laugh.' He flipped the boy upright and pushed his family out the door.

'Just one more call.' He gave his wife a quick kiss on the lips, locked the door behind them and picked up the phone.

'I need a clean line.' His voice slipped back into the tone he preferred. 'The US,' he waited for the familiar connection to another line and then dialled the number.

'Good afternoon, Mr Sutherland,' he said. 'Are you enjoying the holiday season?'

'I am, although I can't seem to tear myself away from the Bloomberg channel. My wife tells me it's my porn.'

Hackman laughed politely. 'It could be worse.'

'Yes, I suppose – I could be naked, rubbing baby oil onto my remote control.'

'Thank you for that visual, I'm about to watch a movie with my kids. Did you read the report I sent you?' Hackman had been waiting for a response for over a week.

'I did. I admire your audacity. You've got some nerve,' Sutherland said. Hackman could hear him flicking through television channels.

'Thank you. We had a stroke of luck – we'd been watching Hassan Ali for a while.'

'Because you thought he was an anti-vaxxer?'

'He'd started saying things at conferences. It sent up a red flag so we put him on our watchlist.'

'That list must be growing,' Sutherland replied, his voice a little more focused.

'Yes, on both sides of the Alliance.'

'Anti-vaxxers on our side of the divide really piss me off, Hackman. They seem to have forgotten the stench of shit in the streets. Ebola has been eradicated *because* of the Global Vaccination Programme – if you stop vaccinating, Ebola returns. These stupid fuckers want to bite the hand that inoculated them. If I read one more letter from "A concerned parent" I'm going to take my rifle down to a community hall and shoot some bleeding hearts straight through their bleeding heart. I'll violate their right to conscientiously object, using my right to bear arms. How do you like that?'

'I think I like that just fine,' Hackman replied.

'The decoy vaccine this Hassan Ali was using – that's a Muslim name right? It's always the Muslims. Is that impolite of me to say? But it *is* always them, isn't it? I still think you should have dropped a bomb on them back then – finished the Middle East, Afghanistan and Pakistan once and for all. You know you would have done that if you weren't so castrated by human rights conventions. That's why I love the corporate sector.'

'I'm sure history will prove you correct, sir,' Hackman replied.

'It usually does. So thanks to this decoy vaccine we have population sets running around the Eastern Alliance who are susceptible to both Ebola and a belief in God. I'm a God-loving, Ebola-fearing man Hackman, but I don't know what's worse.'

'Quite, sir.'

'What did you do with the Mus– the anti-vaxxer? Hassan Ali? I hope you punished him for his efforts to undermine the Immunity Shield.'

'We took care of it.'

'Good. I see you've sent a man to Sri Lanka in search of this elusive ghost. Can we trust him?'

'Of course I trust him.'

'I just mean, is he the right man for the job? He's a little damaged, isn't he? When did his daughter die?'

'It's been two years. We want him to be damaged – if he was fully functional he'd pull that place apart. He's coming to the end of his . . . professional life. I wouldn't have sent him if I didn't think he was right for the job – you know me better than that.'

'You're right, I'm sorry. It's just those damn anti-vaxxers, they put me in a mood. My wife says I need to let it go. But we all worked so hard to crush Ebola. It was a plague sent to test our resolve – and then these people with more sensationalist concerns than robust science are giving us a bad name, forgetting that we fought a war against the virus. We lost people but with God's angels at our side we won the war. There's no way I'm going to lose the peace.'

'No, sir,' Hackman looked at his watch. He'd heard all of this before.

'Do you believe in God, Hackman?'

Hackman stifled a sigh. 'No, sir. I believe in the security of the nation and the inherent strength and weakness of mankind. I'm an orthodox American.'

'You are that indeed. Our country needs men like us both – you protect it and I make it strong and healthy.'

You mean profitable, thought Hackman. *I protect this country – with men like you and from men like you, if necessary.*

'You've been working hard,' the older man said.

'As have you, sir – your energy and commitment is inspiring.'

'The Lord gave me two hands and only one life with which to make a difference,' Sutherland said.

'I'm sure the Lord wishes the rest of us were more dedicated.'

'The Lord loves us all – the believers, the workers, the sinners and even the non-believers like your good self, Hackman. He'll bring you to His bosom one way or the other.'

He could hear Sutherland smiling. Perhaps he'd found the Bloomberg channel. It had been another good day for the biotechs.

'And the breach in Sri Lanka,' Sutherland asked. 'Has it been fully contained?'

'Completely. The Sri Lankans implemented the containment protocols quickly. Deaths were minimal and easily obfuscated.'

'I suspect a lot of things in Sri Lanka are easily obfuscated. It's a good place to do business. That president knows what he wants.'

'He does and he always seems to get it from one of us.' Hackman swept the files on his desk into a pile and began the security sequence to open the cupboard under his desk.

'Not losing your joie de vivre I hope?'

'Not at all – I'm still joyous about life even if I'm not religious.'

'As I said, the Lord will bring you to His bosom one way or another.'

'Will you be joining us in London for the meeting next week?' Hackman asked. 'Neeson has made progress with the new vaccine thanks to your lab upgrade. He's like a kid in a candy store.'

'He deserves it. He's a patriot *and* a believer. I'll be at the meeting. Abre de Libre and Bio have had a productive year together – we should celebrate and set some goals for the future. What do you think?'

'I couldn't agree more. See you then – all the best for the season, sir.'

'You too, Hackman, enjoy your movie.'

He put the phone down and completed the sequence on the bio-metric panel. He placed the files in the cupboard, and after he heard the satisfying click of its locking system, he joined his children in time for the opening credits.

Chapter 17

Noah spent a frustrating day with Khan. Every time he questioned the doctor about his new vaccine, he dismissed him with a 'Later, later . . .'

Although Khan had welcomed him into his personal laboratory, he never left Noah alone for long enough to check samples, even if Garner could get him past the security panels on the refrigerators.

Noah returned to his hotel room, pushed the door open and took his gun from behind his back. He locked the door.

The room was exactly as he'd left it. And yet –

The bathroom door opened.

'I could have killed you!' he snapped.

'Unlikely. You tend to look first. You trust your reflexes. Lesser agents shoot first and look later.' Sahara pulled out a bundle of papers from her bag.

'I thought these might help.' She sat on the bed and began sorting through the documents: articles from Sri Lankan newspapers, patent applications and annual reports from a biotechnology company called Sri Bodhi that was pioneering medical technology in the Eastern Alliance.

Noah sat with her, not looking at the papers. He didn't put his gun away. He studied her face. A stray curl fell forward across her cheek. She pushed it behind her ears and retied the loose bun.

'This one is interesting.' She handed him an article published six months ago.

Sri Bodhi levels the playing field
Executives from Sri Bodhi spoke passionately at today's WHO conference in Mumbai. The conference marked the fifteenth anniversary of the Global Vaccination Programme, established in 2025.

Mr Prakash, CEO, argued for greater access to the medical technology of the West. He noted the increasing number of rumours and now allegations about disparities in the universal indicators of health between the countries of the West and the East. He noted that dropping mortality and morbidity rates and increased life expectancy should not be the privilege of only one part of the world. It should be the 'right of all citizens' he declared to the standing ovation of the audience.

'World War Righteous is over. History has taught us that for peace to prevail, all countries must prosper, all countries must be healthy. Let us move on from history to a future where science and technology can be given to all, can be used by all, and can be benefitted by all.'

Mr Prakash declared that Sri Bodhi would not be held back by the Information Shield and the 'draconian Western Alliance approvals process'. He said he understood why his company, like all companies and citizens of the Eastern Alliance were not allowed to cross the Information Shield. However, he stated that this geographical and digital information divide disadvantaged the Eastern Alliance.

The current policy implemented by the governments of the Western Alliance and the Eastern Alliance was mediated at the end of WWR by the United Nations (shortly thereafter re-constituted as the Central Western Alliance Government) with non-partisan support from the WHO. It was agreed and enshrined in the Armistice Accord that any technology (including but not limited to medical, military and information technology) developed by private sector companies in the Western Alliance must be approved for trade, sale and implementation in the Eastern Alliance by the Department for Biological Integrity.

At the end of the conference, Sri Bodhi declared it will conduct a review of disease control centres to ensure that their equipment is on par with the equipment of similarly densely populated cities in the Western Alliance.

Mr Prakash reiterated, 'Although India is my home, we will begin our work in Sri Lanka. For too long it has been unfairly prejudiced by the stigma of history. And we will not stop at the boundaries of the South Asian Sector. We will assess all countries in the Eastern Alliance. This is a long-term plan for us – and we hope a long-term relationship with the people of the East – in which we will help build the infrastructure and our own capacity to create happy, healthy societies across both the East and the West.'

Mr Prakash's speech was followed by another standing ovation.

'Sri Bodhi, Sri Bodhi,' Noah whispered, flicking through the other articles. There were more of the same: Sri Bodhi arguing for the technological rights of the East. Sri Bodhi meeting with Eastern leaders. Sri Bodhi giving grants and equipment to hospitals, labs and disease control centres.

'The name means "respected tree".' Sahara explained. 'It's the tree Lord Buddha meditated under – where he achieved Enlightenment.'

'I know.' Noah stopped at another article. It showed President Rajasuriya holding up a shovelful of red earth outside Colombo General Hospital. Three children stood beside him, holding trays with flowers, incense and fruit. The traditional offering to the gods.

In the next frame, the children poured the offering into the shallow hole made by Rajasuriya, patches of damp visible under his armpits. It was a consecration ceremony for a memorial to those killed at the hospital during the first pogrom. Standing behind Rajasuriya, in each photograph, was a much younger but unmistakable Prakash.

Sahara leaned over. 'It's dated 13 May 2030. Ten years ago. That's the holy day of Buddha Vesak.'

'Rajasuriya still secretly plans his personal calendar using the ancient dates.' Noah said. 'He's hedging his bets between God and Bio. Sensible. Do you have a hard line from Sri Bodhi to Khan's lab? More than corporate boasting?'

'Corporate accounts, publicly filed at the Mumbai Stock Exchange.' Sahara pulled out a heavy document from the pile and opened it. Noah read the balance sheets.

'If Sri Bodhi funded Khan's lab – do they own him? And who owns Sri Bodhi?'

Sahara shrugged. 'Wear the blue shirt for dinner tonight. The yellow one makes you look old.'

*

Noah stepped out of the car and onto the broken pavement. Khan's tired house was sandwiched between a block of apartments and a shiny convenience store. At the front door he felt a spear of heat strike his back. He reached for his weapon, ducked and turned.

A motorcyclist honked angrily and kept driving. He was wearing a helmet, jeans and a leather jacket. Not a sarong and singlet like most. Noah's hand went to his back. It was wet.

Khan opened the door. 'Welcome, Noah – you're a mess. Chickpea curry I believe.' The old man laughed. He led Noah through a narrow corridor.

'The bathroom is there. I'll be in the kitchen.'

Noah took his shirt off and looked at it. 'Shit.' He soaked the red stain in the sink, rubbing it hard with a cracked bar of soap.

He opened the bathroom cabinet. It was a small pharmacy: several powerful painkillers, anti-nausea medication and steroids. He closed the cabinet.

'I don't think I can save the shirt,' he shouted down the corridor. 'Do you mind if I grab one of yours?'

'Yes, yes – just find something,' Khan shouted back.

Garner directed him through his earpiece. 'First door on the left, sir – his study.'

Noah opened the door gently, revealing a large table covered in papers. He checked the corridor and entered.

'What am I looking for?' he whispered.

'I don't know, sir. Blink twice to activate your lenses and I might be able to help you.'

'Sorry.'

'No problem.' He waited while Garner scanned the room. 'There is audio but no visual surveillance. I didn't know scientists were this messy.'

'Maybe just the mad ones.' He stepped over piles of lab reports, test results and patient files.

'Secure cabinet, left corner.' He followed her instructions and placed his handheld over the fingerprint panel. His copy of Khan's print worked.

'There are hundreds of patient files in here.' He lifted the first one. 'Patient B276; Anuradhapura Clinic.'

He checked the second, third and fourth files. He skipped to the middle and then the back. The patients were all from the same clinic, and the files all contained brain scans. He heard footsteps and closed the cabinet.

Khan stood at the doorway with a shirt.

'I was just looking at your wife. She was very beautiful.'

'She was.' Khan took the photograph from Noah, touching her face. 'This one was taken at the Great Wall of China. I remember thinking: how audacious – to build such a wall.' He laughed. 'Human beings like walls, yes?'

'Sir,' Garner spoke in his earpiece again. 'The photograph of the wife – I've expanded it. Her pendant is that shape – the mandala that Dr Neeson showed you . . . it must be Khan – he must be the ghost.'

Noah looked around the room. 'Doesn't it hurt? To have all these reminders of her – she's everywhere.'

'Yes it hurts, but the mind heals, Noah – science has taught me that. It is an extraordinary thing. We are designed to regenerate and to fight to live.'

And to live to fight. Khan said *designed*. Not: we have *evolved* to regenerate. There was a difference.

'I think if someone I loved died, I couldn't bear seeing her photos,' Noah said. 'I would try to make myself forget. I would purge my home of every reminder.'

'You could do that?' Khan asked.

'I could. I did.' He remembered the little bear she slept with at night, her thumb in her mouth, her fingers tight around its dangling leg. Maggie had wanted to keep it all – she took most of it with her when she left.

He had thrown the rest and then crumbled, weeping onto the filthy ground next to the bin, oblivious to the passers-by who walked around him.

'What happened?' Khan reached out. 'Tell me, son . . .'

Noah shook his head and backed away, as though reluctant to speak, overcome with grief.

'Come then – help me cook,' Khan said. 'That usually makes me feel a little better.'

In the kitchen, Khan measured the mustard and cumin seeds with a spoon from the lab set. He poured them into the pan and stepped back when they spat and sizzled.

'Aisha used to laugh at me. She said cooking is not a science – it is an instinct. She would take a pinch of this and a handful of that. Her food was wonderful. Science is my instinct. I prefer to titrate my curries.'

Noah reached for the peeled onions and garlic. 'Shall I?' he asked. Khan nodded. He chopped them finely the way Maggie had taught him. She was also an excellent chef. 'Tell me when you're ready.' He lifted up the cutting board.

'One minute,' Khan swirled the spices around. 'Now, thank you.'

Noah scraped the food into the pan, inhaling the familiar fragrance.

'You cut well. Can you cook?' Khan asked.

'Yes, but I don't do it much. I drink a lot of shakes now – nutrition boosters. The flavours are okay.' He shrugged. 'It's only me at home and I'm rarely there. Work.'

'Yes, work – you work too much. I can tell. Your mind is always working through something. You should let your mind rest sometimes. Be still.'

Stillness eluded Noah as much as sleep.

'Pass me the prawns.' Khan motioned to a bowl of cleaned prawns in the sink. They were the size of fat figs. 'Shakes, genetically enhanced, tasteless food, *chee chee*.' He shook his head. 'You'll love these, Sri Lanka's finest.'

He threw the prawns into the hot pan and tossed them, coating them in the spice mix, smiling as the grey flesh curled and turned bright orange. He turned off the cooker.

Noah leaned over the pan. 'Looks great, let me help you.' He took the plates and steaming rice to the table. Khan followed him with the prawns and a dhal curry.

They sat together, silent before Khan spoke.

'You know, even when you purge a place of all things connected to that person, even when you remove all trace of their existence and their past, you cannot truly eradicate the memory any more than you can truly eradicate a virus. The memory remains like a sensation, imprinted on the gene, destined to emerge again.

'When my wife died, I looked to science and I searched for a reason. Why this disease, why my wife – why not another disease, or another man's wife, another man's best friend. Why mine?'

'And what did you find?' Noah whispered.

'I found that all life seeks life. The virus seeks a host so it can live.' Khan reached over and heaped rice onto the middle of Noah's plate. A small mound, capped with dhal on top, its saffron-coloured gravy trickled into the prawns on the side. 'Nature has allowed all of us a place here on this planet. We can either seek to eradicate each other or we can find a way to live together.'

'No – we can eradicate or be eradicated.' Noah shook his head. 'How do you live with a disease that destroys you slowly but surely?' Or in the case of his daughter, quickly and ever so painfully. 'You are a virologist. Your job is to eradicate viruses.'

'So you keep telling me,' Khan replied. 'I do look for more robust vaccines and better cures.'

'Like your new vaccine – the one you're trialling . . .' Noah prompted.

'Yes, my new vaccine. But the *why* of my work has changed for me. I don't do it to kill the virus but to find a way to co-exist with it. Animals that feel they are in danger fight back hard. Their response is always disproportionate.' Khan served himself a much smaller portion of food and then put the ladle down.

'The limbic reflex – I'm familiar with it.'

'Indeed. Then you know that behind your eyes is your amygdala. So small but so powerful. All your violence and fear is right there, Noah. Imagine if we didn't feel endangered – if we felt safe. If the virus felt safe it might not strike out at us.'

'You know as well as I do that the virus has no feelings, no consciousness,' Noah retorted. 'It follows its own genetic imperative to kill in order to live.'

'But *we* have feelings and consciousness,' Khan replied. 'And it hasn't helped us. As I said, the virus and humans are not so different from each other. We could learn from each other I think.'

'All the virus would teach us is how to become more efficient killers,' Noah replied, weary and confused. He looked at his untouched food, the melted ghee in the dhal coagulating on the steel plate.

'No, son, we learned to do that all on our own. We don't need to improve that particular skill.'

'Could the doctors do anything to help your wife?' Noah probed.

'No, nothing – they said the sickness had taken hold too deeply. There was nothing I could do for her.'

'Was she comfortable?'

What comfort was there for any of them? He preferred violence to God. It gave him no real comfort but it was something. The Khans had been denied blind faith in a faithless God. Had they known any comfort?

'Yes. She was comfortable with her disease and her death as she was with her life.'

'And you?' Noah asked quietly, respectfully.

'Eventually – yes. Come to my clinic in Anuradhapura and I'll show you why.'

*

Neeson logged on to his computer with the same password he'd used for fifteen years.

```
Aisha:08122025
```

He pulled up Noah's last briefing. He couldn't believe it. How had Khan decoded his virus and engineered a vaccine so quickly? He felt the familiar surge of awe followed by the equally familiar aftertaste of envy.

He wanted Khan's vaccine. He had always wanted what was Khan's.

'Lead us not into temptation,' he whispered. 'But deliver us from evil.'

Neeson picked up the lab phone and dialled Hackman's number.

Chapter 18

Vijay drove them north from Colombo towards the city of Anuradhapura. Noah held onto his seatbelt and braced himself against the dashboard. Vijay looked at him and laughed.

'Eyes on the road, Vijay,' Noah said tersely.

'My eyes are always on the road, sir, even when they're on your worry-worry face.'

He weaved the car between lorries brimming with vegetables, and open trucks with livestock penned inside. He nosed the car less than a metre away from a busload of school children and then hit his horn repeatedly.

Little girls in starched white uniforms, their plaited hair looped and tied with navy blue ribbons, laughed and waved at them. Noah waved back with one hand, his other ready at his hip.

'Why are we slowing down?' he asked.

Vijay jerked the car to the side of the road, narrowly missing a small teashop.

'My cousin owns this shop. I like to help him, bring tourists and friends. You want tea?' he asked. 'Best in Sri Lanka. Best in the world.'

'I suppose so – tea would be good,' Noah replied.

'What's up?' Crawford noted the dilapidated building from the back seat. 'I'm sure Khan has tea sans typhoid – we've only been driving an hour.'

'Sanitation is our salvation,' Garner quoted the WHO Declaration and got out of the car.

'I didn't know you had family here, Vijay?' Noah asked, his left hand reaching for the safety on his weapon. 'You didn't mention it in Colombo.'

Vijay led them inside. 'I'm sorry, sir.'

'Are you?' Noah replied, not taking his eyes from General Rajasuriya, seated at the table. A pit fire in the corner provided the room's only light. Soldiers emerged from the shadows. They took Noah and his team's weapons from them.

'Good afternoon, Dr Williams, have a seat.'

An old man scurried forward with four silver tumblers of tea. It smelled of cardamom and cloves. Maggie would like it. Noah sat opposite the general.

'How was your dinner with Dr Khan?'

'Delicious, thank you.' Noah counted the soldiers. Eleven. 'He's a good cook.'

'And a brilliant scientist. We're very proud of him – and protective. You've been working hard together.'

'There's a lot I'd like to learn from him, General. As you say, he's brilliant.'

'Can you tell that we have been working hard too? After the Global Vaccination Programme was carried out in Sri Lanka, we diligently implemented the Great Purge.' The general blew on his tea before sipping it.

'My soldiers walked through villages and cities, destroying buildings, books and artwork – anything that reminded people of our former ways. We were happy to dispose of the antiquated icons and delirious ramblings of the previous generation.

'Many of these buildings now sit idle and neglected, blending into the background like the majestic palm trees that we no longer notice.'

'Some have clearly been repurposed. Like this teashop.' Noah motioned to a broken piece of stone in the corner of the room, hidden among canisters of fresh milk. It was half a torso. The fulsome belly and unmistakable curve of an elephant's trunk remained, but the god's head was missing.

Garner sat down next to him. 'Was this a . . .?' her voice trailed away, unwilling to say the word here.

Noah spoke softly. 'Yes. You need to look, but they're everywhere. Like when you go to Rome and suddenly realise that you're leaning against a small . . . tribute to Venus while licking a gelato.'

'I can't see you licking a gelato, Chief. Is there a gun strapped to your body in this scenario?' Crawford replied, still standing.

'Why am I here, General?' Noah asked.

'So that I can help you,' the man replied. 'You Westerners would never have made the sacrifices we did. You're far too rights-orientated. It will be your downfall, if you want my advice.'

'I'll pass that on,' Noah replied.

'You make declarations for yourselves that are impossible to keep. You eventually realise that the only way you can preserve the rights you value is to violate them. It creates an impossible moral tension. That is the great failing of the West.'

'There are worse failings than a complex relationship with the rule of law.'

The general laughed. 'The irony is that you hide in the shadows of black ops and black sites so that your leaders can claim the quicksand of a moral high ground they don't deserve.'

A metallic sound rang out behind them. Everyone in the room reached for their weapons. Even though Noah and his team didn't have any.

Three soldiers stepped forward. One drove the butt of his gun into Crawford's back. The other two slammed his body down on a table, pushing his head into its cracked laminate surface.

The general looked at Noah and spoke softly. 'I wouldn't.'

A soldier poked an iron prod at the pit fire and then brought it out to the general. He took it carefully. Its tip glowed red, like a splinter of the sun.

'In 2020, my brother passed a new law. He decreed that people who were not like us should be branded so they would remember whose country they lived in.'

He waved the iron slowly, adjusting its weight, a heavy but comfortable sword in his hand.

'I ordered my soldiers to enter people's homes. We placed a specially designed branding iron over their own kitchen fires and held them down, even the children.' He brought the iron to Crawford's face, hovering it above his cheek.

'No!' Garner screamed, struggling against the soldiers.

'We seared – *I* seared their skin with a wheel.'

'Don't move, Crawford,' Noah ordered.

'Easy . . . for you . . . Chief,' he gasped. His eyes were wide, his body braced for pain as the iron came closer.

The general rested its tip on the table next to Crawford's red face. Smoke curled up into his mouth and eyes. He coughed, saliva hissing as it hit the iron.

'It was the symbol of our old ways and our *righteous* path; a burning tattoo on their forearm. I'm glad those old ways – and those days – are gone.' He lifted the iron and placed it back in the fire.

The soldiers released Crawford. He stood up and staggered. Garner caught him and helped him to a chair. Noah could see she was terrified but she didn't move from her post, between Crawford and the soldiers.

'I'm tired, Dr Williams. I've fought too many wars and buried too many soldiers.'

'You've buried plenty of civilians too.'

'As have you. Don't lecture me. The young – you always think you're better than your elders.'

'I suppose it depends on what our elders are like. My father was better than me. I'm finally learning to be more like him.'

'Your father was a very lucky man then, to have a son like you.'

'Perhaps.'

Metal clattered again, startling him.

The old man was rearranging his metal plates and tumblers on a stone table, around nine small broken statues. It was a crude but effective drying rack.

Nine stones – one for each planet; each planet a powerful demi-god. Noah's father had believed in the planets.

'They are fickle, son,' his father had said, 'worse than people. You must stay on their good side. Appease them. Ask them for their favour. They can bless your life with riches just as easily as they can curse you with tragedy.'

The planets had screwed Noah.

'Get out of Sri Lanka,' the general said. 'The breach has been contained. There's nothing more for you to do here. Tell Hackman I've given him fair warning. I've given *you* fair warning, because I'm a fair man – unlike my brother.'

'Understood. Is that it?' Noah asked. 'Khan's expecting me.'

'Yes, of course. Khan. It's a long and dangerous drive to Anuradhapura.'

The general reached out and took Noah's hand. He pulled him close and whispered in his ear.

'Be careful, the planets are watching you.'

The soldiers stepped back allowing them to return to the car with their weapons.

'I'm sorry, sir, I had no choice,' Vijay whispered.

'We always have a choice, Vijay.'

'My options were . . . limited, sir.'

'What are you going to do, Chief?' Crawford held a water bottle against his face. He was shaken but not burned. Garner's hands trembled as she pulled a chill pack from the medi-kit.

'My options have always been a little fucked,' Noah replied. 'I'm staying. *We* are staying – and Vijay, you're taking us to Anuradhapura.'

'Thank you, sir.' Vijay started the car. 'Seatbelts please. Nine more hours to go.' He accelerated hard, pulling the car back onto the northbound highway.

Noah braced himself once more against the dashboard. It was only later that he wondered how the general, who had received the same vaccine as his soldiers and citizens, could remember the planets.

Chapter 19

The bus lumbered to the left allowing them to pass. Vijay sped around it. A motorcycle overtook the taxi behind them, and darted into his slipstream. Noah watched the bike in the side mirror – one rider, helmet again, grey saddlebags on the back. He swore silently and turned around.

'The motorbike is fine, sir. Taxi good too,' Vijay said. 'Green car – problem.'

A third vehicle swerved into sight again through the mirror. The green sedan, three occupants, broken left headlight, number-plate obscured by dirt. The car had followed them from Colombo.

The bus drifted back, cutting the sedan off. Noah smiled and settled into his seat.

'Nicely done.'

'Thank you, sir,' Vijay replied. 'I am a professional – you tell all your friends. You want driver in Sri Lanka, you call me – I show you all the sights and lose all your tails.'

Vijay shifted gears and headed into the opposite lane. It was clear but they were approaching a blind corner. He honked his horn again.

Crawford jolted awake, hand to weapon, eyes darting.

'It's all good,' Noah laughed. 'Vijay was just signalling. Go back to sleep.'

They drove through the night and arrived at Anuradhapura as the early morning sun filtered through the clouds. Its pink light made the chaos around them seem benign.

Khan's clinic had been built on top of the ruins of the ancient city, once the capital of medieval Sri Lanka, and one of the most sacred places in the Buddhist world.

Vijay parked the car and the team surveyed the crowds: tuk-tuks and taxis, vans packed with medical supplies, minibuses jammed with people.

Noah recognised the motorcycle parked on a side street, no sign of the rider. He reached for the door handle but Vijay stopped him, a tentative hand on his arm.

'Why are we here, sir? I drive without questions – but I ask you now. Why are we here?'

Garner and Crawford stirred at the back, Crawford stretching noisily.

'Khan said he wants to show me something – so I'm here.'

'This place has many stories,' Vijay checked whether the others were listening. 'It is a sad place, sir. No one comes here anymore except Khan and his patients.'

'It's a medical camp, Vijay – all medical camps are sad, with hope trying to breach the perimeter. Is there anything I should know about this particular one?'

Vijay looked through the window nervously. 'No, no – just be careful. Stay with Khan.'

Noah laughed. 'Yes, I'm sure he'll be able to protect me from his patients.' He checked that his weapons were concealed properly.

'No, no – he'll protect you from the ghosts. He's here to help – they won't trouble him.'

Noah shook his head and opened the door. The astringent smell of chlorobicide couldn't quite mask the stench of the open latrine. Crawford coughed beside him, covering his mouth with his hands. Garner raised an eyebrow but said nothing.

Nurses in white coats, gloves and face masks stood at the entrance. They organised the sea of ragged people into queues, conducting Haema Scans and prioritising illnesses. They directed some patients to a fast-moving line.

'Rapture addicts – of course.' Vijay motioned to the emaciated people siphoned off to a separate building.

'Even my son . . . He says it makes him feel complete. They forget to eat and sleep and function. They just drift . . .'

'I'm sorry, Vijay. I didn't know.'

'We all have our burdens, sir.'

Khan walked towards them. 'You made it! I trust you weren't waiting long?' He held out his arms as if he was about to hug Noah and then dropped them awkwardly, acknowledging his gloved hands.

'I'm sorry about the smell – we have excellent sanitation inside the precinct, but on the outside, the toileting is a little more erratic. I've asked the Ministry of Health to apply to the Japanese again.'

'They make outstanding toilets,' Crawford noted.

'They do. How was the drive? It's a long way from Colombo but well worth the trip.'

He led them through a warren of tumbling stone walls and carved pillars. Medical staff rushed by, nodding respectfully at Khan.

They passed small chambers, each converted into examination rooms and filled with doctors, nurses and patients. Noah glimpsed consultations, IV infusions, dental checks and eye tests. Wires ran along the stone corridors and snaked into each room, supplying power for the lights and portable equipment.

Noah stopped abruptly, staring through a small, square window into a room. He recognised the metal tunnel attached to a bed, the monitors and cold lights. Technicians and doctors fussed around the patient inside the machine. There were two soldiers by its side.

'Is that an MRI?' he asked. 'In there?'

'Yes, it is.' Khan dragged Noah past the door. He was surprisingly forceful. 'I had a funder who recognised the need for such diagnostic equipment. Let's keep moving, this way.'

They passed a hall where workers ladled food for lines of men and women.

Crawford eyed the enormous vats of steaming curry and trays of snow-like rice. 'Chief, come on – I'm starving. I didn't get any tea.' He pleaded.

'You're always hungry,' Garner said.

'Do you mind, Amir?' Noah asked. 'They can catch us up later – Crawford gets nasty when he hasn't been fed.'

'Of course, of course – please, make yourself comfortable. Noah and I will be at the stupa – ask anyone for directions.'

Noah nodded at Crawford and left. They were a good team.

Khan pulled him through the mire of people and up a flight of stairs, out into an open courtyard made of stone, so black and shiny it looked like the surface of a lake.

A massive white stucco dome stood in the centre of the courtyard, like an egg rising from the black lake. At its peak was a spire of gold, pointing accusingly to the heavens.

'In our old language, we called this a stupa. It was very important to the first civilisations of Sri Lanka.'

Noah knew what it was. The stupas held religious objects – this one had stored Lord Buddha's clavicle bone. The Bio file reported that President Rajasuriya now kept it for himself, in his bedside table.

He had seen pictures of Anuradhapura before it was purged. A sprawling labyrinth of ruins: palaces, temples and man-made lakes. It was adorned by parades of stone lions, armed with swords, ready to fight for the Buddha.

What remained of the ruins had been battered by soldiers – Eastern Alliance on the instruction of Western Alliance. Statues smashed beyond recognition, the relics and possessions of Lord Buddha stolen, hidden or destroyed.

'The people who come here – who are they?' Noah asked. 'I was expecting a rural vaccination clinic. Booster shots and blood scans.'

'We do a lot of that here. Walk with me,' Khan gestured ahead. 'We also have a rehabilitation clinic on the other side. I'll take you there later. In the Eastern Alliance, immunity is no longer our main health issue.'

'Drug addiction,' Noah said.

'Yes – Rapture, in particular, but anything that enhances mood. After the sadness of the war, people are hungry for happiness, I suppose.

'We also do preventative medicine, diagnosis and referral, public health education – the usual work . . .'

He led Noah inside the stupa, both of them bending to clear its low doorway and then straightening up as they emerged into a small domed hall, arranged like a hospital ward. An aisle down the middle, a row of ten beds on either side.

'And some unusual work . . .'

'What's going on here?' Noah asked. Men and women rested calmly, some sitting up to smile at Khan. At the back of the hall, MRI, CT and X-ray footage covered an illuminated wall, like an avant-garde mosaic. From that distance Noah couldn't read the tones of grey and black, only the familiar outline of brain scan after brain scan. And tumour after tumour. Uniform and painfully familiar.

Khan smiled but didn't leave the doorway.

'What's wrong with these people?' Noah asked again.

'Nothing is wrong with them. They're dying. There is nothing we need to do for them. In modern medical terms I suppose you would call this section a palliative care clinic.'

Noah narrowed his eyes, trying to decipher the scans at the end of the room. The people around him looked underweight, their eyes shadowed a little, their lips dehydrated. But they didn't look profoundly sick.

'What are they dying of?' Noah asked.

'There are many kinds of illnesses, Noah. We don't heal them. We comfort them, we feed their bodies and their . . . we make them strong enough to face the final part of their journey. We teach them not to fear their sickness but to embrace it.'

'I don't understand what you're talking about. What sickness do these people have? What sickness could you possibly accept?'

'Why must you classify everything? You're such a virologist.' Khan laughed.

'I am. So are you. We're trained to identify and classify disease so we can find a cure for it. If you're not curing these people what are you doing to them? Are you experimenting on them? With your new vaccine?'

'I don't experiment on people, Noah. My patients know what's going on – for the first time since the war, they know what's going on. I'm not hurting them. I've identified a disease – a new one that should not be cured. It should be accepted and explored.'

'All diseases should be cured!'

'No, take it from an old virologist. Some diseases *must* be cured. Ebola must be cured. Tuberculosis, AIDS and malaria too. We have cures for some of our plagues, but not all. We should keep looking. These diseases – they are the simple ones. The ones we can see with our microscopes, scan with our machines and treat with our drugs. We are explorers. We should go further than what we can see, scan and treat.'

'We are scientists, not explorers. What other diseases are there?' Noah asked angrily.

'Life is a sickness. It's killing us from the day we're born.' Khan leaned in and dropped his voice. 'Life without belief in something higher, something greater than yourself. That is sickness. These people – they finally know who they are and where they're going.'

Belief. How did Khan even know the word, let alone the meaning – or its absence?

And then Khan spoke normally, as though he hadn't whispered anything at all, making Noah doubt he'd heard it.

'A vaccine won't eradicate a virus – a virus can never be truly eradicated. It mutates in order to survive.'

Noah didn't know which disease Khan was talking about now.

'Ebola, Noah –' Khan replied, as if answering him. 'One or more strains of Ebola still live happily in the world. We just don't see them very often. I'd hide too if I could. But there are too many cameras as you know.

'We're part of a fragile but resilient ecosystem. It's finely balanced – there are consequences if you remove even one part.'

'That's ridiculous,' Noah replied. 'If all life – human and viral – should be allowed to exist according to some natural law we haven't identified yet, then how do you explain why Nature gave one life such superior survival skills?'

'The virus isn't just a random act of Nature, Noah. It's an act of evolution. I remember a poem, or fragments of it anyway. My memory is so poor these days but these words keep coming back to me.' Khan closed his eyes, searching for the words from a hidden corner of his mind.

'Whenever there is decay of righteousness . . .
and a rise of unrighteousness,
then I manifest myself.
For the protection of the good,
for the destruction of the wicked and

for the establishment of righteousness,

I am born in every age.'

The old man opened his eyes. 'I can't remember the rest. I don't even know who wrote it. But I think the virus has a purpose – all disease has a purpose. It manifests at a particular time in a particular person – or a particular place – for a reason.'

Noah was silent. His head full of questions: *What was the purpose of my daughter's disease? How were the good protected and the wicked destroyed?*

He didn't ask Khan anything.

Instead, he repeated his words: 'For the establishment of righteousness.'

Khan nodded.

Could he be talking about the Sixth Virus – remembering it? Feeling it? He had said *belief*, Noah was sure of it now.

Crawford and Garner caught up with them at the mouth of the stupa.

'You all right, Chief?' Crawford asked.

'I was just explaining to Noah that, in ancient times, this structure was used to house important objects,' Khan said. 'Although no one knows what kind of objects. When we found it, it had already been raided and emptied; local robbers no doubt.'

'We should go, sir,' Garner said. She'd found something.

'Thank you for coming, Noah. I'm glad I got the chance to show you what we do. I must attend to my patients, there are so many today.'

Khan departed with his customary awkward nod of the head and then stopped, stripping off his gloves and shoving them in his pocket. He walked back to Noah and put his arms around him, holding him tight. Noah hugged him back and then laughed to disguise his confusion and comfort, before pushing the old man away.

Chapter 20

Inside the car, Garner rolled out her laptop and talked fast. 'We went back to the MRI room, sir – it was General Rajasuriya in the scanner. He was having an MRI of his brain done. We couldn't see him at first but then the bed moved out of the tunnel and – it was him.'

She typed as she talked. 'I can't access his Haema Scans or medical results. His records are within their high security firewall. Let me try something else . . .'

'What is he doing here with Khan?' Crawford asked.

Noah thought about Khan's palliative care ward. 'Did he see you?'

'What?'

'Garner. Stop typing for a minute, you won't be able to touch those records. Did he see you?' Noah repeated.

'I don't think so – no, Chief. We were at the door – there were people everywhere. He couldn't have seen us,' Crawford answered. 'But can we get out of here, before that changes?'

Vijay drove them past the cluster of small buildings that Khan had converted into clinics.

They went deeper into the ruins, the jungle on one side and the remains of ancient palaces on the other.

'Slow down, Vijay. If we climb up there,' Noah pointed to a building, 'we could get a good view of the entire complex.' Noah remembered something his father had told him about the Buddhist kings of Sri Lanka – they were called the reservoir kings because they had excelled at hydrology, taming water to feed their people. Water, in a dry country, was power. Noah was curious to see what remained. Vijay eased the car to the side of the unpitched road. He got out and looked around.

'We walk from here, please.' He guided them onto a damaged stone staircase. 'We climb to the top, three storeys.' He pointed up and then along. 'Each building is connected to another by stone bridges in the sky. See –'

He motioned to the tall grey arches between the buildings. Each one was made of a single piece of carved stone, long and heavy.

Noah couldn't fathom the engineering that would have been required to lift stone like that. Human ingenuity was limitless when it came to palaces and temples.

And war.

Vijay was leading them somewhere. Noah and Crawford took big strides to keep up with him. Garner held back, often stopping to take photos.

Tree roots had pushed through the broken stones, warping their path. One side was flanked by a wall of granite. It was discoloured – as though someone had tried to scrub away a layer of paint but couldn't obliterate it from the pores of the stone.

'This must have been very beautiful once.' Noah traced the faint lines of what would have been a mural depicting the life of the Buddha.

'It was, sir, my grandfather told me. He said our people used to have folk tales and legends. They passed on their stories through art.

'Some of the older people – they remember what it looked like before the war. There are no photographs or records so we must guess. I think a great king lived here.'

'It's so vast, I suspect many great kings lived here – generations of kings and their subjects,' Noah replied. The afternoon heat had intensified. Sweat pooled under his armpits and his shirt clung to his body. He opened his water bottle and grimaced at its iodised taste.

'Yes, a long time ago we were a proud and accomplished civilisation. So many stories.'

'Do people talk about this place?' Noah asked.

'People try not to talk about anything. Talking is dangerous. Walking is better for health.'

Vijay started up the last segment of stairs. He leaned against a broken column at the top, before stepping over the threshold onto a wide platform that overlooked the hills around them.

Noah followed him, his hand on his side-arm. The platform formed the hub of a giant wheel. Long stone bridges radiated outwards like spokes, towards the rooftops of other buildings. He turned and counted them – eight bridges connecting eight buildings. It was impossible to see the mathematical perfection of the design from the ground. From the sky it would look magnificent – the Buddhist wheel of righteousness built out of stone.

A massive tree towered over them from the centre of the platform, its roots clawing through the earth, creeping up its trunk, like a tangled mass of veins and entrails.

'This is Sri Maha Bodhi,' Vijay slipped into his tour guide persona. Noah looked up sharply at the name.

'A sapling of a great tree in India was brought here to this island and planted thousands of years ago.'

'Why?' Noah asked.

'I don't know, sir.'

Noah knew. It was a sapling from the tree under which the Buddha had achieved Enlightenment: the tree of liberty.

'Do you like the view, sir?' Vijay asked.

From this vantage point, they were surrounded by the anatomy of an old city and its temples, some parts subsumed by the encroaching jungle. But sometimes bones jutted out defiantly, wanting to be seen. The complex extended for kilometres.

As his eyes adjusted to the glare, Noah noticed large pits of freshly turned earth between the ruins. He focused his binoculars on one and then another. The binoculars' scale function gave him numbers in the corner of his vision. The pits were as big as tennis courts. There was a rusted bulldozer next to them.

'What's that over there, Vijay?' He handed the binoculars to the driver and pointed. 'Past the aqueduct – see the bulldozer? Are they excavating the site?'

Vijay looked through the binoculars and then muttered under his breath. 'New ones.'

He pushed the binoculars back at Noah.

'New ones? New what? What am I looking at?' he demanded. Crawford and Garner stood beside him, their own binoculars focused on the patchwork of fresh earth, the dark pigment contrasting against the green skin of the jungle.

'Four new graves,' Vijay whispered. 'No one comes here anymore, except Khan and his patients. And sometimes the army. The smell was too strong. I knew as soon as we arrived.' He shook his head. 'You explore here, sir, or rest for a while. I need to check the car. Make sure she is ready for drive back to Colombo.'

Vijay turned and scrambled down the steps before Noah could reply.

He recognised the squares of darkness now, the purpose of the bulldozer. He'd been a part of that purpose before. He had dug the earth more than once when he was young. Rolling bodies into a pit, a mask hiding his shame.

'The army has been here.' Noah repeated Vijay's words.

'Doing what?' Crawford asked.

'Hiding the dead. This is where they put the bodies.' He turned back towards the team. 'You two get back to the car. Make sure Vijay is okay.'

'Anything wrong, sir?'

'No, all good. I'll meet you down there.'

He looked at the graves again through his binoculars. Panning east, there were at least ten more stupa domes, white and red, rising from the earth like welts. Each one had been a place of worship only fifteen years before.

Worship. He stood under the tree and closed his eyes, but he refused to pray the way his father had taught him. Instead he chanted the names of the dead: the people he'd killed, the lives he'd ruined; always starting with his father's name and always ending with his daughter's. He wore their deaths like a penance.

A voice barked in his earpiece.

It was Crawford. 'He's gone!'

Noah's eyes snapped open. 'Repeat!'

'The car, it's gone. Vijay's gone – tracks leading back the way we came.'

Noah jumped up and ran to the edge of the platform, stopping at the first bridge. He saw the plume of dust trailing behind the green sedan as it hurtled towards them, closing the distance rapidly.

'Incoming. Green sedan.' He raised the binoculars. 'Three passengers, armed. Take cover, I'm coming down.'

'Shit. Weapons hot, Garner,' he heard Crawford shout. 'Where the fuck is Vijay?'

'Crawford, take cover,' he repeated. 'Evasive action only, we're barely armed.'

'Got it, Chief,' Garner replied in his ear. 'They've seen us. Three men.' He could hear her running as she spoke. 'Heading to the scrub, south-east of your location.'

He drew his weapon and turned towards the stairwell. Footsteps coming fast. Someone shouting commands. He turned back towards the bridge and holstered his gun. He would need both hands if he fell. If he could get across it, he could escape through the connected building. He ran hard, heart pounding, his lungs sucking in air.

He crossed the first bridge without looking down, skidding to a halt on the second platform. In the corner of his eye he saw someone emerge under the boughs of the tree. Only one bridge between them. The man stepped onto it tentatively, arms stretched out. He inched forward and shouted.

Noah didn't stop. He turned and bolted along the rim of the wheel, across to the next platform. He found the stairwell and plunged down. The first bullet hit the stone behind him. And then another, but he was gone. Running; scared but in control.

He reached the bottom of the landing just as a shadow fell across it. Noah saw the man first and didn't break the rhythm of his run, charging forward instead. The man's face turned from surprise to fear, his hands lifting but not in time. Noah grabbed him by the shirt, drove his knee into the man's gut and heard the air whistle out. The man groaned but held onto his weapon. He raised it in both hands. Noah gripped the man's wrists together and pushed them away as the gun fired by the side of his head, deafening him for a moment, the silence replaced by a ringing in his ears.

He smashed the man's hands against the unforgiving stone of the stairwell and kicked the gun away. The man tried to follow it, bending down. Noah dropped his elbow between the L3 and L4 vertebrae, heard the familiar crack, and shoved the man out through the swinging shutter that covered the window opening.

He didn't look back, already moving through the room, arms outstretched, his gun an extension of his body, his finger ready to pull the trigger as soon as he detected movement.

He remembered something Sahara had said: *You look first and then shoot. You trust your reflexes.*

He took refuge against a pillar, the coolness of the stone comforting against his sweaty back. Across the room he could see another staircase to another bridge, another part of the wheel rim. To reach it he would have to expose himself to whoever was still out there. Two more people, definitely armed, hopefully short range. The ringing in his ears subsided. He could hear the sound of his own breathing again.

He wiped the sweat from his forehead and eyes with one hand. He checked the gun and pulled out his second weapon from his ankle holster. That was his nervous tic. Check and check again. It calmed him. Three deep breaths and he ran.

He was halfway across the room, lunging behind broken statues, when bullets ripped through, spraying shards of stone and wood around him. He ducked and ran, firing his gun and then diving behind a heavy wooden table that lay on its side. He used it to shield himself, shooting towards the origin of gunfire. Bullets came back. He listened, waited, then fired once and listened again. The shooter moved. Shooters. He heard heavy, even footsteps and a shuffle. One man was dragging an injury. Noah's odds were improving. He turned his body, threw a hand above the table and shot again, twice. One gun out, the other ready. He swapped, listened and waited – one, two, three steps closer. Patience. Four steps. He shot.

A man screamed, another shouted. Someone called for help. And then the staccato sound of bullets again, only one source now but ricocheting in every direction. Wild, panicked fire, not targeted. Even so, any bullet could be fatal.

He reached the stairs and slipped, a mistake that saved his life as another barrage of bullets and shrapnel hit the wall next to him.

Leaning on his right side, not lifting his head, he fired two rounds in the direction of the shooter, not sure if he hit anyone.

A fleeting regret for what he was destroying once again. Then a fire ripping across the nerves on his left side as one bullet and another slashed him carelessly. He stumbled again, crying out in pain and anger, feeling the warmth of fast-flowing blood, the cold rush of adrenaline as his brain urged his body to flee. It hurt to breathe. Bruised ribs were acceptable. Blood was not.

Gunfire again – but this time the low, muffled sound of a silencer. And then another one. That wasn't right.

He pressed his earpiece. 'Garner, there's another shooter. Can you see anything? I need eyes, I'm hit.'

'Negative. I'm looking.'

He scrambled up the stairs, his hands still gripped around his weapons in a rictus of fear but not panic. He didn't panic. Fear would drive him forward. Fear would get him from the stairs, three flights to the platform to the bridge. There was an aqueduct near the fourth spoke of the wheel – if he could reach it, he could dive into the lake below.

Or he had to run back now and take out the rest of these men – two, maybe three. He didn't have enough bullets. He needed to keep going. At the top of the first landing, he stopped. The stairwell was not like the others. It had caved in on itself. It led nowhere.

Shit.

He looked around the room searching for a way out.

Another shot – again, like a bullet passing through water or the metal cylinder of a silencer. He ducked as he heard a man scream below him.

Another bullet, close range; the crying stopped. He turned to the stairwell, gun raised. He controlled the tremor. He waited for the shooter. He was ready.

Garner's voice came through his earpiece, loud but calm. 'I see you, sir, you're on the first floor.'

'Exit to the roof blocked,' he whispered.

'North-west window. It opens onto scrub not stone. You can jump. We'll be there.' He ran to the window, his side burning.

It was jammed shut. He dropped his guns, turned his body on one leg, lifting the other simultaneously, breaking through the rotten wood and pushing out half the frame with it.

He ignored the pain surging through his side. The room lurched. He bent down and grabbed his weapons. One empty, one half empty. He shoved them back in their holsters. He wouldn't die unarmed. He had felt a silencer to his head before. Execution was no way to go.

He pulled himself onto the ledge, stopping just in time to judge the distance to the ground. Not too far to jump but he needed the scrub. Ten metres to the left. Not exactly *under* the window. He cocked his head for a moment, listening for footsteps rushing into the room. He couldn't hear anything above the sound of his own heavy breathing, a blood beat hammering in his ears. Where was the last man? What was he waiting for?

He had to move. He pushed his body against the wall, the heels of his boots pressed into the stone, his arms and hands splayed to grip and balance himself, feet shifting quickly but carefully towards the corner of the building. He left a thick stain, a comet's tail of brilliant red against the wall. He stopped at the corner – underneath him was a large cluster of banana trees, their fan-like leaves reaching up towards him.

The voice in his ear shouted, 'Jump, Chief – now!'

He jumped, the leaves catching and collapsing under his weight but buffering his fall. The pain in his side radiated up towards his chest. A car screamed towards him. He tried to roll himself out of its path but floundered in the crushed branches and fruit, its sugary mucus sticking to his body. He was blinded by the headlights and tried one more time, desperately, to roll left.

*

Sahara stood at the edge of the window and peered out. She saw the car brake hard and a door fling open. Crawford was dragging Noah and shoving him inside. Vijay was swearing. Someone barely closed the door before the car accelerated, skidded past the spot where she had hidden her motorcycle and then blazed down the dirt road of the ruins, towards the highway.

He was alive, she was sure of it. For the first time in many years, it mattered to her. She relaxed her shoulders and allowed her right arm to drop to her side, the silencer cold and heavy in her hand.

Chapter 21

Noah collapsed on the back seat of the car. Crawford threw him a bottle of water. Garner pulled out her blade and cut the shirt from his body, the strips heavy with blood. She moved his arms and torso around, feeling him methodically for more injuries.

'Gently,' he choked. He took a gulp of water and emptied the bottle on the main wound, crying out, then gritting his teeth.

'All clear,' she said tersely. Noah thought he could hear a slight tremor in her voice. Crawford opened the medi-kit for her. She ignored Noah's pain and began cleaning. 'No entry or exit wound. Flesh tear only. Three strikes.'

'And you're out,' he whispered, drinking heavily from a second bottle.

'A lot of whining for a flesh wound,' Crawford noted. The corner of Garner's mouth twitched as she strapped a dressing to Noah's left side.

'Getting old.' Noah tried to turn back to see if they were being followed. He gasped loudly at the stabbing pain in his lower chest.

'Getting soft. I'll need to tape that,' Garner replied. 'Bruised ribs, maybe one broken.' Her fingers expertly felt the ridges of his chest. 'Most likely bruised. Stop crying.'

He nodded. 'Where were you?' he asked Vijay.

'Washing the car.'

'Washing the car?'

'He was, sir. We found him whistling and washing by the aqueduct,' Crawford said.

Noah stared out the window. One more strike and Vijay was out, if not already.

They drove back in silence, all three of them with hands on weapons, breathing hard, bodies rigid with tension.

Vijay kept to the back roads. He constantly checked his mirrors; his hands tight around the steering wheel. He didn't ask any questions and Noah wasn't sure he had any answers.

One thing was certain: he and his team had seen too much at Anuradhapura.

At the hotel, the front desk was unusually empty. Anything out of the ordinary made Garner reach for her weapon.

Most things made Crawford reach for his. 'I'll go first.' He stepped forward, gun out.

Vijay threw his coat over Noah's bloodstained body. Garner wedged herself under his shoulder and helped him up the stairs. He tried to push her away but she caught him each time he stumbled. They heard a bedroom door open. He felt her tense beside him.

The hotel manager emerged from a room, flushed and sweaty. He rolled his sleeve down but not before they saw the bruised puncture mark on his forearm. He hid his Rapture addiction well.

When he saw Noah, he nodded and kept walking, his glazed eyes averted. He knew better than to stop.

Inside Noah's room, they dragged him to the bed. Crawford threw him a fresh shirt. Garner swept the room.

'It's all clear,' she said.

'Sweep it again – we're missing something,' Noah said.

Garner looked back at him. 'Sure.'

'I'm not criticising – I just want to be sure. I need to talk to London.'

'Sure,' Garner repeated. She and Crawford walked the room in a grid, doubling over each other's steps, checking and checking again.

'It's clear – sir,' Garner said.

'She means, *still*, sir.'

'Yes, thank you, Crawford. I can read her pauses too. Okay, let me do this call and then we'll meet in Garner's room in twenty minutes. Sweep that twice too. Be ready – we should expect trouble.'

'Are we staying, Chief?'

'I don't know – I'm not done yet. Twenty minutes,' he repeated.

They left the room.

Noah inserted the battery into his satellite phone and called Hackman.

'What the fuck just happened?' Hackman yelled. 'Drone footage shows gunfire. Gunfire! First you jump into a civilian protest and now you start a fire fight. You're supposed to be with the WHO. What the hell is going through your head?'

'The WHO hasn't been fired on in two decades,' Noah replied. 'Thanks for your concern.'

'Are you okay?' Hackman asked.

'No major injuries. The team is secure. Any thoughts on who that was?'

'Your guess is as good as mine.'

'My guess is Rajasuriya – we're being watched everywhere we go. Today we saw something he might want to keep quiet.'

'What?'

'Mass graves.' Noah paused. He didn't say anything about the general.

'We all have those, Noah – burial of the Ebola dead wasn't always done the way people would have liked. But we did it the best we could at the time. We chose containment and hygiene over culturally acceptable last rites.'

'I know that.' Noah's father was taken away in a truck. 'This wasn't Ebola. There were fresh graves – fresh and large. Rajasuriya sure does like his privacy on this side of the Information Shield.'

'We don't interfere with another sovereign nation.'

'Since when?' His head ached. Every part of him ached. Since when had they courted monsters? Since when had they not?

'Sri Lanka is peaceful – that's what matters.'

'It's called negative peace, Hack.'

'What?'

'Negative peace – where conflict has ended but structural violence still exists, leading to unequal power relations –'

'Institutional abuses, unequal life opportunities and conflict once again. I know the definition of negative peace. You're a spy not a poli-sci professor. Institutional abuse is our modus operandi too – just because you don't like the way *he* does it, doesn't give you the right to shoot your mouth or your gun off. Rajasuriya's been on the phone for the last hour. He wants you out. Frankly, so would I if I were him. This is a colossal cock-up. He says the hospital outbreak has been contained, the WHO can go home and there's certainly no need for Bio to be there shooting at people.'

'They fired first. We just stopped for some sightseeing.'

'After you visited Khan's outreach clinic in Anuradhapura!'

'You asked me to get close to him – that's what I was doing.'

'Then give me something – before Rajasuriya's soldiers storm in to your hotel and march you to the airport, or worse. Do you have his new vaccine?'

'We're colleagues, not blood donors.'

'Get a sample, Noah.'

'I need more time.' Noah fumbled with the buttons of his shirt. 'I'm getting closer to him. I think he wants to share it with me . . .'

'Because you're not blood donors but you are *friends*?'

'Something like that,' Noah replied. 'He talks to me about . . . things, but I don't know if it's because he trusts me or . . .'

'Or what? Maybe he's manipulating you. Can we at least conclude he's responsible for the Immunity Shield breaches? Do we know which other population sets he's breached?' Hackman asked.

'I don't know – he's just not what I was expecting. We've been looking for the usual suspects – a bioterrorist, or an anti-vaxxer who thought the Global Vaccination Programme was either detrimental to public health, a violation of personal choice or part of a terrible pharma conspiracy. He's not any of those. Sometimes I think he's trying to tell me something – like he's been expecting me. Sometimes I think he's just talking to himself, unaware that I'm there, assessing him.'

'Has he suggested a philosophy as yet? I know how you like to understand a man's philosophy before you –'

'Before I kill him? Yes. That's my preferred approach although it hasn't always worked out that way.'

'You need to let go of the past, Noah – it's holding your career back. Anyway – Khan's philosophy – what does he say?'

'He suggested the virus is an evolutionary culling mechanism – that its existence is normal and from time to time it performs a vital service. An act of evolution.'

'An act of evolution or an act of God?'

'He didn't say God,' Noah replied. It was almost the truth.

He wasn't ready to tell Hackman about the patients at Khan's clinic either. Or the poem. He recognised it immediately – it was from Chapter IV of the *Bhagavad Gita*. His father quoted the Hindu scripture all the time. It was beautiful in Sanskrit and terrifying in English.

'He's not the first person to suggest there is a cycle to life that's sometimes expedited by Nature. There's a certain logic to it,' said Hackman.

'There's no scientific basis for it. And only organisms with a consciousness have logic. Nature has no logic at its disposal. Hence the phrase "random acts of Nature".'

'God has logic,' Hackman replied. 'If Khan was a God-fearing or a God-loving man, he might see Ebola as a divine plague sent to cull the wicked.'

Khan had been clear. The words of the *Bhagavad Gita* were clear. God manifested himself on Earth from time to time to destroy the wicked and restore righteousness.

'God is dead, deaf or indifferent,' Noah covered for the old man.

'So you say. Khan might think differently. Does he remember God or a God-like power?'

'Asked and answered, Hackman – he hasn't mentioned anything godly.' Noah wanted more time before he decided what to do.

'Is he developing a virus to perform this evolutionary cull? That would be the obvious path for a man of his skills.'

'No – he's not a killer.'

'How can you be so sure?' *Because I'm a killer*, Noah thought. *I can always recognise them.*

'He wants to save lives through science – that is very clear. We're scanning his hard drive daily. So far the science is all about developing multi-strain vaccines and cures. And before you ask, every life is important to him. He's not one of those "sacrifice one to save the rest" kind of guys.'

'You mean like me. Do you think he's the ghost?'

'I – no. He's building up to something but I don't know what it is. I don't think he's good for the decoy vaccine.'

'But he's good for something else – find out what it is and then make the call. You either turn him over to Rajasuriya so he can deal with him in his usual way, or if you think he's undermining herd immunity, then you know what to do with him. Are we clear?'

'Very.'

'Are you sure, Noah, because you don't seem yourself. You know I trust you. You've always been solid, despite everything you've been through.'

'I'm solid. I'll turn him over or I'll take care of it myself. What about the president?'

'I think I can buy you forty-eight hours,' Hackman replied. 'I still have some currency with him.'

Hackman disconnected the phone.

Noah put the phone back in its hiding place. He thought better of it and shoved the phone in his belt under his shirt. He unlocked the bathroom window – not that a lock would stop her. Nor did he want it to. He found himself looking for her often – wanting her to be there.

'Sahara, if you're listening, the men who attacked us at Anuradhapura. Can you access the surveillance footage on the green sedan? It will take my guys time to hack the Sri Lankan Government's facial re-cog programme. I want to know who they are and who they're working for. I'm going next door – see you there, if you can make it.'

He spoke to an empty room.

*

Noah paced the dark floorboards and then sat down abruptly on Garner's bed, breathing deeply.

'Let me change the dressing sir, it needs to be kept clean.' Garner pulled away from her computer. Crawford sat at the table next to her, scanning through data on two screens.

'Keep working, I'm fine.' He went to the window that looked over an alley behind their hotel. That would be Sahara's most discreet entry point. She was good at not leaving surveillance footprints unless she wanted to.

'Expecting someone?' Crawford asked.

'Sort of – let's narrow the search.'

They were researching Sri Bodhi, the company that had funded Khan's laboratory. 'I want to know who owns Sri Bodhi and who runs it – they are reaching into disease control centres in the region for a reason.

'Crawford – look at everyone from mid-level execs and scientists to the CEO. Crosscheck their names and any comms with Khan and all of the vaxxers who were involved in the breaches. Check emails, phone records and funding applications. What are the degrees of separation between these people? Find out where they might have met, even casually. Start with conferences or meetings that were held in the four cities where the Immunity Shield was breached – and Colombo.'

He paced back. 'Garner – pull Sri Bodhi apart. Who's higher up that food chain? Who owns it and who does it own? I want to see the family tree.'

Crawford sifted through hours of surveillance footage of WHO and biotech conferences. He identified interactions between the vaxxers who were involved in the shield breaches – they all knew each other and they all worked at hospitals that were heavily funded by Sri Bodhi. However, none of them had any connection with Khan.

Garner mapped out Sri Bodhi's corporate family tree but Sri Bodhi was its highest point in the Eastern Alliance. It had thirteen subsidiaries which, like Sri Bodhi, had made financial contributions to Eastern governments, hospitals and labs. The focus of their funding was disease control and epidemiology.

She shook her head. 'We still don't know who owns Sri Bodhi. There is a mother company somewhere – but not on this side of the shield. It looks like it's the subsidiary of a Western Alliance company. Look at its financials – only four percent of its budget is spent on research and development. Most of its budget is operations and manufacturing – on actually making the equipment.'

'You're saying this is a shell company for the technology. They make and distribute it – they're not developing it on this side?' Noah asked.

'Not unless some other unrelated Eastern Alliance company is developing it for them and they're buying it whole. But their acquisitions are factories, land and equipment to make more equipment. When you probe into who they do business with in the East, it looks like the transaction history of a supplier, not a developer. Their business partners are just smaller suppliers. They provide the small parts *to* Sri Bodhi or they are distributors *for* Sri Bodhi.'

'That can't be right.' Noah started pacing again. 'We're right back at the original problem. If this technology is coming from the West to Sri Bodhi and then to Khan, it has to pass through the Bio approvals process.'

Bio.

Noah stopped pacing. He pulled out his satellite phone, punched in his access code and dialled the number he called more often than Maggie or his mother.

'Patrice, how goes it?'

'Noah, this is a surprise. Shall I connect you to him?'

'No, I was calling you.'

'Me?' He could hear the surprise in her voice. The worried pause. He waited, listening for the telltale sounds of other people coming on the line. The call would be recorded as a matter of standard protocol.

'Yes, you – I think I'm almost done here. Can you look something up for me, please? It's always the way, isn't it – when I'm on our side I want info I can only get from the other side.'

She laughed. 'What do you need?' Her voice relaxed a little.

'Sri Bodhi.' He could hear her fingers moving on the keyboard, searching as he spoke. 'It's a biotechnology company here. Got its roots tangled up in every hospital and lab. Best friends with all the people at disease control too. I want to know who owns it. Can you run a check – simple one really, I could do it myself if I was there. I can't even get the New York Stock Exchange directory from here and that's probably all I need.'

He waited.

'If you've got time – I'd also like to see every application the parent company has made to Bio for technology they want to export to the East.'

'Unfortunately it's a little more complicated, Noah – can I work on it and call you back? I have access to your line.'

'Sure. I understand, corporate veils and all. I owe you. Is there anything you'd like me to bring back? More tropical fruit perhaps?'

'Raw turmeric, actually. It's supposed to stave off Alzheimer's. Good for your immunity too. We only get the processed powder on this side but, ideally, you're supposed to steep the raw root in water and drink it.'

'Like tea?'

'Exactly like tea. When you get back, let's have a cup of tea together,' she said. 'There's never enough time these days, don't you find?'

'I couldn't agree more. Turmeric and tea it is, thank you, Patrice. Tell Hack I'll call him later, I don't want to be late for work.' He disconnected the phone.

He wasn't sure what disappointed him more – Patrice's deflection or Sahara's failure to show up.

'Sir, take a look at this.' Garner turned one of her screens towards him. 'The staff lists for Sri Bodhi and two of its subsidiaries. This is their Visiting Fellow, seven tours of duty over the last fifteen years, some more than just a brief visit.'

The face on the screen was Neese – Dr Jack Neeson, Head of Immunology at Bio.

'Check the location of his fellowships,' Noah replied, too sharply. He swallowed hard.

'He was at the four Ground Zeroes, six to twelve months before the gaps in herd immunity were detected there.'

'Look for points of connection between Neese – Neeson and the vaxxers.'

Garner searched again. 'Nothing obvious between them, sir – wait . . . here: they've attended some of the same conferences and select focus groups, but no recorded interactions or meetings. That's odd – it's like one or both of them have made an effort not to leave a contact trail behind.'

'What about Khan and Neeson?'

She looked again. 'Numerous points of contact – a joint fellowship, research papers together . . . I'll collate this for you.'

'This is all wrong,' Noah murmured to himself. He remembered the Bodhi tree at Anuradhapura: its thick, muscular trunk with roots that crawled up its body and fanned out in a wide radius, gripping and strangling the branches as they reached for the sun. Roots tangled everywhere. The tree of liberty.

Blood had seeped through his bandages. He looked down at his chest, not recognising the wound for a moment.

'You need to see this, sir.' Garner touched the screen to open a document. 'This is a requisition form – twelve months ago, Neeson asked Sri Bodhi to provide the AILA Reina to Khan's lab. Why would he do that? Are you okay, sir?' Garner asked.

He didn't answer for a moment. Traitors never looked like traitors.

Chapter 22

Noah sat down heavily on his bed, one arm against his blood-soaked bandages. He kicked off his boots without unlacing them. Lifting his shirt, he wiped the blood and sweat with a towel. He took out a bottle of water from the minibar and drank quickly, not stopping until he had drained it.

'I need a shower and then we can talk – should I sweep the room?'

Sahara smiled and stepped out of the bathroom. 'It's all taken care of. I hope you don't mind but even Garner and Crawford can't hear us.'

'That's fine as long as you aren't going to kill me.'

'No, not yet.' She smiled sweetly. She had a bag slung over her shoulder which she set down on the table. It was large enough for at least five weapons. 'Let me help you.' She followed him back into the bathroom.

They stood chest to chest, Noah poised for an assault. She peeled his shirt away from the wet bandages and pulled it over his head. For a moment he was blinded by the fabric, his abdomen tense, waiting for the cold insertion of metal. Nothing.

She surveyed his body critically, shaking her head at the wound. She took a small knife from her pocket and cut the bandages away, ripping the dressing from his skin. He cried out and reached for the wall. Sahara stepped closer and held him up.

'Quiet, I wouldn't want Garner to get the wrong idea about us. She'll burst through that door, guns blazing.'

'I don't think she's interested,' he replied. She was close enough for him to lean down and touch her lips with his.

'She's not but she cares for you. They both do. They care for each other too,' she mused, 'although neither will admit it.'

'I'm sure Crawford would admit it,' he said, his lips barely parted. The side of his body felt scorched.

'Crawford makes it sound like he's attracted to her. He'd never admit that he's actually in love with her. No place for love in our line of work. He probably learnt that from you.'

Noah swayed forward. She held him against her body, bearing his weight.

He bent his head and placed it on the top of her shoulder. They were the pieces of a puzzle. He had loved once. He kissed her. He never wanted to stop.

His mind flashed between images, present and remembered.

Her eyes closed, her skin wet and slippery as he pushed her gently against the shower wall, his arms on either side of her, one hand reaching up to turn the water away from them.

She laughed, pulling her lips away. 'I'm cold now.'

He laughed back. 'Let me warm you up.'

'Predictable, but if you must.'

The curve of her scapula to her clavicle, her hammering heart, the strong ridges and plates of bone that protected her, the softness of flesh and tautness of muscle.

He followed his memory down.

To her pelvis, slender but strong enough to cradle their child. Her body changed in his hands and he traced the trail of darkened pigment and hair. He knelt and rested his head there, against the swell of her belly, shining and hard. Skin stretched to its limit. She put her arms around him and held him close. He wept.

A rush of cold water cut through the darkness.

Black sandalwood hair spilled over him.

'Shower quickly and I'll patch that up.' Sahara turned and left him on his knees, half naked. He slumped against the shower wall and slid to the floor. He sat among his torn clothes and bandages, until the room stopped spinning and the water washed away his blood.

*

Sahara assembled the contents of her shoulder bag on the table. Noah sat on a stool opposite her as she methodically set to work with gloved hands. She dabbed the wound dry with sterile gauze and then poured hydrogen peroxide over it. He cried out.

She shook her head disdainfully. 'What kind of pain training do they give you people these days? You ought to be able to sew this up yourself.' She sprayed an anaesthetic over the open flesh and surrounding skin, muttering to herself. He caught the word 'baby'.

Kneeling beside him, she threaded the curved suture needle and held the shaft with the forceps. He knew the drill: needle straight down into the tissue, curve the wrist, get the right depth, take the needle across and pull – tight but gentle traction, join the edges of the skin together, not too tight or you buckle it. The first tie is always a double. Suture knotted. And then again and again and again: needle down, curve and pull.

'You're fast.' He winced. The anaesthetic could have been stronger.

'I don't usually have much time when I'm doing this.'

'Do this a lot, do you?'

She laughed, not breaking the rhythm of her needle.

'Done.' She inspected her work and then covered it with a new dressing. She wrapped a fresh thick bandage around his waist, reaching behind him to take the roll around his back, and then in front of him, across his stomach. With each turn of the bandage, her hair brushed against his chest, her breath against his arm.

If he dropped his arms he could touch her. He could place his hands around her waist and pull her into him. He could hold her; and be held.

'Finished.' She pinned the bandage tightly. 'Ask Garner to change the dressing in four hours. You'll have three lines of a scar.'

'I've got worse. You heard the conversation with Khan?'

'Of course, I tapped in through your handheld.'

'Who else heard it?'

'Does it matter? They'll hear it eventually.'

'I just want to know how quickly you report these things back to Hackman.'

'I want to know why you didn't tell him the entire conversation.'

'I didn't think it was relevant.'

'Really. *Paritranaya sadhunam, vinasaya ca duskrtam*,' she quoted the verse from the scripture that Khan had recited at Anuradhapura. She knew it in Sanskrit and English.

'*Dharma-samsthapanarthaya, sambhavami yuge yuge*,' Noah finished for her.

'Very good, you *do* know your Hinduism. I find that attractive in a man.'

'My father taught me.'

'To answer your question, I can't report in real time. I call him or I wait for him to call me on a sat phone, like the one you have. The Information Shield works for us and against us. It's not easy for me – or you – to get information out. Sometimes I just take the intel and make a decision myself.'

'And what decision would you make in this situation?' Noah asked.

'I would wait until Hackman called me. I would watch each of the players in this long, twisted game and I would wait.' She stood up and ran her fingers through his wet hair. Leaning forward, she kissed him slowly. He lifted a hand but she shoved it back down to his side. She touched his face and studied his injuries and scars, tracing them with her fingertips and then her mouth. Their lips connected and disconnected – parting to parry and chase each other. And connect again.

Yearning rushed through him. Too much adrenaline in his body. Not enough blood in his brain.

He held her back and pushed the hair from her face.

'Let me look at you.'

'Not too closely, Noah. You won't like what you see. Keep moving, stay in the shadows. Isn't that what they say?'

'I prefer the sunlight.'

'We don't deserve the sunlight,' she said, sudden tears in her eyes.

'Everyone deserves the sunlight,' he replied.

She kissed him again. 'I've wanted to do that for a while.'

'You're attracted to damage?'

'I am damaged.' She smiled a crooked, wistful smile. 'Sleep. I'll watch over you.' She helped him up and led him to his bed.

Chapter 23

Hackman surveyed the group gathered around the polished oak table: Neeson from Bio on one side, and the contingent from Abre de Libre on the other.

Alec Sutherland had brought his inner circle: the chief financial officer – a fearsome woman, ironically called Angela Rose; Adrian Reid, the head of research and development, who jumped every time Sutherland questioned him and looked like he preferred the laboratory to the boardroom; and Christopher Tolley, the head of strategy, a man who may have been born in a boardroom.

Hackman had toyed with the idea of bringing more staff but Sutherland didn't need to be patronised with window dressing – he knew the right people were in the room or listening to the room.

Neeson touched the large screen at the front and pulled up a map.

'As you know, we haven't had a naturally occurring Ebola outbreak in thirteen years. The last was a brief resurgence in Syria shortly after the end of World War R. It wasn't even a resurgence – we hadn't fully eradicated the virus in the Middle Eastern Section.'

'You can't blame yourself for that, Dr Neeson – after what those people did to the Holy Land, they had it coming to them. ISIS were a bunch of savages and if millions of Muslims had to die with them so the world could be free of that tyranny, then so be it. "The Lord will make pestilence cling to you until He has consumed you from the land where you are entering to possess it."'

'Deuteronomy? Old school. A lot of smiting, blighting and perishing in that book,' Hackman remarked, his face unreadable.

'You know your Bible and yet you don't believe it.' Sutherland shook his head.

'It's not my Bible – but I do respect it, sir. Dr Neeson, you were saying?'

Neeson was staring at Sutherland, distracted. 'Um, yes – the Middle East, no,' he picked up his papers and then put them down, turning back to the map.

'No naturally occurring outbreaks in thirteen years,' Hackman prompted. 'We've had a clean bill of health since the end of the war.'

'Yes, thank you. Ebola is no longer a threat. The virus has not mutated or naturally resurged. Our monthly Haema Scan results and quarterly spot checks have been consistent. Herd immunity is stronger than it's ever been, I'm pleased and relieved.'

'Thank you, Dr Neeson,' Hackman said. 'I think I speak for all of us when I say I am extremely relieved when you are relieved.'

'That's right,' Sutherland laughed. 'When you're worried, Doctor, I start stocking up on antivirals, broad-spectrum antibiotics and bottled water. How did you go with the false positives?' Sutherland always made it sound like a pregnancy test.

'We feigned an Ebola 47 outbreak in Ciudad la Paz, Mexico. It was completely plausible that this remote village had missed vaccination boosters. The local herbalist was doling out traditional medicines too, which was helpful. We framed it as local complacency. The body count was low – five families, heading for the nearest hospital in the back of a truck. We picked them up three miles from home. We could show they'd been isolated en route and hadn't infected others.'

'Yes, you don't want to start a panic. I saw the photos – what did you give them?'

'Just a mild haemorrhagic fever, not Ebola-related at all, but identical symptoms.' Neeson replied.

'"Just a mild haemorrhagic fever"? I didn't know there were degrees.'

'There are degrees of everything,' Hackman said. Like degrees of market capitalisation.

'It was a waterborne bacteria,' Neeson explained. 'We inserted a Catholic priest into the village and one Sunday, at the end of mass, he gave the selected families a special communion. We were able to localise the infection that way. The village had recently experienced the flu so we used that in our messaging too.'

'What was the message?' Sutherland asked.

'The usual – Ebola still exists and it follows its own life cycle that we can't predict. Hence vaccination and the three-year boosters are our best line of defence. The flu can undermine the body's ability to fight Ebola, etc., etc.'

'So make sure you take your Ebola booster and your flu vaccination on time? Genius. You should work in marketing, Doctor, not science.'

Neeson smiled weakly. Sutherland didn't notice.

ADL prescribed an aggressive programme of regular booster shots that protected herd immunity, *and* generated an eternal pipeline of revenue in a world terrified of disease. It worked well for them, Hackman thought. Sutherland was a genius, of sorts.

'The second outbreak – in India – that was good work, both of you.' Sutherland flicked through the file.

'Thank you. We thought it was the . . .' Neeson swallowed hard.

'Smart thing to do, wasn't it, Dr Neeson?' Hackman jumped in. 'Once we had interrogated Hassan Ali and his colleagues, we returned the vaxxers to their lab. Then we infected it with the Ebola Strain 50 we developed with you. We'd been looking for a safe test site. The laboratory in India was perfect. Lockdown was instantaneous and impenetrable.'

'Excellent. Ebola 50's military application is promising, once we have a vaccine of course,' Sutherland added quickly.

'The president will approve the virus when we are certain we can protect our own people from it,' Hackman repeated the words of the Secretary of Defence.

'Yes, yes,' Sutherland dismissed him. 'Ebola 50 is a breakthrough in engineering. I feel quite fatherly about it.'

'It is a breakthrough – it works quickly,' Hackman agreed. 'We placed Hassan and his colleagues in the lab, infected all three and withdrew. They made contact with staff by 8.17 am; they were symptomatic twenty-eight minutes later and three minutes after that the place was locked down. They died by lunchtime – the entire lab. The Indian government was so terrified of the fallout, they asked us to handle the clean-up – alone. No questions asked about the source.'

'Excellent. The test is very promising. Ebola 50 is a fine example of what can happen when government and science come together to protect the people.' Sutherland raised his hands as if to applaud Neeson, and then locked his fingers together in a gesture of half-prayer.

'You all deserve to be congratulated.' He looked at Neeson and his own head, Adrian Reid. Neither looked like they wanted to be congratulated.

'I know it's hard to focus on the bigger picture here – the vision that Hackman and I have for a safe society. But I want you to keep reminding yourselves: society needs to be ever-alert to the risks that surround us. People are too easily strayed, too easily relaxed. We now find ourselves dealing with petitions and protests. These groups – Concerned Mothers Against Vaccination, Stop the Corporate Injection, the Anti-Vaxxer Network or Forum or whatever it is –' he disconnected his hands and unfurled his fingers as he listed the groups, his hand shaped like a gun pointed accusingly at Hackman.

'They're lobbying to repeal compulsory vaccination. They want exemption clauses – exemption clauses! On the basis of philosophy, conscience and religion, of all things. Where in the Bible does it say you should deny your children life-saving immunisations? Those vaccination exemptions were abolished twenty years ago for a reason – because all of those conscientious objectors gave kids measles in Disneyland, years after it should have been eradicated.

'And where were those conscientious objectors when Ebola was ripping through their town?' Sutherland vented. 'They were stepping over the bodies of the dead, and pushing their loved ones out of the way to get in line for the trial jabs.

'If people can't be trusted to act for the greater good, then they must be forced to act for the greater good. They should wear their vaccination welts with pride – with *pride* not self-righteous indignation. I told you, Hackman, when they started all this "right to choose" bullshit – I told you to shut them down!'

'The government can't storm the offices of community groups on behalf of biotech companies. That's just not how a democracy works,' Hackman answered wearily.

'Don't tell me how democracy works,' Sutherland slapped his hands down on the oak, sending a ripple through the meniscus of its red surface. 'It's my money and my company that's invested in ensuring the safety of this democracy.'

'It's my agents on the frontline,' Hackman replied.

'Don't forget who invented the vaccine. Five years of war and disease – the world was dying and I stepped in with a solution.

I gave them back their lives, their wellbeing. Now I have to listen to those bleeding hearts at the WHO, with all of their rhetoric about public health and responsibility. Don't you forget who started this,' he said menacingly.

Hackman was well-practised at dissembling. He nodded agreeably but he was certain none of them would ever forget.

'No, sir,' Neeson spoke slowly and clearly, diffusing the diatribe. 'As a scientist, I am indebted to you. I will never forget your contribution to public health and safety.

'As a Christian, I am inspired by you,' Neeson continued. 'You're doing God's work and we should all be grateful. "I testify unto every man that heareth the words of the prophecy of this book. If any man shall add unto them, God shall add unto him the plagues which are written in this book."'

Hackman saw the muscles in Sutherland's jaw relax. The blotches of red on his neck remained but didn't crawl further up. Hackman found himself surprised by Neeson, for the first time in a while.

'Good man. Good man,' Sutherland said. 'We need more men like you.'

'I trust you were pleased with the outbreaks,' Neeson said. 'They were controlled and completely untraceable. You need men like Hackman for that.' He turned to Hackman who nodded.

'Thank you, Dr Neeson – and you, Hackman,' Sutherland replied. 'I was pleased. We saw people heading back to the clinics to get their boosters on time. Mission accomplished. I'm sorry people had to die to achieve it – I pray for all those poor souls. They're martyrs even if they don't know it.'

You also saw an immediate spike in share price and investor confidence, Hackman thought.

'Let's talk about the Sixth Virus now,' Sutherland said.

'The eradication policy is going well. We see no resurgence of religion or faith in the Eastern Alliance,' Hackman replied.

'That's not entirely true – the ghost has tapped into a network of vaxxers who ...' Sutherland flicked through the file in his hands again and quoted: 'Who feel an energy inside them that's guiding them to administer a decoy vaccine.'

'There are two issues there – the ghost and –'

'I want to deal with that first,' Sutherland interrupted.

'Of course,' Hackman replied smoothly. 'Our target, Khan, has the expertise and the equipment. He even told our agent the virus is Nature's way of culling.'

Sutherland laughed genuinely for the first time. 'Clever man. Has he published any papers on that? We couldn't have asked for a better ghost. He'll make a fine bioterrorist; or perhaps a disgruntled virologist turned anti-vaxxer. Either way he'll be hated and remembered.'

'Indeed. We're very optimistic about him.'

'What about this new vaccine he's working on? I presume you'll end that when you end him?'

'Of course. Vaccine development is the purview of Bio and ADL – and no one else.'

'I'm glad to hear it,' Sutherland said. 'And the second issue – the unnamed energy. What the hell is that? A Rapture addiction gone too far? Those vaxxers all sounded like they'd been cooking their own chemical compounds, if you know what I mean.'

'Yes, sir.' Hackman laughed in spite of himself. 'We have no idea what they're talking about. There is a consistent philosophical motivation with all of the vaxxers who reached out to the ghost. They are driven by this same energy, it wants to be loved, it wants to be remembered –'

'I read the transcripts too.' Sutherland cut him off again. 'I want to know what *you* think it is.'

'I don't know. We're investigating. Our man is getting closer.'

'Yes, your man. Is he investigating this Khan or is he trying to turn him? He's meant to be laying breadcrumbs, not charging into ex-religious sites and teashops. You said he was sub-functional – this looks more like malfunctional. Call him off.'

'What?' Hackman and Neeson looked up sharply. Noah had never been called off a mission.

'You heard me. Call him off.'

'I can't. He'll know something's wrong.' Hackman knew Noah was already suspicious, but he kept that to himself. He and Noah went back a long way. Even Neeson and Noah. Perhaps they were getting sentimental in their old age. Perhaps they were just getting old.

'So what if he gets suspicious? He's paid to execute that job, not question it. Call him off or I will tell Rajasuriya to take care of it. I'm sure he'd be only too happy to.'

He stood up and cleared his throat. 'Thank you for the update and the coffee, this has been helpful. I have another appointment but the rest of the team will take over now. Why don't you walk me out, Hackman?'

'Of course, sir.' Hackman stood up quickly.

Sutherland nodded at his R&D director. 'Adrian, show Dr Neeson our new fertility scanner. You'll like this one, Doctor – it's all about going forth and multiplying.'

Hackman led Sutherland out of the conference room towards the elevator. Inside, he pressed L and stepped back next to the older man.

'A fertility scanner?'

'Our data mining of the Haema Scans and other medical records indicates that reproduction rates have flatlined but our Fertility Booster vitamin range is still one of our best sellers.'

'As good as your Deca-Vit injections or the Immunity Builders?'

'No, of course not. And nothing surpasses EBL-47. My vaccine is still our number one.'

'Of course,' Hackman replied. Abre de Libre's sales of Rapture in the Eastern Alliance were doing very well too – but they were strictly off the balance sheet. Sutherland found a way to profit from most health concerns.

'People want more babies than they're making,' Sutherland said. 'The fertility scanner aids the process. It takes human error out of the equation.'

'I seem to remember that was part of the fun, sir. Should I call your driver?'

'No, he'll be waiting for me.'

At the lobby, Sutherland walked through the automatic glass doors first. His driver held the door to the limousine open for him.

'Don't let me down, Hackman – and don't let your man down.' Sutherland spoke to him through the window. 'Lock in the ghost and then get your team out of there. We can't be responsible for everyone. How was the movie?'

'Sir?' Hackman queried.

'*The Goonies*. Did the kids like it?'

'They loved it. It's an American classic.' Hackman hadn't told Sutherland what movie his children were watching.

'It sure is. I'll see you next time.' Sutherland knocked on the window and his driver started the car.

Hackman put his hands in his pockets and shuddered as a cold wind swept off the Thames.

Neeson joined him, more prepared with his winter coat, collar up. 'He's gone back to his five-star rectory?' he asked, voice neutral, eyes ahead.

Hackman laughed. 'He has. I had no idea you were so Bible-literate.'

'You can talk. I'm literate in many religious scriptures, it's not just the Bible for me anymore.'

'Diversifying your faith portfolio?'

'Hedging my bets?' Neeson laughed. 'There is a God and all religions, if followed properly and lovingly, will take you to Him eventually.'

'I'm surprised. You used to be so . . . monogamous.'

'The wisdom of age, I suppose. I like to read and quote scriptures . . . more promiscuously now. My favourite is the *Bhagavad Gita*; it's a Hindu text.'

'I know what it is. So you're a scientist by day and a multi-faith scholar by night.'

'Khan used to say religion and science are just different methodologies for deconstructing our shared reality, and understanding the same universal truths. I think he was right.'

'Jesus, now you're scaring me.'

Neeson laughed and then replied, 'Here's a quote for you, from the Gita. I want you to remember this one: "Now I am become Death, the destroyer of worlds."'

'You made that up – isn't there some rule against making up religious doctrine?'

'There ought to be, but I didn't make that up. In 1945, Robert Oppenheimer said he thought about that verse when he watched the first testing of the atomic bomb he created. He saw the tremendous fireball rise into the sky and the words of the god Krishna came to his mind: *Now I am become Death, the destroyer of worlds.*'

Hackman shivered. 'Anyway, thanks – back there. You didn't have to step in. I've handled worse.'

'I know. I wasn't trying to help you. I just prefer science to the greedy, narcissistic ravings of a self-appointed messiah.' Neeson kept his voice low.

'Don't talk about Jesus like that,' Hackman teased.

'Jesus loves you too, Michael.'

'That's what Sutherland tells me.' He laughed as they headed back to the warmth of the Bio Building.

Chapter 24

Noah woke up, his wound dressed, his body bruised and still tired. Through the haze of the muslin net around the bed he could see Sahara. She had positioned the armchair next to him, facing the door, with a clear shot if she needed it.

'The men who attacked you . . . they won't come again, at least not today. You killed one and the other two are off the payroll indefinitely.' She pulled the net back for him.

'There was another shooter too. Whose payroll?' he asked.

'President Rajasuriya's. He's trying to encourage you to stick to your job. No more excursions. Just complete the investigation into Khan, confirm he's the ghost and then get out.'

'Are those instructions from the president or Hackman? Because they sound like Hackman's and the last time I checked Bio wasn't working for Rajasuriya.' He pushed himself up from the bed and shifted his legs over the side to the floor.

'It's hard to say who's working for who.'

'Who are you working for?' he demanded. He stretched his torso, getting a sense of his pain and range of movement.

'I work for stability.'

'Stability. I've been hearing that word a lot lately.'

'It's a good word – a good idea if you've seen the opposite.'

'We've all seen some instability in our lives. I'm not sure the compromises we keep making to fend it off are worth it.'

'You wouldn't say that if you were here when it all started. Instability looked a lot like carnage.'

'Explain it to me then, Sahara – help me understand why this is all worth it. I won't judge.'

She looked at him sadly. 'You *should* judge. It was such a long time ago but I see it . . . all the time.'

'Tell me –' He reached for her but she moved to the window, peering through a gap in the shutters.

'Sri Lanka – the great Buddhist nation,' she whispered.

'The keeper of the faith?' he asked.

'Indeed,' she said bitterly. 'Man sensed God and yearned to love him. To understand him.'

'I used to feel it too,' Noah whispered.

'The Buddhist monks had a power over the people that Rajasuriya couldn't compete with. A deep and primal hold that was born hundreds of years before democracy.'

Noah nodded. 'Men worshipped monks because God hadn't shown himself for so many years.'

'That's right. God seems absent except when he rains down death on us, like a divine drone strike. But monks are no more than men who yearn for influence and power. Rajasuriya allowed them to translate their bigotry into laws.'

'General Rajasuriya told me about the brandings . . .'

'Yes, the brandings – even the Jews shuddered at that one. They remembered a different time, and a different tattoo on the forearms of their forefathers.

'But the brandings came later – first the monks insisted that Muslim women must dress like all other citizens. The president conceded and Muslim women were required to remove their covering. When they failed to do so, they had it removed for them. Such a simple thing: a piece of cloth, the kind you'd buy at a fabric store anywhere.' She paused, lost in thought.

'What happened?'

She told the story she had lived and tried to forget:

'A Muslim woman, a Sri Lankan citizen, entered the public hospital where she worked. She was completely covered by her traditional garb. She walked past the security guard and smiled, her eyes behind the gauzy veil were warm. And every day of the previous four years that she had worked there, this security guard had nodded his head happily and smiled back.

'But on this particular day – 12 January 2020 – he was different. He had been briefed and then reprimanded and then warned. If he did not enforce the new hospital rule, a regulation mandated by national law, he would be fired alongside her.

'When I interviewed him later, he asked me, what could he do? He had a family, he needed his job. He said he approached the nurse. He asked her once, twice and then a third time to remove her face covering. She refused. He called a female guard. He was careful not to touch the nurse himself, respectful as he was of what he understood to be her customs.

'He looked at her. He said that her naked face was as beautiful as her eyes. Not a conventional beauty but an unassuming symmetry of pleasing, calm features.

'He briefly thought it was a shame that such a peaceful face was not seen by the patients she served. He thought they would be comforted by it and there was so little comfort in the world.

'The nurse left the building and returned home. She never worked in the hospital again although she was needed soon enough. Little is known about what happened to her afterwards.

'Perhaps the city had been waiting for the right moment. Perhaps the world had been waiting for that moment whether it was right or not. A meeting was held at the main mosque in

Colombo that night. Only the men gathered: old and young, the weak and the strong, all of them angry.

'They decided that they would accompany their women to work and the next time one was asked to remove her covering and shame herself in front of others, they would defend her honour – with force.

'And so it began. The Muslims pulled out sticks and the Buddhists pulled out knives. The army watched for a long time, letting the mobs do their killing until they could stand it no longer. They were desperate to kill too.

'India watched across the narrow Palk Strait, wringing its hands. Its citizens were Hindus, Muslims and Buddhists. Its neighbours were Muslims. They lived side by side, uneasy and on guard. It stepped into the fray, backing the Hindus. Pakistan stepped in, backing the Muslims. Neither particularly cared about Sri Lanka, both simply wanted a naval base in the Indian ocean.

'Most of the world dismissed it as yet another conflict in Sri Lanka. But then Malaysia, Indonesia, the Middle East . . . the Middle East intervened to assist its Muslim brethren.'

She looked at Noah sadly.

The rest was history. The past that determined their present. The conflict had escalated across Asia and then the West faster than any biological pandemic could.

'I was training at Rochester when it started. Westerners and US military bases attacked in the East. Then retaliatory attacks in the West against completely unrelated Islamic communities. You know that all Christians think that all bearded dark-skinned men are Muslims, don't you?'

She almost smiled. 'It's not just the Christians. The beards confuse bigots generally.'

'Why did you stay?'

'I don't know – a misguided sense of duty perhaps. Maybe trauma.' She shrugged self-consciously. 'I keep returning to the scene, reliving it, trying to redo it – trying to undo it. I don't know. I keep seeing the women and the children . . .'

He knew. He saw them too.

'Contagion.' She shuddered. 'Neighbours, friends, colleagues – Sri Lankans who had known each other their whole lives, grown up together, whose children played together – they hunted and slaughtered each other in the streets.'

'Rage is infectious, particularly when the patient's underlying immunity is weakened by the racism that's inherent in us all.'

Sahara nodded.

'How did you survive?' he asked.

'I copied the Hindus. I painted the Buddhist wheel of dharma on my door and waited. The Hindus joined the conflict eventually. They had an unsettled score . . .'

'There are other ways to settle a score.' Noah knew he was wrong as soon as he'd said it. In their world, there was only one way to settle a score.

'I should have tried harder,' she said.

'To do what?'

'Make the agency listen. I was young but I wasn't naïve. I understood the politics of this region, the bloodlust that sits patiently underneath the veneer of peaceful religions. It was fermenting, a hidden cyst waiting to erupt and poison the bloodstream.'

'Don't tell me you feel responsible.' He wanted to hold her shaking hands; her tense and weary body.

'We are all responsible.'

'No – this one is on the monks and Rajasuriya. Not you and not us – we are responsible for a lot of the world's problems but not this one.'

'No?' she replied. 'This one was predictable from the start. We protected Rajasuriya. He'd already slaughtered one ethnic group and he was simply moving onto the next, like any other methodical tyrant. We knew what was happening and we all ignored his savagery because we were so desperate to have an ally in this region. We needed him and he knew it.'

There was nothing Noah could say. He had heard it all before, straight from Rajasuriya's own mouth. He'd read it all before in history books about other countries, with other dictators. The same outcome.

No, not the same outcome, he thought. WWR was so much worse.

'I reported back – about the monks and the riots, the police. I kept telling the agency to intervene, to talk to Rajasuriya, to tie conditions to the aid they were pouring into the country, to impose sanctions – anything. Anything,' she repeated.

'What did they say?' he asked, afraid of the answer.

'My orders were to stay out of matters of territorial sovereignty.' She laughed harshly.

'I could have gone higher up the chain of command but I was afraid, unsure – you're trained to follow that chain no matter what, to trust your superiors. To doubt them ... well you just don't, do you?'

He didn't answer.

'Western troops were eventually deployed in the East and it might have ended there. But something else happened to weaken us all.'

'Ebola.' Noah replied. It started with war but ended with Ebola.

She looked towards the door. A shadow passed under it but no one came.

'I think maybe they wanted the Buddhists and the Muslims to slaughter each other. Or they wanted things to escalate here, to justify an intervention and settle things once and for all.'

'Maybe they just underestimated how badly things would turn out,' Noah said. 'That religion and Ebola would feed each other's rage and take all of us to the brink of annihilation.'

'Maybe,' she walked over and held his face in her hands. 'Be careful, Noah. You're Hackman's man, but Rajasuriya belongs to Bio. They need him here. He maintains the status quo – the *stability* they've created – so they maintain him.'

She spoke one last time before she kissed him: 'They protect him in a way they would never protect you – or me – even though one day we will both die for them.'

She pulled away.

'Stay with me – please,' he asked.

She shook her head.

'Where are you going?'

'Out your bathroom window, across the wall and then up two floors.' She slung her bag over her shoulder. 'I can access the rooftop from there and jump to the building next door. That way I don't trigger Garner's perimeter alarm.'

'You can make that distance?'

'Just. It's the landing that hurts. I think of it as my daily strength training.'

'Daily?'

'Yes, I like to pop in every day and check on you, sometimes while you're sleeping.'

He laughed and stood up slowly. He took her hand and placed it against his face again.

'Thank you for what you did for me today. I know that was you at Anuradhapura.'

Sahara shrugged. 'There's a car outside the hotel and outside your balcony window. Plus the cameras in the corridor, elevator and foyer. The hotel manager is on Rajasuriya's payroll too, even though he looks away for you guys.

'Everyone has a price or a fear, Noah. See you soon. Get some rest, you look terrible.'

Chapter 25

Noah recognised the sloped silhouette of the man sitting on the bench. The hospital garden was deserted except for the crows that danced around Khan. He threw the fried chickpeas further away and laughed as they fought dishonourably for each remnant.

Noah sat next to him. 'You seem very popular with the locals.'

'They're just using me.'

'All people use each other, even friends.'

'I can see why your wife left you.' Khan laughed and then stopped when he saw the cuts on Noah's face.

'Shaving accident. Nothing to worry about. Do you come here often?'

'I like to sit on this bench.' Khan studied his face. 'I feed the birds and organise my thoughts before work. What happened?'

'I like benches too.'

'You're far too young. Bench-sitting is an old man's game.'

'I feel old.' He took a handful of chickpeas. The oil was seeping through the bag. 'I have a bench in London. I sit there and watch people.'

An orderly pushed a heavy bin through the glass doors into the courtyard. There were three bins in the garden. It wasn't needed. He brought it out anyway.

Noah scattered the rest of the chickpeas at the birds and stood up. 'Are you ready to work?' He dusted the salt from his trousers and watched the orderly, who tried not to watch them.

'I was born ready,' Khan replied, laughing.

*

Noah pulled the protective suit on gently. The cuts on his body were healing but stung against the friction of the synthetic.

'It's been over fifteen years since you went to the West – do you remember much of it, or miss it?' Noah asked.

'I'm old, not senile,' Khan replied. 'Of course I remember it. I miss some things – like Italian coffee. And my old colleagues. I'd like to see them again. You might know one – Jack Neeson. We used to call him Neese.'

'Yes, I know him well.' Noah was certain now he didn't know Neeson well at all.

'Do you work with him?' Khan's eyes brightened.

'I do – he was my mentor and supervisor for my PhD. He's based at the . . . Bio headquarters in London. He's done very well there.'

'Yes, he is a great scientist. We wrote papers together in our youth and shared much of our research. I did an infectious diseases fellowship with him in London. Virology can be a competitive field – there's money to be made in cures for certain diseases. But Neese was always in it for the science – he enjoyed the exploration, the search for answers as much as I do. I miss him.'

When Neeson had identified Khan as a possible ghost, he had given Noah the Bio file on the man, but no personal insights.

'He's a prolific publisher – I don't know how he finds the time.'

'Yes,' Noah remembered something. 'He's always sending me papers. I don't read all of them and then I get in trouble.'

'You should do as he tells you. Ask him what he thinks about the importance of viruses in ecosystem rebalancing. In fact, he's probably already sent you a paper on it. He believes in one hundred percent herd immunity but he doesn't think total eradication is the key – co-existence is.'

'You mean you're not the only crazy one?'

'That's exactly what I mean. When you see Neese, please do tell him I miss working with him. I have something for him, a gift I think he'd find useful. I've been meaning to get clearance for months. Perhaps you could take it back with you?'

Khan stood up. Noah looked at him expectantly. 'My wife was very fond of him too. Now, is your precious Western body suitably protected?'

'Yes, thank you,' Noah replied, confused.

'Good – Devi is going to show us something special. Devi,' Khan called.

'Good morning, sir. I've prepared the samples, just as you instructed.'

'Thank you.' Khan turned to Noah. 'For the last ten months Devi and I have been developing a specific form of gene modification.

'I've had the idea for a while but it was only when Devi arrived that I could catalogue, locate and shape the precise amino acids I needed to create different structural permutations of proteins. Devi has vision and precision, far beyond mine.'

'Thank you, sir,' Devi said.

'No, thank you, Devi – the process might have taken me years which I don't have.'

'We've done it together, sir. However, the artistry has been all yours.'

'What does she mean by that?' Noah asked.

'I mean, sir,' Devi answered for Khan, 'that once I identify the right combination of amino acids, they need to be bonded and arranged in particular three-dimensional patterns. This requires two hands and knowledge of virology, molecular biology, immunology and genetic modification. It requires specific knowledge and patience.'

Khan tapped Devi's metal hand affectionately. 'She's become like a friend to me. Few people share my obsession. I think that's partly why I was so happy to meet you.'

'I'm flattered – and confused.'

'You saw what happened to Baby Karthik. You know how important this work is. But it was largely theoretical until the hospital outbreak took place.'

'What do you mean?' Noah asked. Perhaps Hackman had been right – maybe Khan was a threat even if he wasn't the ghost.

'I've created hundreds of thousands of new antibodies – permutations of potential vaccines. But the WHO and Western Alliance governments won't allow us access to a live Ebola virus.

'I've never been able to test my antibodies until the hospital outbreak happened and I cultured the Ebola variant from the children and the monkeys.'

'You know that's illegal – you said you hadn't violated the protocol. You said –'

'I know it's against the law and I take full responsibility for it. I don't think Devi would last forty-eight hours in prison.'

'I appreciate that, sir,' Devi said.

'I can understand why the West doesn't trust us with a live Ebola virus,' Khan said. 'But in order to develop better vaccines and cures, I need the live species.'

'We *have* a vaccine – our vaccine, EBL-47,' Noah replied.

'Yes, but it only creates immunity for Ebola 47 and the strains whose mutation *preceded* it. Ebola 47 will mutate and improve – we saw that in the hospital outbreak.'

'Ebola 47 has been eradicated by the Global Vaccination Programme,' Noah answered automatically.

'No, it hasn't. Ebola re-emerges – not just at the hospital. There was a village in Mexico recently, and a lab in India last week. Total eradication of any virus is impossible – you could eradicate a species before you eradicated a virus, and it's very hard to eradicate a species.'

The lab in India had been the work of his Wet Team. Hassan and his colleagues, the entire lab had been eradicated. Noah forced himself to focus.

'The human race has done that to countless species.'

'None as strong as a virus or the human race itself. But we digress. I haven't shown you the best part.' Khan stood at his computer and talked as he worked.

'Devi, have you prepared the tissue cultures? Face mask on, Noah.' Khan wore the bodysuit to protect against transfer, but he had refused the head gear and face mask.

'Of course, sir – all of the samples are ready. Which Ebola strains would you like to use first?' Her hand moved towards the largest refrigerator in the lab.

'Let's use the first three – Ebola A, B and C. I used the hospital Ebola to create new strains. And then I tested our different antibodies against the new strains.'

'You've *invented* new strains of Ebola?' Noah would have no choice but to remove Khan now. He swallowed hard.

'New strains and new *vaccines*. New vaccines, Noah,' Khan repeated. He paused to make sure he had his full attention.

'One test vaccine was particularly effective – it is more important than all of my others.

'Watch what happens – and stop interrupting. Devi will perform the experiments under the scope but she'll expand the image up there for us. On the big screen.'

He moved two stools over for them as though they were at the movies. Noah couldn't sit.

'The tissue culture has been given my new vaccine – can you see it?' Khan asked.

Noah nodded.

'Now watch – Devi will transfect the tissue culture with the new strains of Ebola. These three are the strongest. They don't need an incubation period. As soon as they come into contact with the host they begin attacking it. Watch, watch, watch,' he clapped his hands together in delight.

The vaccine began expressing antibodies and counterattacked Khan's engineered viruses.

'You've created a powerful multi-strain vaccine,' Noah said.

'No – keep watching the vaccine.' Khan smiled behind his mask. His hand gripped Noah's arm, his eyes were on the screen. 'EBL-47 is multi-strain – it vaccinates us against Ebola 47 and all of its ancestral strains. This one is better than that. It vaccinates us against all of Ebola's future strains.'

Noah watched the vaccine change – as each Ebola strain attacked the tissue culture, the vaccine rearranged the structure of the antibody to protect it. The vaccine was evolving.

'Oh my G–' Noah stopped himself.

'It's incredible, isn't it? The vaccine is sentient. It adjusts to the virus mutations and changes its own structure to fight it. It has a life, a will of its own – it is conscious.'

'That's impossible.' Noah shook his head.

'All organisms have a consciousness. Why not then, the vaccine too?'

'It's impossible,' Noah repeated. 'How did you . . .?'

'I don't know. At first I thought it was an accident – so much of scientific discovery is accidental. But these last few months have been incredible. I am a different man – guided and changed by what is happening to me.'

'What is happening to you?'

Khan ignored him, mesmerised by the sight of the vaccine on the screen in front of them, changing, adjusting and manoeuvring the structure of the antibodies it expressed, constantly regenerating its protein base.

'I call this one the Devi Vaccine – she is all-powerful. She is the mother of all my vaccines. She can protect us from unforeseen mutations, even weaponised ones.'

'The mother . . . what about the babies?' Noah asked suddenly.

'What?'

'The babies at the ICU ward here – the outbreak. Baby Karthik,' the words tumbled out. He needed to slow down.

'It was too late,' Khan said simply. 'By the time I got to them, the virus had already carved a path of destruction through all of their major systems. The vaccine is not an antiviral cure. It's only a vaccine. It slowed the virus down a little but that's all. I tried so hard. Baby Karthik's antibodies helped me improve this vaccine though. His death was not in vain.'

'What will you do with it, Amir?'

'I'll share it, of course. It still needs to go through a live trials process. I'm not sure how to do that. The WHO and the East – we are not always honest with each other, I think.'

'How do you mean?' Noah asked.

'We are dependent on the WHO and the Western Alliance to provide us with our vaccine – our Immunity Shield. I trust the WHO to always act in our best interests as long as *our* best interests are aligned with *their* best interests.'

'The WHO safeguards global health,' Noah replied.

'Ebola had been killing people for years, since the first outbreak in 2013. Black people, people who were going to die anyway. The West only took notice of Ebola in 2022 because the virus had devoured Africa and was seeking a host in Europe. The West put its money and its best minds into developing a vaccine to protect itself. And still there is no cure. Some things can't be cured.

'I trust in scientists like Neeson to keep inventing vaccines – but I trust the virus to keep inventing itself. One day there will be an Ebola 48, 49 and so on. I want to be ready for it when it comes again.'

'So you want to share all of this,' Noah pointed to the images of the Devi Vaccine on the screen, 'with the world?'

'Yes, indeed – why else?' Khan asked, confused. And then he realised. 'Is that why you're here? To discover if I am a criminal and a killer? Perhaps you thought I was responsible for the deaths of those children?'

'No – I never thought you hurt those children. I don't think you want to hurt anyone.'

'I want to help people, Noah. You know me now. Let me show you – Devi,' Khan called out again. 'Put up Abre de Libre's vaccine, on maximum magnification.'

He turned to Noah. 'Devi has shown me its two components. Look, look . . .'

Another image flashed on the screen – Noah knew it well. It was EBL-47-E.ALL, the vaccine given to the East, with the core vector EBL-47 and the Faith Inhibitor strand.

'This section –' Khan pulled the Faith Inhibitor off the screen and turned its 3D image over in his hands.

'This is damaging the brain, Noah. It's taken me a decade of study but with Devi's help I have finally worked it out.' He clapped his hands shut, returning the image to the screen.

'It damages the brain, here,' he tapped the front of his head. 'It damages all of us who take this vaccine – we are affected, possibly beyond repair. It's reducing us in some way. The vaccine is trying to help us but it is also hurting us. This place,' he touched his head again. 'It contains so much of value, son – so much of who we are is right here. And so much of that has been taken away from us.'

'Why don't you remove the strand from the vaccine if it adds no immunity value? You could engineer a vaccine with just the EBL-47 vector.' Noah's throat felt dry and tight.

'No, I tried that. The Haema Scanners are looking for Ebola antibodies *and* this strand – the WHO or Bio or someone wants it there for a reason.

'When Devi and I engineered the Devi Vaccine, we included a shadow or passive strand – it exists in the body but doesn't hurt it. It's a placebo – I used a gene-mining technique an old friend taught me.' He paused to look at Noah, placing a hand on his arm.

'My vaccine and I are trapped – we are samples on a Petri dish, struggling to find a way out; a way to reach the people who need us. I want to help – surely you can see that?' he asked with his sad eyes. 'I feel something inside me – something strong that has helped me answer these questions I've had for so long. In the last year, I've had greater clarity than ever before – I am being guided to help others.'

'Yes, it's the strangest thing,' Noah answered, more to himself. His chest was starting to ache.

'Strange that I should want to help people? Most of us want to help each other. Most of us see that we are more alike than we are different.'

Noah shook Khan's hand away. 'When my father was dying, *most people* refused to come near our home. I couldn't take him to the hospital without help. The neighbours – people who had known and loved him for decades – wouldn't open their doors to me. I lined up in endless queues for nothing better than paracetamol to ease his pain. Yes, we are more alike than we are different – we are weak and selfish. You said before that this virus is an act of evolution, a necessary and natural cull – perhaps you're right because I have no doubt that we deserve it.'

'I'm so sorry, Noah. I never meant to say that your father or his death was . . .' Khan's voice faltered.

'I know you didn't. His death was . . . despite the horror of it, he never lost his . . .' Noah stopped.

'He never lost his what?'

Noah didn't know what to say. What word described faith better than faith? What word could he use in this country where faith had been prohibited and then eradicated?

'I need to check in with my team.' His head was spinning. He could feel his shirt, damp against his wound. He couldn't tell if it was blood or sweat.

'Yes, yes – and you should rest. You look more tired than usual. Sri Lanka is a good place to close your eyes for a while.'

'Thank you, Amir. I'll see you tomorrow.' Noah left the lab, grateful for the mask that hid his face.

Chapter 26

Noah opened the door to his hotel room with his right arm, his left held tightly against his throbbing side. He took off his shirt awkwardly and wiped the sweat from his body with it, assessing the bandages in the mirror – there were three small patches of blood seeping through.

'You said sometimes you just take the intel and make a decision yourself. What would you do now?' Noah didn't even look for her as he spoke.

'I would still wait.' Sahara stepped forward and began unwrapping the bandages.

'*Wait*? Khan's super-vaccine doesn't carry the Faith Inhibitor, at least not an active form of it.'

'I heard the same thing you did, Noah. His vaccine also provides full immunity against any number of Ebola strains. So he could breach the Immunity Shield against the Sixth Virus – without risking herd immunity to Ebola.'

'An evolving, sentient vaccine – that he tested against his own engineered Ebola virus. You don't think that merits a call to Hackman on the old sat phone? Or did he say "Don't call me, I'll call you?"'

'Something like that.' She opened her medi-kit. 'We have a little time. Khan said he'll go through a proper trials process. He's a scientist first, a rebel second.'

'What if he tried to smuggle the vaccine out of the East? He's constructed it with enough of the right markers to pass the Haema Scanner.'

'It's not fresh fruit, Noah. You can't just put it in a cooler box and catch a plane with it. Someone will notice. The next call you make to Hackman is the last one. Khan knows the Faith Inhibitor is damaging the frontal lobe – but is he the supplier? Is he the ghost?'

Noah shook his head. 'We're looking at two different decoys but only one – Khan's – protects people against Ebola.'

He gasped as she peeled off the dressing and cleaned his stitches. When she finished redressing the wound, he opened the muslin net around his bed and sat down.

'Maybe Khan hadn't got that far yet but thought Hassan Ali could test it for him. Khan would need clinical trials at some point – maybe this was it,' she suggested.

'No. Khan wants his vaccine to *immunise* people. Full herd immunity. He would never risk the lives of people on a premature trial.'

'Is he trying to bring back the Sixth Virus with his new vaccine? He thinks he's being guided. Just like the other vaxxers.'

'He thinks he was guided to create his new vaccine. I doubt he's thought beyond that.'

Sahara was quiet for a moment. 'You don't believe in much of anything, Noah, and yet here you are having faith in him; protecting him.'

'I'm not protecting him – I just don't think he's being instructed by a higher energy to bring that energy back. He is being *instructed*, if you want to call it that, to aid the Global Vaccination Programme.'

'Maybe this energy is using standard tradecraft – each piece in the link doesn't know about the other pieces, or their objectives, except for the piece directly next to it,' she said.

'Yes, I'm sure this energy has read Bio's manual. What do we do next?' he asked.

'We wait for Hackman.' She walked over to the bed and stood in front of him. She reached out, first inspecting the small welt on his left arm, where repeated vaccinations had thickened the skin. Then her fingers were on his face, tracing the line of his jaw, an eyebrow and, finally, in his tangled hair, pushing it out of his eyes. She locked her hands there and tilted his head back, exposing his neck.

He placed his hands on either side of her hips, drawing her closer. She released his head and he rested it on her chest. Her arms wrapped around him tightly, gently. He could hear the steady rhythm of her heart, the resigned rise and fall of her breath. He moved his hands under her shirt, feeling the warmth of her skin.

He kissed her and this time she stayed, pulling the soft muslin around them both.

*

Sahara left Noah, still asleep. She returned to her apartment and locked the door before she opened the freezer. It was still there. A small container hidden behind three packets of frozen rotis. She checked the thermometer. It read minus twenty degrees, the acceptable temperature for medium-term live virus storage. She didn't know why she had kept it.

She did the maths again. Twenty-five millilitres divided by five babies equalled five millilitres each. She had given them three millilitres each, leaving her a vial of ten millilitres in her freezer, behind the rotis, next to the frozen chicken curry and the pistachio ice-cream.

She had no plans to use it. She wasn't stupid. She just wanted to have it. Just in case. She scratched the swelling on her left arm. It was small and red, disguised among the many mosquito bites on her body. She remembered how she got it, at the end of the war fifteen years ago.

It was the monsoon season in the north of the island, and although she should have been afraid of malaria, she knew there were worse diseases out there.

'Stop scratching,' the commander ordered.

'Sorry, sir, I can't help it.' She touched the welt, reassured by its presence. The whole platoon had them, a tattoo that bound them together.

'You're sure the vaccine works?' she asked.

'It's not your job to doubt us. But for the record, I'm one hundred percent sure,' he replied. 'Our scientists stateside have tested it — a compressed longitudinal study, given the urgency. But the live trials were successful even after prolonged exposure to Ebola, strains 1 through to 47. It's already been added to this season's flu jab at home, the UK and as much of Europe as we can reach — two vaccines for the price of one.' He didn't smile.

It was the greatest medical breakthrough of their time but its existence hadn't been made public yet.

'You are immune — we all are.' He motioned to the Western Alliance soldiers around him. They were dressed in WHO uniforms.

'We are — but they aren't?' she asked, looking at the charts spread across the table. Maps of the countries that would soon become known as the Eastern Alliance. Red indicated Ebola, blue indicated war. Many countries had both colours. Some, like Sri Lanka, had only one — pockets of blue. The entire continent of Africa was ablaze in red, the Middle East in blue.

'Not yet – we'll give it to them eventually. For now, we let Nature take its course. And we help it. Listen up, soldiers,' the commander walked to the front of the room. He stood at the head of the table, his feet apart, shoulders square and strong. His eyes were unrelenting. Soldiers always remembered his eyes.

'I'm only going to say this once. We are about to implement a cull and control strategy – my strategy.

'I sense hesitation and concern from some of you. There is no place for it in this unit. If you want out of this mission, I can arrange for you to be humanely executed, which is more than you deserve.

'This is war. We have intelligence from the Middle East – factions there are funding the armed militia in Asia to defend the Muslim communities here. Pakistan, Bangladesh, Indonesia and Malaysia have enough Muslims to keep this thing going for a while. We also know that the governments of India, Sri Lanka, Burma and Thailand are getting better at killing their minorities.'

The commander's voice was raised but he never shouted. He spoke clearly and slowly. Like he was reading the Bible in church.

'The Ground Force Depletion Report puts the Western Alliance body count in India, Pakistan and Sri Lanka at 40,000. The potential losses across the rest of Asia are far greater and that's before we send a seventh battalion to Afghanistan and Syria. We need to get control of these regions and finish this war. This way is faster and safer.'

For us, she thought but didn't say.

'You know what to do. I don't expect it to be easy for you.' He almost sounded empathetic. 'But I do expect you to get it right. You'll go to separate medical camps. Each unit will carry the weapon in a different jab – the flu, tetanus, hepatitis. Some in blood packs. Each weapon has been engineered to incubate and manifest at different times. We don't want our Patients Zero to be connected to a clinic or a particular immunisation. It has to look like normal transmission.'

He looked directly at Sahara. 'You've been in this hellhole since the beginning. You've seen what this war is doing to people. I expect you to understand. You're assigned to the Sivanadana Caves.' He motioned to a temple complex at the northern tip of the island. Sivanadana – the dance of Lord Shiva, the destroyer.

'There are hundreds of refugees there. A Hindu priest has set up a makeshift camp around the temple. You will provide food packs and health checks, including a cholera jab which contains the weapon. Once they're infected, we'll send another unit in to purge the temple. It has to be shut down.'

Sahara felt her hands shake. She tried to control it but the commander saw.

'Staying in the conflict full-scale is not an option for us anymore. This way is safer.' He looked at her directly. 'Do you understand?'

'I understand, Commander Hackman,' she replied.

She repacked the freezer and shut the door. Her hands were still shaking.

Chapter 27

Noah knocked loudly. 'Open up.'

Garner opened her door, weapon drawn.

Crawford was at one of the computers. 'You asked us to look into Khan's full medical records, and the other vaxxers who were involved in the breaches. We can get everything on them – but still nothing on General Rajasuriya.'

'Forget the general for now. What do you know about the others?' Noah stood over Crawford's shoulder.

'From their Haema Scans we could tell they had cancer but we couldn't identify what kind.'

'Yes, yes,' Noah said impatiently. 'What types of cancer are we looking at?'

'Only one – a frontal lobe tumour.'

Noah's mind reeled. He inhaled deeply and squared his shoulders. 'Give me the headlines.'

Crawford brought up the individual scans on one screen and the medicals on another. 'They all have exactly the same kind of tumour in exactly the same place.'

'The periodic scans indicate comparable rates of growth in this cerebral zone, with no metastasising elsewhere,' Garner added. 'Symptoms include migraines, some vision weakening, fatigue and dizziness.'

'I know what the symptoms are,' Noah said tersely.

'Yes, sir, sorry. This section here –' she pointed to the screen. 'These are the glial tissue neurons – the packaging cells that repair the brain. That shading tells us those cells are multiplying exponentially.'

'Increasing repair and facilitating the speed of information transmission.'

'Exactly. Which is why the patients all appear to have full intellectual and physical faculties. They've all refused treatment too. For a tumour of this size in this location, the usual treatment would be surgery and then radiotherapy – possibly chemo as well.'

'They've refused treatment?' Noah repeated. He thought about the patients he had seen at Khan's clinic. And the general. 'Is there a prognosis for any of them?'

'One year at most given that there's no mental attrition. Most likely six months.'

'They're all dead men walking.'

'Correct. Early treatment would most likely prolong life – possibly even save it.'

'Have you checked the literature – are these symptoms normal?' Noah leaned over Crawford to begin a search on his computer. Crawford pushed him away.

'No, Chief – the literature would indicate that these symptoms are highly *abnormal*. The literature predicts a far greater loss of mental and physical faculties. This is the frontal lobe we're talking about.'

'Do their doctors comment on that?' Noah asked.

'Yes,' Garner replied. 'A number of them requested permission to write up their case studies. Examples of malignant, terminal tumours that do not cause loss of function and interact almost benignly with the brain are hard to come by.'

'Have the case studies been published yet?' Noah asked.

'Some. Most neurologists are waiting to track the progress of the tumour – they don't want to publish until they see what happens.'

'Can't talk about a benign tumour that betrays them in the end and has them feeding and shitting through a tube, I suppose.'

'That's right, sir – it's important to know your enemy first.'

'Indeed, Garner.' Noah smiled. 'That's why you are a great agent.'

'Actually it's the confluence of intellect, powers of analysis, eidetic memory and proficiency in all areas of field training, including bomb disarmament.'

'How are you still single?' Crawford asked.

'That's good work, both of you. Anything else?'

'Thank you, sir. We've been having a little trouble with our surveillance computer motherboard – the local power surges are overheating it. The relay from our cameras keeps crashing.'

'It's annoying,' Crawford said. 'We could separate the cameras onto two or three motherboards if we could – you know, borrow a few more from our WHO friends?'

'How many cameras do you have? I know you like big lenses.' Noah laughed.

'Six – two on the road, one on each door and two others,' Crawford replied.

'It's fine, sir. Something to remember for next time. It's hard to enter the Eastern Alliance inconspicuously with that much gear. One more thing –' Garner paused, apparently uncertain whether to tell Noah the next part.

'Yes?'

'From the scans we've seen, the tumours are also exactly the same *shape*. This isn't your typical amorphous mass that creeps into whatever healthy tissue it can find. Tumours, like all diseases, tend to colonise and feed randomly with only their own perpetuation as the principle driver for growth. Hence the growth is expedient. The growth of these ones – it doesn't look expedient. The shape of the tumour is quite specific and, in each case, identical. I know that must sound stupid.'

'Garner, very little that comes out of your mouth sounds stupid. Let's see it.' He leaned towards her screen to inspect the tumour. She clicked on the scan enlarging it and increasing the image resolution. He pulled back sharply.

The tumour started at the same location, a small central mass that radiated tiny arms out towards points in the frontal lobe, covering some parts but avoiding others. It furled around the faith zones but bypassed the other executive function zones. It followed a specific path. A path Noah recognised.

But was it a deliberate one? he wondered. His heart beat wildly in his chest.

'Sir?' Garner prompted him.

He pulled his eyes away from the screen reluctantly and looked down at Garner. 'Run a check for me – look at the Haema Scans and neurological tests across Sri Lanka and India that match the exact diagnosis of these vaxxers. We'll start with those two countries and see what comes up.'

'Do you think there might be more cases? The exact same tumour, sir?'

'Maybe.' He didn't trust himself to say more. He had to find Khan.

*

Noah stepped out of the tuk-tuk and paid the man more than the meter fare. The driver smiled back with gappy, betel-stained teeth but there was something about him: the striped sarong wasn't creased, the white singlet wasn't sweat-stained, the leather slippers were dusty but too expensive.

'I wait for you, sir?' The man tucked the money into a belt around his waist. It was a nice touch.

'No – it's late. I'll be a while. You can go.'

'Come back later for you? Tell me time,' the man tried again.

'No, thank you – that's very kind of you.' Noah walked towards Khan's house. The front door was slightly ajar. The man stalled the vehicle a few times. Noah waved goodbye with one hand, his other reaching behind for his gun. The tuk-tuk coughed angrily and started down the street.

Noah turned, weapon drawn. He pushed lightly against the door. The corridor was empty and dark.

He inched into the first room on the left, Khan's spare bedroom. The belly of the mattress had been sliced open, its cotton entrails and springs spilling out; clothes thrown from the cupboards.

He saw a large boot print across a paper on the floor, its fine red dust pointing out to the corridor. The intruder had kept going.

No sign of life. He stepped back into the corridor, raising his gun to his chest at the sudden sound in the next room – Khan's study. He heard furniture dragged, a man straining. Muffled footsteps towards him. He exhaled and forced himself to wait. *Come closer, come closer, sweetheart.*

He extended his arms and pivoted into the doorway, moving the gun to the left just in time. The shot rang loudly in the small room, hitting the wall above Khan who dropped the broken chair leg and ducked, his hands over his head.

'I could have killed you!' Noah shouted.

'That's what happens when you carry a gun!' Khan shouted back, surprising both of them. He picked up his glasses from his feet and fumbled them back onto his face.

'What are you doing here, son?' he asked. 'Is everything all right?'

'Is everything *all right*? Are you serious? What happened here?'

He looked around. There were papers everywhere, torn; books thrown from the bookcase; photo frames smashed. Khan's secure filing cabinet was empty but some of the brain scans were scattered on the floor.

'I don't know – I came back from work, late as usual, and the house was like this. This room is the worst. I think they were looking for something in here.' He looked at his filing cabinet.

'Who?' Noah asked. Only soldiers wore boots in a country like Sri Lanka.

'I don't know, son.' Khan sat down at the table. He swept the papers that covered it into a pile and pushed it to one side. Noah's eyes fell on a back issue of the *New England Journal of Medicine*. The feature article was called 'Mining the shadows' – by Dr Amir Khan and Dr Jack Neeson.

Noah handed Khan the broken photograph of his wife.

'Thank you.' He pulled a handkerchief from his shirt pocket and wiped his face. 'I'm too old for this.'

'Has anyone ever threatened you? Or a competitor perhaps, who wants to steal your work?'

'No – I'm no threat to anyone. I share my work with my profession. I've never even patented a single gene sequence. Besides,' he said, 'all of my work is now done through Devi. Everything from the last year has been stored on her hard drive. Once our new vaccine is ready I'm going to share that too.' He looked at the filing cabinet again.

Noah tucked his gun at the back of his belt and sat down.

'How are you, Amir?'

The old man patted Noah's hand and then held it for a moment. 'I'm okay – it's just things ... Just things.' He picked up the photograph of his wife again.

'Rest a moment. I'll fix you some tea and then we can tidy up, if you like?'

'Tea would be good, thank you.'

Noah stood up. 'My masala chai is pretty average but condensed milk fixes most things.'

Noah returned a few moments later with the spicy tea. Fat from the milk sat in oily droplets on its surface.

Khan hadn't moved or released the photograph, a shard of glass emerging dangerously from the frame. Cardamom-scented steam filled the silence. Noah took the photograph from him. Khan wrapped his hands around the cup and spoke, finally.

'Tell me more about your father, Noah. I felt bad about our last discussion. I think I would have liked him.'

'You would have liked each other. He had great respect for scientists. He thought science, mathematics and re–... philosophy sought to explain the cardinal organisation of all life.'

'They do – they aren't contradictory despite what many people think. They are all by-products of a search for meaning in our world of chaos. Those disciplines are different pathways to peace, I think. Your father was very wise – did you listen to him?'

'Not always – not enough.' Noah looked around at the mess in Khan's study. 'In 2023, when Ebola crossed the Atlantic . . . he didn't survive.

'It spread so quickly. The West lost twenty percent of its population but . . . it could have been much worse, I suppose.' He blinked back tears.

'Yes, I suppose. Africa and the Middle East lost more than seventy percent. The vaccine was developed by the US – you should be very proud of your country.'

Noah shrugged. 'Outbreaks are sporadic but cyclical now.'

'Cyclical . . .'

'Research by the WHO and Bio indicates that the virus emerges in a cycle. Like the one in Mexico recently – you knew about that one.'

'Yes, information about outbreaks is available to us – it reminds us of the importance of the Global Vaccination Programme.' Khan smiled. 'I read the full report on the WHO portal. Apparently the village had been weakened by a particularly virulent strain of the flu. I've never been a believer in the Weakened Immunity Hypothesis.'

'What?'

'You heard me. You need to read more, Noah.' Khan smiled again. 'When Ebola spread into the West, the WHO told us that people who suffered from the flu were weakened by it and less able to fight off Ebola. Of course this created a predictable response – people rushed to get the flu jab.'

'And the data showed that in the West where there was a higher rate of flu vaccination, there was also a lower rate of Ebola penetration,' Noah interrupted.

'Temporal sequence is often vital to causality, but not *always* an indicator of it. At least not in the way that we often assume.'

Noah shook his head. 'All epidemiological studies indicated that once you adjusted for factors such as better hygiene and nutrition in the West, greater influenza immunity through the flu jab slowed the spread of Ebola in that region.'

Khan refused to be dissuaded. 'The hypothesis is wrong because influenza sends the body into full-fight mode. Influenza is a superb killer but our bodies have learned to fight back, producing thousands of antibodies every hour to combat it. Many of those same antibodies would have been useful to fend off Ebola. Its pathology is similar. Sufferers of the flu are, in my opinion, more likely to be able to survive an Ebola outbreak. I wrote a paper on it, but it wasn't allowed over to your side. I'm sure you have special access – you should read it the next time you are sitting on a bench somewhere.'

'And the Mexico outbreak?'

'Was deeply tragic, barbaric even. We don't respect the flu enough. People fear Ebola but they have forgotten the flu. It wasn't that long ago that it was used by colonising forces to wipe out millions of people in their own homes, their own countries.'

'The flu wasn't *used*. Like smallpox, it was just something that came along for the ride when people went from one country to another.'

'Conveniently so for all those Spanish, Portuguese, British, Dutch and even American settlers, wasn't it? They showed up, coughed and sneezed a lot, and "unwittingly" destroyed entire indigenous communities. They didn't have to waste a bullet. Or a single Western life. The flu is very efficient. I'm surprised we didn't learn more from that.'

Noah stared at Khan in shocked silence. He didn't seem to notice.

'A cyclical occurrence,' he quoted. 'There are all kinds of cycles in this world, Noah, not all of them natural. Use your scientist's eye to observe them carefully.' He took his glasses off and pressed his fingers against his temples.

'May I?' Noah reached forward and placed both hands on either side of Khan's head. He inserted his thumb into the eye socket pressure points, his index fingers at both temples, and then splayed the rest of his fingers around the zygomatic bone, near the auriculotemporal nerves. He pressed down with increasing pressure from finger to finger, pain zone to pain zone, as Khan exhaled into his grip. Noah bypassed the kill zone, held Khan for a few more moments and then let go.

'How did you know?' Khan asked.

'I've seen it before. Terminal?'

'We're all terminal, I'm just on a faster track than most.'

'Most – not all. My daughter,' Noah began. There was no need; Khan had told him everything he needed to know. And yet he wanted to tell him.

'My daughter – she was four years old. Inoperable, small secondaries but aggressive growth of the primary throughout both sides of the frontal lobe. She lost gross motor functions within six weeks. Speech and feeding by twelve weeks. The doctors said they hadn't seen one that fast in a long time.'

'I'm sorry, Noah. What was her name?'

'Seraphina – Sera, after the angel.' He closed his eyes.

'I'm so sorry,' Khan repeated.

'I'm sorry too.' Noah opened his eyes. 'How much time do you have?'

'Four months, five at most. Enough to refine the Devi Vaccine. I won't be able to conduct the trials. But Devi has catalogued everything I know— she will be able to help another, better scientist test and perfect it.'

'There are treatments you can try: chemo, new immuno-therapies, ultrasonic aspirators –'

'Maybe it's saving me,' Khan interrupted him. 'Life is killing all of us. Everything that is born must die.'

'Everything that is born must be given a chance to live,' Noah said, his voice choking.

'Is that how you have lived, Noah? Have you given everything in your life a chance to live?'

He looked at Khan sharply, afraid that the old man knew him too well.

'This tumour has helped me see the virus in a way that I had never seen it before. It guides my hand and tells me what to do. It is urging me to share scientific truths with people, telling me to help people while I still can.'

'Those people in your clinic at Anuradhapura,' Noah said. 'They have the same tumour – it's killing them too, isn't it?'

Khan shook his head and went to the filing cabinet. He picked up an MRI scan from the floor. Noah quickly folded the journal into a tight roll and hid it inside his jacket.

'Life without meaning is killing them.' Khan showed Noah the scan.

'And what's the cure?' Noah felt like someone was strangling him. He remembered the wall of MRI and CT scans at the clinic showing the brains of men and women, the same grey mass blooming within each one. He remembered the general. How could all of those people have the same tumour? And yet he didn't doubt it.

'The tumour is the cure – it is healing us in some way. I told you the vaccine was hurting us. The tumour is evolving, adapting to the vaccine and fighting back. It is *giving* back what the vaccine took away. It is teaching us who we are and why we're here.'

'You can't just give up.' Even in the final moments of his daughter's life, Noah had kept waiting for something.

'The tumour is giving me much more than it's taking away. The cure for a life without meaning is death. Like me, all of those people at Anuradhapura have chosen a shorter life with . . . with faith – than a lifetime without it.'

Noah's chest tightened. He felt old emotions stir and swirl around him.

'I will miss my morning swim, Noah. But I don't fight the current anymore. I let it find me and carry me towards the lifebuoy.'

Khan picked up Noah's hands and placed them at his temples again. He had said *faith*. Hackman's orders were clear: if the threat could not be contained it must be destroyed.

'I'm not afraid. We all have to die – some of us can choose how we live. What a privilege it is to know that there is something within us, a current that carries us gently towards itself, if only we would let it.'

Noah knew what he should do. He took a breath and tightened his hold on Khan.

'Do you think . . . do you think my daughter felt the world differently too? Did she see what you see?' Noah whispered.

Her world was darkness and dulled pain at the end. Was she frightened? Or did the waves put their arms around her and guide her home?

He let go of Khan and stood up abruptly. 'You tidy up in here, I'll make a start on the spare bedroom.'

Chapter 28

Noah got out of the tuk-tuk. The surveillance car was still parked outside his hotel. Seven cars behind that he saw Sahara.

He pulled out his sat phone from his bag. It was 4 am in London but he called anyway.

'Hello . . .' her voice was thick and confused with sleep.

'It's me – sorry to wake you.'

'Noah? Is everything okay?' She was awake now. 'What's wrong?'

'Nothing, Maggie. I just wanted to hear your voice. I'm almost done here. I'll be back soon.'

'Noah . . .'

'Do you remember that raggedy bear Sera used to sleep with? Its leg kept falling off. You had to sew it back on. Six times, I think.'

'Seven times, damn bear.'

'Damn bear.' It hurt to breathe. 'Do you still have it?'

'Of course I still have it. I have everything.'

'Could I maybe have it sometime? Not to keep – just to see it.'

'You want the bear?'

'I just want to see it . . . Does it still smell like her?' He closed his eyes and tried to recall it. Recall her.

'A bit. You can see the bear. You can keep it. Or we could share it. Noah . . .'

'You don't need to say anything. I just wanted to hear your voice. I'm sorry to disturb you. Good night, Maggie.'

'Good night, Noah.' The phone went dead. He dropped it back in the bag as he passed the hotel manager's desk.

Later, he would remember that the desk was empty.

*

Noah secured all the windows and doors. He looked through the brain scans Crawford had sent to his handheld, his finger flicking the screen faster and faster. He studied each brain tumour, expanding it and then focusing on different segments.

The tumour was located in the specific area of the brain where faith was generated — the specific area that should have been damaged by the vaccine given to the Eastern Alliance.

What if Khan was right? What if the brain was adapting to the Faith Inhibitor, treating it like a virus and fighting it off with this tumour?

Noah knew that region of the brain intimately. He had memorised his daughter's scans. He knew the contours and shades of her frontal lobe, the tumour and the oedema, as well as he knew the lines of her lips when she laughed, the creases on her hands when she played.

He knew the colours: the pinks, reds and blues of this section of the brain too, when he opened the heads of men who wouldn't give him answers.

Noah traced the lines of the tumour across his own forehead.

What if the tumour was the body's adaptive immunity response — its way of protecting the frontal lobe from the Faith Inhibitor — and maybe even regenerating the parts damaged by it?

He remembered Hassan Ali's words: 'It yearns to be felt by others ... It wants to be loved again. It told me what to do. It wants to come back.'

There was a name for 'It'. In the Eastern Alliance, before the Armistice and the Faith Inhibitor, there had been many names. He had called them out in reverence, and then when his daughter was dying, in despair and anger.

He picked up his handheld and checked the shape of the tumour again. As Garner had identified, the tumour was not the typical amorphous mass that was expected from such cancers. It was a shape, a pattern — a familiar intricate circle. A cosmic design that spoke of a universal energy. A malignant growth, its blackness weaving through a man's brain, killing him but restoring his faith.

*

Noah pulled out the crumpled *New England Journal of Medicine* from his jacket.

'Mining the shadows' by Dr Amir Khan and Dr Jack Neeson. They wrote it while completing a fellowship in London together.

'The thesis of this paper is that the structure of any cell can be replicated to create an imitation or "decoy" that operates in the host as though it were the original cell.'

Noah turned back to the front page of the journal — it was published in April 2018, two years before World War R began. Seven years before the borders came down; before the Armistice and the Global Vaccination Programme. He kept reading:

'All cells have a DNA and a shadow DNA which is identical in shape but neutered in power, hence the name "shadow". If properly extracted or mined, the shadow components of DNA can be used to develop complex structures that mimic their predecessor's presence in the host without harming it.'

The process had failed, but twenty years later, technology had evolved, giving Khan the ability to do this with Devi. Technology had also given that ability to Neeson.

At the front of the article, there was a photograph of the two scientists seated at a lab desk. They were smiling the exultant smile of men who had discovered something; the easy smile of men who were friends.

Noah flicked to the conclusion of the article. In an insert box was a polemic titled 'Eradication is impossible; why immunity should always be maintained'. He recognised Khan's words, or were they Neeson's?

'The virus has a place and a purpose in our ecosystem. It is Nature's culling mechanism – it should be respected not feared . . .'

He wished now that he had read all the papers Neeson had sent him over the years. He turned pages quickly, trying to find the Ebola case study. There it was – a photograph of the test vaccine that Neeson and Khan had tried to create.

He remembered Neeson calling his attention to the structural tag attached to Hassan Ali's decoy vaccine – the ornate circle that led him to Khan in the first place. Neeson had asked him if the ghost was just leaving a signature or if he was trying to communicate with them.

The photograph in the old journal needed far greater magnification – but Noah was certain that if he could have expanded the image in front of him, he would see the tag: the scientists' shared signature of a mandala.

Chapter 29

Noah logged on to the WHO portal and typed in a quick search. Nine papers came up, written by Neeson, many with research contributions from Khan. None of them were about DNA mining.

He knocked on Crawford's door.

'What's up?'

'Can you access any of Khan's old research papers? Is there a database at Colombo General or an archive somewhere in the Eastern Alliance system that you could have a look at quietly?'

'We're always quiet, Chief, except for Garner – in my imagination she's loud. Efficient but loud.'

'Keep talking like that and it will only ever be in your imagination. Answer the question.'

'Is there something in particular you're looking for or do you want every paper Khan's written?'

'Not every paper, I don't have time.'

'What exactly are you looking for?'

'Research on DNA mining and cell replication. Also, any submissions for live trials that he's made. And any applications for patents for new drugs. Also, Devi – I want to know why Neeson would requisition the new AILA for Khan? I think Sri Bodhi's parent company is Abre de Libre but I'm not sure.' Patrice had never called him back.

'You mean the ADL that supplies the world with everybody's favourite humanity-saving vaccine?'

'The very same. If you have time, I want to see any research that refutes the Weakened Immunity Hypothesis.'

'Chief?'

'It's just something Khan said. I want to look at the relationship between the flu jab and the containment of Ebola in the West during the Great Pandemic. Check Khan's papers here – and Neeson's when we get back home.'

'I'll look into it. We're supposed to join the WHO team in an hour – they're swabbing the maternity ward one last time. Perhaps I could pass and work on all this for you?'

'Check in with the hospital first. Hackman's called us back. Wheels up in less than nine hours.'

'I saw that – he could have sent a nicer plane.'

'Next time,' Noah laughed.

'I'll have that intel for you in a couple of hours. What are you thinking, Chief – is Khan good for it?'

'I think a lot of effort has gone into making him look like he's good for it. I'll catch up with you later.'

*

Noah went back to his room and inserted the battery into his sat phone. He paused before dialling the number. It was 5.07 am in London.

'Neeson, it's me.'

'Noah, what a surprise. Is everything all right?' Neeson's day started early. Noah waited and listened again.

'Everything's fine. I'm getting to know Khan. He mentioned he did his fellowship with you. I asked him what he missed about the West and he said working with you.'

'That's lovely – I miss him too. He has a great mind. I asked him to move here, when we knew that the wall was going up. I wanted to keep working with him. We could have achieved . . . a lot together.'

'Why didn't he move?' Noah asked.

'Loyalty, duty I suppose – he and his wife were dedicated. She was a virologist too – although not as obsessed as him.'

'Obsessed is a good word for him. He talks about his wife a lot.'

'Aisha was very special. Beautiful and gentle. She would nudge him out of the lab and bring him back to the world. They were very lucky to have each other. She understood him . . .' Neeson's voice trailed away.

'You must have known her well too.'

'Yes, she was in London with him. Her death was very sad.'

'Death often is. You've still managed to work with Khan, despite the shield – I had a look on the WHO portal.'

'We communicate a little, whatever's allowed after Bio screens the comms. I've been working on an adaptive antibiotic, using case studies from around the world. Khan likes to contribute to the progress of medicine.'

'Yes, I can tell.' Noah knew the call was being listened to. What could he say? What would he say if he was alone with Neeson?

'Speaking of the progress of medicine,' Neeson continued. 'I've sent you various papers from the Christian Coalition. I think you'll find them interesting. One is about the effect of prayer on the brain – it thickens and strengthens it.'

'The Christian Coalition? Jesus, Neese, are you still trying to convert me?'

Neeson laughed. 'I don't like the Christian Coalition either – who wants to be lectured about the decline of God in the West?

They remind me of my ex-mother-in-law. She was a miserable woman. But they're the only ones funding neurotheosophy anymore.'

'Neurotheosophy? Is that a word?' It was Noah's turn to laugh.

'If you read the papers I sent you, you'd know that it's the study of religious experience through science.'

'So you're using science to convert me? And quoting the Christian Coalition – what has our new world come to?'

'Even extremists have a place.'

'Yes – on watchlists and in prison.'

'No, fool. Extremists remind the rest of us about the virtue of moderation. Khan was a great moderate in his youth.'

'He still is. Have you seen his lab? It's very well-equipped,' Noah prompted.

'Hackman showed me your initial notes – he seems to have acquired the AILA Reina – it was the prototype for Roberta, her grandmother if you will. He should be able to do great things with that technology.'

'Yes, perhaps.'

'I hope so. The robotic arm still has unprecedented fine and gross motor skills. The cohesion of intellect and movement makes these artificial intelligence models far superior to any human being.'

'Surely not superior to you.'

'I'm an old man, Noah. I find even the easiest experiments difficult now. I use Roberta for everything – I'd train her to light a cigarette for me if I wasn't worried she'd get addicted.'

'Is Khan's AILA as good as yours?' Noah asked.

'No, but his will achieve more.'

'Roberta is two models ahead, what's holding her back?' Noah's tone was casual. If Neeson could lie effortlessly to him, Noah wouldn't reveal it had shocked him.

'I am – as I said, I'm an old man, with arthritic fingers and an atrophying brain. Roberta could do much better than me. In fact, when you return, you should come over and get to know her. I hear rumours you want to retire – you could work with her. She'd like you.'

'I'm flattered and a little alarmed you're trying to set me up with your robotic lab assistant. I should be back soon – is there anything you want me to bring you from here?' Noah asked. 'As long as it's not horrible like durian.'

Neeson laughed. 'Thank you, Noah, that's really kind of you. I never make it over there anymore.'

'When was the last time you were in Sri Lanka?'

'Fifteen years ago – just after the Armistice. I came to supervise the GVP – the early years were difficult so I was in and out of the Eastern Alliance a lot.'

'Did you see Khan?' Noah gave Neeson another chance.

'Some. Sri Lanka implemented the GVP very efficiently. They were keen to comply after everything that happened there. We had more push back in other Eastern countries and we needed to refine the vaccine on-site at times, in some cases adding a much stronger memory inhibitor to the mix. That had its own side effects which I had to manage. I was needed elsewhere, not in Sri Lanka.'

'How much stronger?' Noah kept his voice even.

'Strong enough for the Purge to be completed in that zone; for the Faith Inhibitor to do its work and kill the faith centre. The impulse to worship was strong in some places. We hadn't fully accounted for that. The memory inhibitor wore off eventually. In the majority of cases the side effects weren't permanently damaging. It was deemed a better solution than others.'

Other solutions involved executing those who challenged the GVP or didn't respond to the vaccine.

'I miss lychees – real, fresh lychees from a tree – not genetically engineered in a greenhouse,' Neeson said. 'I used to love peeling back the prickly red skin to reveal the translucent flesh underneath. There's something satisfying about having to work for your food. It heightens the pleasure of that sweetness.'

'Work for your food? Come on now, you're shelling fruit, not hunting boar. I'll bring you back a bag of lychees, as much as they'll let me carry.'

'Thank you, Noah, I'd like that. He's a good man – Khan. A much better man than me.'

'I've met worse than you. See you on the other side, Neese.' Noah disconnected the phone.

Chapter 30

Noah entered Khan's private laboratory cautiously. It was dark, the only light coming from equipment blinking like lost satellites in a black and endless universe. He turned on all of the lights. The tables were empty, the computers gone, the refrigerators bound with metal ropes and padlocked. Only Devi remained untouched.

'Good morning, Dr Williams,' she said. He found her neutral tone comforting.

'Noah,' he corrected automatically. 'What happened here? Is Dr Khan in yet?' He looked around for signs of the older man.

'No, sir.'

'He should be.'

'Yes, he should be, but human beings are capricious.'

'Is Khan capricious?' Noah asked.

'No, sir,' she sounded troubled.

'No, I didn't think so. What happened?' he repeated.

'Soldiers, sir. They arrived before Dr Khan and took much of the equipment. They said they would come back for me with a technician. I'm too complicated to move.'

He inserted his earpiece.

'Garner, talk to me.' There was no reply. He tried again – nothing.

He pulled out his phone, dialled Crawford and waited – no reply. Twice more.

'I think you should go, sir. They will be back soon – I sense they may harm you.'

'Your senses are perceptive. Where do you think Khan is, Devi?'

'I hope he's late, sir.'

'I don't think so. Connect me to my hotel, Kunchar House on Harmers Avenue. The manager seems to live in the lobby.' Noah knew the call would send up a red flag but he had to find them. 'Direct the call to my phone if you can.'

'Of course, sir, doing that for you right now.'

He waited.

'The lobby phone is disconnected.'

'Shit.'

'Sir?'

'Try another room in the hotel – any room.' He waited.

'No response, sir. All lines to the hotel rooms have been disconnected. Lanka Telcom indicates that those numbers should still be active.'

'Fuck. Devi – if Khan calls tell him to stay visible. Stay with people, crowded places – in fact, tell him to go to the maternity ward. The rest of the WHO delegation is there, wrapping up.'

'Wrapping up, sir?'

'Yes – we're leaving. Wheels up in eight hours. Tell him to stay with the delegation, I'll be back for him.'

'I will, sir, thank you. Are you worried?'

'I'm always worried.'

Minutes later he was ripping the keys from Vijay's hands and weaving through the streets of Colombo back to his hotel. He didn't try to lose the surveillance car – there wasn't time.

At Jayewardene Avenue he became mired in the gridlock of morning traffic. He swore and hit the steering wheel and then the horn repeatedly, achieving nothing, not even the attention of the cars and street vendors around him. There was no way out. He reversed as much as he could and then slammed the accelerator. Cars noticed him now as he forced a pathway, crushing the front of Vijay's car with each thrust. He escaped the main road and checked his mirrors for police vehicles as he hurtled through the side streets.

Finally, he came upon the hotel building from the alley behind it. Attached to the gate was an electromagnetic circuit-jacker. He had used units like it before – it could complete the circuit on the boundary trip-wire. Garner and Crawford wouldn't have known anyone was coming. He pulled out his side-arm and released the safety. His palms were wet. He breathed deeply three times and moved forward.

The back door to the hotel pulsed slowly in the ocean wind. The lock had been prised open. He moved in, checking the kitchen and dining room, his gun sweeping in the arc and grid motion that had become as much a part of his intuition as breathing. He could smell tear gas but not cordite. He moved towards the front door and his footsteps slowed. The lobby was deserted, the manager gone.

He crept up the stairs to Garner's room. They used hers as the control room; she said Crawford was too untidy. Two screens should have shown three sub-screens each, one for every micro-camera that was hidden around the boundary and the front door. Instead, the screens showed the static of disrupted camera relay.

There would have been a van parked less than fifty metres from the building, just outside the range of the first cameras that watched the road. Inside, someone had hacked into the feed from all six cameras and, when he was ready, he would have signalled to the group leader and then cut the feed simultaneously.

The group leader and his men – he wouldn't have needed many – would have approached the gate, attached the circuit-jacker and secured the trip-wire.

Crawford and Garner would have seen the static and assumed another overload on their surveillance motherboard. They would have been rebooting the computer, their backs turned to the door, unaware that the trip-wire had been broken and the gate opened. They wouldn't have had time to even draw their weapons.

Their screens were all in place but the hard drives gone. All of their research, papers, files, memory sticks – all gone. Noah started running, checking the remaining rooms, looking for signs of struggle, looking for blood, for bodies. There was nothing.

'Fuck, fuck, fuck,' he whispered under his breath. 'Where are you?' The building was clean. 'Garner! Crawford! Answer me goddamn it!' He shouted, his voice hoarse and, for the first time in his life, unrecognisable to him.

His heart pounded hard against his rib cage. He was pouring with sweat in the thick air, but he felt encased in ice.

'Where are you?' he tried to say again, but his tongue was heavy, like he was having an allergic reaction and he couldn't form the words. He was starting to panic. He hadn't done that for a long time, not since a doctor gave him an unthinkable verdict.

He ran back down the stairs and out into the garden. He was almost at the back gate when he saw the well in the corner, hidden behind a lattice of thick ferns. He bolted towards it, noticing the crushed anthuriums on the path, the drag marks on the wet earth, and finally the flecks of dark blood staining the leaves of the hibiscus tree, its twisted branches hugging the stone base of the well and then rising like a gentle canopy over it. The opening was covered by a rusted metal plate. There were graze marks on the stone around it.

'Please, God, please, God,' he whispered.

He pushed against it. It groaned but didn't move. He shoved his gun into his belt and pushed against the plate with both hands. He inhaled the ferrous smell of blood, and something else, something acrid. As the plate shifted, his eyes began to sting and tear. Wisps of grey fumes rose from the well. He pulled back, coughing.

'Garner – talk to me!' he shouted.

He stretched his shirt sleeve over one hand and covered his mouth, grabbing his torch from a trouser pocket with the other. He took a breath in and leaned forward again. His eyes blurred but followed the light down to the bottom of the well. He saw a bloodied handprint on the wall. And another, reaching up towards the sky. They were trying to climb up.

'I'm here. I'm here, guys. Hang on.' He needed rope. He needed help.

Grey smoke emanated from the stone, as if a fire burned deep within it. He fell back and coughed, doubled over, hands on his knees. The mask. He always carried a mask. He pulled it from his side pocket and covered his mouth, forcing his face into the fumes once more, directing the torch beam to the base this time.

He saw Crawford first – partially submerged under the acid that was dissolving him. Then he saw Garner. They were lying together, their bodies entwined and mingled, broken and contorted. Pieces of flesh falling off them and floating to the surface, pieces of bone jutting out towards his light. The fluid came up to their mid-torso and they were sinking deeper into it as it ate through them. Garner was slumped in what remained of Crawford's embrace, her head down against her chest.

Crawford's face was turned up to the opening, his eyes dead to the sunlight that filtered through the hibiscus branches above.

Noah staggered blindly, his fingers missing the stone support of the well. He collapsed to the ground on his hands and knees, vomiting. He couldn't breathe or see clearly. It could have been the acid or the tears. He pulled himself a few paces down the path. By the time he heard the footsteps it was too late. He reached for his gun but a frighteningly merciful darkness fell before he could touch its cold, familiar metal.

Chapter 31

Noah woke up but kept his eyes closed, his head limp. If they wanted to kill him, he'd be dead by now. He listened to the muted conversation in the corner. It was in English. He caught words: West, agent, Khan.

He took a quick inventory of his injuries. His hands were cuffed behind his back but there was no significant pain. He couldn't move his arms but he could tell nothing was broken. That pain was different. His head hurt, his stitches were intact and his rib cage hadn't been touched yet. He exhaled, relieved. His right eye was swollen and obscured, the lid drooping like a shade. He would need to protect his left side.

He heard footsteps approach him from behind. He tensed. Cold water hit him. He pulled against the restraints, flinching as they cut his wrists. He rocked on the chair and then stopped, splaying his unfettered legs on the grey cement floor. He blinked hard, the light in his face blinded him. He dropped his head and then raised it again, gradually, allowing his eyes to focus. The shapes on the edge of the room formed people.

He recognised one – Rajasuriya. He smelled sweat, his own, the president's, the soldiers' around him. Rajasuriya walked towards him, the soldiers forming a protective barrier. Noah smiled. He was tied to a chair, bruised and battered. They were heavily armed.

'As you would have realised, Noah, you are in an impromptu interrogation room. I know you'll be comfortable here, you've seen hundreds of them before. Ours isn't as well-equipped as yours but it will do for now. Look at me when I'm talking to you.'

Noah raised his head higher, ignoring the throbbing. The room was simple: sparse, no windows – just lights, chairs and appliances.

'I don't usually participate in these kinds of things.' The president lifted the golden trim of his white sarong up, away from the light red water that pooled at his feet.

Noah wasn't bleeding. Whose pain had been washed away before him? Where was he – and where was Khan?

'But I'm here because you're special. I like you, Noah. You're smart, dedicated and focused. I wish I had more people like you. In fact, if you weren't so dedicated, I'd recruit you, but we both know you'd never turn. You might spend years pretending to be on my side, and then, when I least expected it, after I'd invited you into my home, my hearth, my family weddings and funerals, what would you do?'

'I'd slit your throat and then wipe the blade on your fancy white shirt, not mine,' Noah replied. It hurt to talk but it felt good.

'Yes, because you think you're so much better than me. You all –' he motioned expansively to the 'all' of the West, 'think you're so much better than us. But I think *we're* better because we're more honest about who we are. We're more comfortable with it. We understand the sacrifices that are made by our own people –'

'You mean the sacrifices you make *of* your people,' Noah interrupted. He shifted in his chair and relaxed his body into the shackles. He loosened up his arms behind him. If he wanted to he could stand up but there was nowhere to go.

'Please, it's the same thing. Great leaders must be willing to sacrifice their own people as well as those who attack their people, in order to secure the nation. Every government that ever sent other people's children to war made that decision. You remember what Jefferson said: the tree of liberty must be refreshed.'

'I'm not talking about war – I'm talking about those graves. They were new.'

'They are indeed. But before you judge me *again*, please do remember that most of our best weapons were developed and delivered to us from *your* side of the wall.'

Sahara was right, they had protected Rajasuriya. They played their part in his crimes. He was their Frankenstein's monster. *Sahara* – he hoped she was safe.

'I do what I must to maintain the stability of my country. The West knows that. When it churns their stomachs, they look away, but they don't dare try to stop me.'

He leaned closer to Noah. A few centimetres more and Noah could crack the president's skull with his own forehead, stand, pick up the chair behind him, spin and thrust one of its legs into the man's thick neck.

Rajasuriya saw his face. 'Tie him up better – I'd like to talk to him alone.'

The soldiers hesitated. One of them spoke, 'Sir, the general was very clear – we were to stay with you . . . and him, at all times.'

'Are you refusing to obey me?'

'No, no – of course not.' Another soldier hurried forward and roped Noah's arms and legs to the chair. They left the room.

'That's better. Now we can talk like friends.'

'Tie all of your friends up, do you?'

The president ignored him. 'You talk about sacrifice. Imagine if you'd asked any man on the street – one of your streets – to sacrifice his right to worship God, his right to love God, to follow a religion of his choice. What would the average American or European say to that? Your civil rights advocates would be up in arms, defending the right to privacy, to freedom of expression – what else? There must be at least three other rights that cover religion.'

'It's been a while since I read our Bill of Rights.'

'The shame of it is you selfishly kept God for your own people but the majority of you ignored him anyway. Like a child that wanted something for Christmas but then got bored by New Year's. That's another advantage of living on this side of the shield by the way – we don't have to do Christmas anymore, thank God.'

The president laughed to himself. 'No, your people prefer to worship the gods of materialism and consumption, vanity and celebrity. You don't deserve God.'

'We don't *deserve* God? God doesn't deserve *us*,' Noah replied contemptuously.

'Hush, Noah, he might hear you. You have a very unhealthy relationship with God, and we should explore that some other time.'

Rajasuriya called the soldiers back. 'Untie him,' he commanded. 'I'd like you to help me with something. Hackman tells me you have many talents.'

Noah rubbed his wrists and flexed his shoulders and upper torso.

'I hope we didn't hurt you too much? I apologise – we had to get you out of there quickly, before they returned for you. You're better off with us.'

They. We. They.

'I'm sorry about your team. We don't operate like that, despite your interference in our business. I told you when we first met, Sri Lanka is a sovereign nation,' Rajasuriya echoed Hackman's defence. 'We reserve the right to implement our global commitments in our own way.'

'My team . . .' Noah cleared his throat.

'Yes, yes, your team. It was a little over-the-top, but they're like that.'

'Who?' Noah demanded.

'This is my interrogation, not yours.'

'Who,' Noah tried to control his voice. 'If it wasn't you, who did it? Please.'

'Does it matter? They're dead all the same. And dead is dead, as you know.'

'It matters to me. It won't help them, but it matters to me.'

The president raised an eyebrow. 'You really are ready for retirement.'

Rajasuriya bent towards him, his lips near Noah's ear. Noah saw the soldiers around the president tense, weapons ready. 'Tell me something,' Rajasuriya asked softly, 'do you believe in ghosts?'

Chapter 32

The soldiers stepped back. He heard the door behind him open and the sound of a body being dragged in. He knew that sound well. He looked up, just as they dumped Khan's limp form onto the chair in front of him.

General Rajasuriya was with him. 'Bind him, he can't stay up. Water.'

They tied Khan's chest to the chair and poured water on him.

The scientist shook his head and gasped, rocking with sudden violence.

'Don't move,' Noah said, reflexively. 'It hurts when you fall with the chair. Be still if you can, I'm here.'

'Noah – thank . . .' Khan stopped, grasping for a word, just beyond the horizon of his memory.

'Why are you here? What's happening?' the old man asked. His shirt was torn and bloodstained. His left ear dangled by a thin strip of skin.

'Who,' Noah whispered. 'Who did this to you?'

'The general's men – the hospital lobby. I didn't even make it to the lab. Devi must be worried. Did you go to the lab?'

'I did – they've taken your work, hard drives, everything except Devi – they didn't touch her.'

'Thank . . .' Khan stopped.

'Thank who?' General Rajasuriya asked.

'I don't know,' Khan said hoarsely. 'I don't know who . . .'

'Dr Khan, you have been accused by the Department for Biological Integrity of developing a decoy vaccine.' The general spoke to Khan but looked at Noah.

'Your friend Dr Williams here has been investigating whether you are responsible for four breaches of the Immunity Shield that have taken place in the Eastern Alliance recently.

'You have been questioned by us and you have denied the allegations – is that correct?'

Khan looked at the general and shook his head.

'Dr Khan – conspiracy to undermine the Immunity Shield is a national and international crime, punishable by death in Sri Lanka. How do you answer these charges?'

Khan's words stumbled. 'I would never do that. One hundred percent herd immunity is vital for our survival . . . Ebola is out there, waiting for its moment.' He coughed and took a deep breath. 'I've only ever developed vaccines to help us. I tried telling them, Noah, but they showed me pictures of this vaccine. It's not mine –'

'Enough!' the president stepped forward. He thrust images in Khan's face. Enlarged photographs of the vaccine used by Hassan Ali. He fired off questions and reloaded with more. 'Why did you make this? Who did you give it to? Tell me who you're working for. I want the names of your vaxxers. I want the population sets you've breached.'

'I told you, sir. I told your brother so many times.' Khan cried as he looked at the photographs again. 'I know this vaccine – but it isn't mine. It is beautifully crafted but not complete. I would never leave something unfinished, you know that.' He looked at Noah.

'Son, he needs to do better. The vaccine won't work – no Ebola immunity. Mine is better. Full immunity, with a passive strand – so it won't hurt anyone. I wish I had more time. I wanted to extrapolate more vaccines. We worked much better together. Aisha always said that together we were the genetically perfect virologist.' He tried to laugh but grimaced with pain instead. 'I could finish it with him if I had more time. Devi knows what to do. She wants to help too.'

Noah's heart raced. Khan sounded delirious but he wasn't. Noah had seen pain drive men mad – this was clarity not madness.

Where did Rajasuriya get the pictures from? No one had those except Bio. *Fuck you, Hackman. I told you I would contain Khan when I was certain. I told you I wasn't sure.* Khan was something – but not the ghost. Why had Hackman turned him in to Rajasuriya?

'Calm down, Amir, please. You need to calm down.' Noah looked at the soldiers around them. 'How do you recognise the vaccine? Where have you seen it before? Think carefully.'

'How do I recognise . . .? Of course I recognise all exceptional virology. I even recognised the Ebola strain in the hospital outbreak. It was perfect; just what I needed. If you paid more attention you'd recognise it too,' Khan replied.

'You're scolding me? Now?'

'I won't have much time to scold you in the future.' Khan smiled, tears in his eyes. 'That vaccine isn't mine – I swear to you. Mine is better. Take it back to him. He'll know what to do. Trust *him* – you need to have faith, Noah.'

'Who is he talking about?' Rajasuriya turned to Noah. 'Who is he talking about?'

The president leaned in to Khan. 'God?' he whispered. 'Are you talking to God now?'

'God,' Khan whispered the name and closed his eyes.

The president stepped back and nodded at a soldier. He raised his handgun and smacked Khan across the face, sending his body towards the floor. Noah jumped up and caught him in his arms. He heard Khan's ragged breathing in his ear. Ancient Sanskrit words found their way from some lost cavern in the old man's brain, mumbled and mispronounced, but immediately recognisable to Noah.

He set the chair and Khan firmly upright. Then he turned around and drove his boot into the soldier's knee, welcoming the sound of bones breaking, tendons severing.

Soldiers shouted and raised their weapons to his head. He put his arms up, hearing someone step up behind him. He relaxed his body for the blow to his back that was coming. Impact hurt less if your muscles were relaxed. Of course a spinal break was something else.

There it was. Badly placed to the left kidney. He sank to his knees, hands on the ground, waiting for the follow-up. He needed to outlast this beating and work out what to do.

'Wait!' the general shouted. 'Wait. Get him up.' Hands dragged him up and onto his chair. He heard the chime of handcuffs and the click as it bound him. Hands in front this time. Better.

'Noah,' Khan whispered. 'Noah, please don't worry about me.'

'Isn't that touching? Tell me, Doctor, who paid you to develop this vaccine?' President Rajasuriya asked.

Khan looked up at Rajasuriya, confused. 'I didn't develop it – no one paid me. I work for you – for Sri Lanka, for its people. I'm trying to help you.'

'Help us? With a vaccine that doesn't work? A vaccine that undermines herd immunity and invites death on all of us?'

'No, no, no,' Khan wept. 'I told you. My vaccine – the one I'm working on – will provide immunity for Ebola and future strains of the virus. It could change everything.'

'Change is rarely stable,' the president replied. 'Let's talk about your other vaccine in a moment. My people will disconnect that computerised-arm machine in your lab. I presume that your work will be recorded on its hard drive?'

'Devi.'

'What?'

'I call her Devi. Please don't hurt her. She can help you if you work with her.'

'I'll keep that in mind when we bring her here and look inside her artificially intelligent brain. Who are you working for?'

'I don't know what you're talking about,' Khan repeated wearily.

President Rajasuriya's right hand twitched slightly. A soldier stepped forward with a short stick, like a riding crop, in his hand. He slapped Noah across the face, left side, whipping his head back. He tasted a rush of blood in his mouth. Noise, like waves breaking, in his ears. The eye was still intact.

'No, no – I said, not his face.' The president shook his head. 'He needs to talk – and Hackman might want to see him before he trades. Body blows only. Something we can dress up later.'

'Hack –' His lip was split but functional. He swallowed hard and tried again.

'Hackman won't trade me. I'm expendable.'

'Don't talk about yourself like that, Noah. You're special.'

He turned back to Khan. 'Finger or nail?'

'What?' Khan asked. Noah felt his blood chill. He'd asked that question before.

'Finger or nail – what would you prefer?'

'Don't do it – he's a crazy old man with strange theories about evolution. An obsessed scientist. He isn't trying to breach the shield.'

'Then why did he create that vaccine? You heard him, he recognised the photographs – he said he can fix it. Where did it come from? Who are you working for?' The president was shouting into Khan's face, spittle flying from his enraged mouth.

'Finger or nail,' he screamed.

'Nail, nail, nail,' Noah shouted, stamping his feet at Khan. It was painful but fast. It grew back eventually if the nail bed wasn't damaged too badly.

A soldier behind Noah grabbed his wrists. Shocked, Noah clenched his fists. People always clenched their fists. They always did it and it was always futile. Hands pried his fingers apart. He screamed a loud primal cry from the base of his chest as the nail was torn out of its bed.

He rocked forward and back on the chair, his chest thrashed against the pain. He put his legs out and planted his feet on the ground to steady himself. His nerve endings were raw and cold to the hot room around him.

'No – hurt me, hurt me! Noah!' Khan cried, lunging in his chair towards him. He fell over. A soldier threw him back upright.

'Again – I ask you. Who are you working for?' The president shouted. 'He has plenty more of those, Dr Khan, and unfortunately for him, he's good at pain. He'll be conscious for most of it.'

'No one. Please, I beg you,' Khan half cried, half talked.

Noah breathed in and out of his mouth rapidly. Grunting like a speared animal, he tried to shake himself out of the pain chaos.

'Take a moment to compose yourself, Noah, we've got time.' Rajasuriya sat down on a chair and crossed his legs elegantly, as if settling back for a chat.

'Were you commissioned to create the vaccine or did you work alone?' he asked.

Khan shook his head.

'He's telling the truth. Jesus, I mean –' Noah caught himself. 'Why are you doing this? He's telling the truth.'

'No. He's not.' Rajasuriya motioned to the soldier behind Noah and he felt hands on his wrists and chest again.

This time he pulled himself up and the chair came with him, plastered to his body with his sweat. It dropped, clattering to the ground. The soldiers were on top of him. One grabbed the chair and turned it up. Others pushed down on his shoulders, forcing him back into it. Another punched him in the stomach so he hunched over, breathless. A belt was strapped around his chest; the leather tightened, squeezing the air from his lungs.

Hands gripped his wrists at the side of the chair again. He saw the pliers this time. A crocodile's snout. The teeth. Small but strong. Anything you bought at the local hardware store would do. He preferred German steel.

Pain bolted through him like electricity. He threw his head back and screamed louder for the second nail and then clenched his jaw, muffling his cry through his teeth for the third and fourth one. He convulsed forward, trying to hit his head on the men around him, trying to knock himself out. They moved back and let him fall over with the chair. He was stranded on his side, his cheek pressed against the water and the blood on the cold floor.

'Stop, stop – I beg you!' Khan cried.

'Like you begged me last time?' The president sneered. Khan looked up sharply, his eyes full of a deeper pain than Noah's.

'Yes, you begged me to show mercy but there was nothing you could do for your lovely wife. We've been watching your clinic at Anuradhapura. I don't know how you put up with that smell. I imagine you're drawn to it, aren't you, Doctor? The smell of death. The fragrance of your wife? Her last resting place. Her final moments. Do you wonder what they were like? Was she terrified? Was she in pain? Would you like me to tell you?'

'No,' Khan whispered. 'She knew whose she was. She knew where she was going.'

'A sweet sentiment. Did you discover that while meditating under a Bodhi tree?' the president taunted. 'When the hospital outbreak happened, I suspected you at first. I thought you might be seeking revenge for her death. You're an accomplished virologist. You could have hidden old stores of contaminated blood.'

He looked at Noah to make sure he hadn't passed out, and then turned back to Khan.

'But I was wrong about you – I was wrong from the beginning. It's more than mere revenge, isn't it? I think you've been working on something far more powerful.'

Noah could see Khan processing the president's words. He knew this man now, knew what he looked like when he was working through a problem.

'Finger or nail, Noah – you choose this time.'

Noah tensed instinctively and then exhaled. He relaxed his fingers.

'Nail.'

'Enough, I'll tell you,' Khan spoke clearly but quietly. Everyone in the room looked at him. The general moved closer.

Khan looked at Noah. 'I did it. I developed the placebo vaccine. For Aisha. And because I've been remembering things – I knew the vaccine was changing us. I told you, part of its structure is damaging us.

'I couldn't understand its purpose but I tried to stop it. I developed a completely ineffective vaccine that passes the scanners – you would never know who was immune and who wasn't. I found vaxxers who didn't believe in the vaccination programme anymore. I ran four trials – I would have done more but then you came, son.'

He paused to catch his breath. 'Water,' he whispered. The general nodded and a soldier stepped forward with a canister. Khan gulped erratically, almost choking.

'Enough.' The president intervened. 'You said four trials – I don't believe you. There must be more. Tell me where the breaches are or we can play with Noah's fingers a little more.'

Khan shook his head. 'If I had more time, I would have done more,' he repeated.

'Who did you work with?'

'No one. I worked alone – as you said, I'm a skilled virologist. My expertise is unsurpassed. If you'd read any of my papers you'd know that. I don't need anyone's assistance. Just Devi.'

He looked at Noah. 'I'm sorry if I disappointed you, son. When this is over, you should go back to Devi. Tell her what happened to me – don't tell her everything. She's very sensitive, I know she doesn't look it. Tell her I learnt a great deal from her. Tell her I said goodbye. Would you do that for me, please, Noah – it's important.'

'When this is over you should tell her yourself. She doesn't like me very much.'

'That's not true – she likes you. And she trusts you as much as I do. She just thinks you're a lazy scientist. She doesn't like to see potential wasted. There was more you could have learnt, if we had time. You should read more, study more, think more. Fight less. Learn from your father, he was very wise. An explorer.'

'Like you.' Noah winced as the cut on his lip widened. 'Talk to Devi yourself – we're getting out of this soon.'

He had no idea how.

Khan lifted his head with difficulty and looked at him squarely. 'No, I'm not. I've been dying a long time. I've seen more death in my life than life. I know when it's near.'

'Don't be so optimistic, Dr Khan,' The president replied. 'I want the new vaccine you've developed.'

'You can have it – the samples are all in the lab. My research is there too. Some virologists could recreate and improve it just using the sample. It needs refinement but I think you can manage that.' Khan smiled at Noah.

The general spoke. 'I think you've served your purpose, Noah.' He waved his hands at the soldiers and they unbuckled his chest restraints.

'No, let me stay with him.' Noah struggled.

'You don't want to see this,' the general replied.

'I've done worse.'

'Perhaps,' he dropped his voice. 'But it's always different when it's someone you love.'

Noah looked up at the camera in the corner of the room.

'Do what you have to do – but let me stay with him,' he said. 'I don't want him to be alone.'

'Noah, don't you realise yet?' Khan said. 'We are never alone. I have never been alone – I feel it everywhere. If you could let go a little, you would feel it again too.'

The soldiers lifted Noah up by the shoulders.

'Wait, let me say goodbye.' He pulled away from them. A young soldier looked at the general questioningly. The general looked at the camera in the ceiling and nodded.

'You should check with them first,' the president warned.

The general shrugged. 'Sri Lanka is a sovereign nation. Do it – leave his cuffs on.'

The soldiers lifted Khan and dragged him closer to Noah. He reached forward and straightened the old man's clothing. He kissed Khan on the cheek, smelling blood and sweat. He kissed him again on the other side, and bent down, resting his head on the man's shoulder.

Khan leaned into him. 'Thank you,' he whispered.

Noah nodded. He stepped away a little, giving himself enough room. He took that particular breath in. Then he flicked his head back and forward, hard into the bridge of Khan's nose, smashing it. Thousands of synapses fired and tears blurred his eyes.

His brain registered the impact and pain in his forehead instantaneously. The soldiers took longer. Before they realised what he was doing, he straightened his body, raised his cuffed hands, fingers back, palm forward, and slammed it into Khan's broken nose cartilage, driving it hard like a blade into his brain. The older man slumped on him, ribbons of blood winding around them both.

Chapter 33

There was silence for a moment, and then shouting. Soldiers pulled him away. Khan fell to the floor heavily, slipping on the blood that pooled at their feet. He was gone. Noah didn't doubt it.

A soldier raised the butt of his gun. Noah dropped his left shoulder and charged forward, knocking the man off his feet and over Noah's shoulder. Another soldier swung at him. Noah ducked, sliding in the blood. He steadied himself, brought his knee into the man's stomach and then barrelled him out of the way. He heard a rifle cock.

'Don't kill him, just stop him,' General Rajasuriya shouted.

Noah took a step forward. There was nowhere to go. Even if he made it to the door, he didn't know what was behind it. But steps forward were always better than steps back.

There were three men on him now, punching and kicking. He kept standing and swept the legs of one man from under him, plunging a heavy foot into his face as he hit the ground.

'Enough – Noah!' A voice he recognised was shouting at him. She sounded afraid. He'd never heard that in her before.

'I said enough!' the voice repeated, more authoritatively this time. 'Mr President, General – you've had the opportunity you asked for. He got your confession, we expect you to honour your agreement.'

He looked up to see a woman in a grey military bodysuit. Her hair was pulled back in a tight braid. She wore her shoulder holster in plain sight, and Bio credentials around her neck.

'Sahara . . .' She looked so different. Her eyes coldly assessed the room. Two Bio agents stood behind her, their faces impassive. She motioned to them and they moved towards him, as the soldiers retreated into a wide circle.

'Keys?' Sahara raised her hand. One of the soldiers looked at the president who nodded. He threw the keys at her.

'You can't be all that expendable, Noah.' He smoothed his moustache and then his clothing. 'Hackman's instructions were specific. You were to do your job and then you were to go home. He thought I should just let you loose on Khan. Give you back the tools of your trade and see how long before the old man disintegrated. But I think our approach worked better, don't you?'

When Noah didn't answer, the president continued. 'He was right about you – you are his best. You took longer than I expected but you got there in the end.'

He moved closer to Noah but ensured there were two soldiers between them. 'A joint covert operation between the Eastern and Western Alliance uncovers plot by traitorous scientist to breach the Immunity Shield in the East.' He spoke as if quoting a headline. 'The investigation into the degree of shield violation is ongoing.' He paused and smiled. 'It has an exciting ring to it. Maybe they'll make a movie in years to come. Tell Hackman I'm sorry if we ruined your pretty face.'

'Not my face, just my manicure.'

Rajasuriya laughed. 'I like you, Noah. I have work for you here if you ever decide to go freelance.'

'Come on, sir,' one of the Bio agents prompted firmly. Together they dragged and guided him out of the room until he could walk by himself. They followed Sahara in silence as she swiped her pass card and punched in codes at every door. Noah realised where they were – in Colombo General Hospital, the basement floors.

'Take me to his lab.' He pushed past the agents and grabbed her arm. 'They'll be pulling Devi out of the wall any moment now. I want to see her.'

'Don't be ridiculous – I need to get you to the airport. There's a chartered flight leaving in an hour. Special delivery, courtesy of Hackman.'

'Then we have time – quickly.' He stood, hunched over her. Pain radiated from his fingertips to his shoulder, like barbed wire threaded through his veins.

She touched his face gently. 'What did they do to you?'

'What I deserved. You know about my team – Crawford and Garner.' It wasn't a question.

She nodded.

'Could you have stopped it?'

'No – my orders were to protect you. I'm always a safe distance behind you, not them. I'm sorry, Noah. It's hard, losing your people.'

'It has to be for something. Take me to his lab. Please.'

She turned to the others. 'Wait for me in the lobby but take your time getting there. Take the stairs – two flights up. Your credentials will work in this part of the hospital.' They were unwilling to leave Noah's side.

'I'll be fine – I'll meet you at the airport,' he reassured them. 'Go,' he ordered. 'No, wait,' he called out. 'Lychees – I promised Neeson I'd get him lychees. Could you?'

Sahara shook her head. 'I'm sure they can. Anything else – something more useful like a flak jacket and a side-arm perhaps?

Let's go, quickly,' she repeated, dragging him into the nearest lift and pressing the button to Khan's floor.

'Who are you?' he asked.

'A friend.'

'I don't have any friends.'

'So you keep saying.'

'Who do you work for?'

'Does it matter which country, which allegiance? People only ever work for themselves.'

'They've all seen your face now. If you don't work for them, they know who you are.'

'Maybe it's time I went home too.' The lift came to a halt and the doors opened. 'I don't know – I still prefer it here.'

'It's not safe for you here.'

She shrugged her shoulders. 'Nowhere is truly safe. I'll take my chances a while longer. I think things will get more interesting in this part of the world.'

'More interesting?' He shook his head. 'I need boring. I need a rest. I need . . .'

'What?'

'I don't know – something other than this. More life, less death,' he said, thinking of Khan.

'Life is killing all of us. Your security passes have been revoked so we'll have to use mine.'

'You have passes for this section?' he asked.

'Sometimes, it depends – today I have a pass.'

She guided him quickly through the doors that took them to Khan's lab. Devi was still there. He walked around the room, trying to work out what it was that Khan had left for him.

'Good afternoon, Dr Williams,' Devi's voice echoed around the room.

'You really should call me Noah, Devi. It's time we were friends.'

'We are friends.'

'I thought you said you didn't have any friends,' Sahara remarked, stepping over torn papers.

'Dr Khan says Dr Williams always underestimates himself,' Devi replied.

'Dr Khan says you think I'm a lazy scientist,' Noah retorted.

'You are a lazy scientist. Did Dr Khan have any other messages for me?'

Noah's throat tightened. He opened his mouth but the words wouldn't come out. He sat on Khan's stool and pulled it close to the old man's gamma counter, touching the re-calibration switch.

'Don't play with his stuff,' Devi said kindly.

'Sorry. I just –' he paused. 'Amir said to tell you goodbye. He said he learnt a lot from you. He was grateful.'

'Thank you for that message, Noah. You were with him at the end?'

'Yes.'

'He wanted me to show you something. Take the control pad and watch the screen.'

Devi's arm slid down from behind the scope and moved gracefully towards him, holding Khan's control pad. As he made contact with her, he felt a small but deep prick on his palm. He winced and nearly dropped the pad. He was about to inspect his hand, when he stopped.

'Careful, it's delicate,' she said.

He looked at her and then at Sahara who hadn't noticed anything. Underneath the pad, he rubbed his palm gently, feeling blood and the uneven graze of broken and punctured skin.

Suddenly, the screen on the wall illuminated. It flashed and was then filled with photographs of a younger Khan with his wife. Noah leaned back in the seat as Devi flicked through the slide show. Khan and Aisha in London, at a conference in Atlanta, at a church in Geneva.

'He said it's important to remember the happy times we were given,' Devi said. 'Some things, some memories, can't be eradicated.'

'She was very beautiful, wasn't she?'

'Yes. I think he grieves – grieved – every day but he also remembered and laughed. He suggested you do the same after your morning exercise and swim.'

'After my morning exercise and swim?'

'Yes. He said you should swim more. It relaxes the mind.'

Noah laughed, the pain almost obscuring the things his eyes would normally notice immediately: the detail of their lives on the enormous screen. The smile, the hands held, the way their bodies turned towards each other, the sunlight glinting off the gold medallion she wore in every photograph, a gold circle with fine geometric shapes inside it. The perfect mandala.

'It's time to go, Noah,' Devi said. The photographs disappeared, leaving the screen empty, save for Devi's last command to herself.

```
<DELETE FILES>
```

'We need to get out of here now,' Noah pulled himself to his feet.

'You've only just worked that out? I can't believe *you're* Hackman's best. Let's go.' Sahara led the way, back out the three doors and down the corridor to the stairs. An alarm rang behind them. The elevator door opened. He heard the pounding of boots: soldiers.

'Against the wall, quickly.' She pushed him away from the stairwell. 'Here,' she opened the first door and ran through, her hand on her gun. He was right behind her. She skidded short, seeing the soldiers coming towards them. He nearly knocked her over. They turned simultaneously and ran. She stopped halfway down the corridor, turned back to the soldiers and shot at a trolley of oxygen tanks. They collapsed in a landslide of metal.

He grabbed her hand, crying out as the raw and torn nerve endings in his nail beds touched her skin.

'This way,' he shouted. Heavy feet running behind him and screams as staff and patients hit the floor. She stopped in a doorway and bent down to pull out her second weapon from her ankle holster.

'Can you use it?'

'I'm fine.' He pushed his bloodied finger through the trigger guard, gasping when he made contact with the metal. He pulled back the slide. 'I'm fine,' he repeated.

'This way, try to keep up.' She bolted down the corridor and through large doors into an operating room. Doctors and nurses stood over a patient, retractors and clamps in place, scalpels poised, open skin revealing the fleshy mass of a distended bowel.

Some people raised their hands, others hovered protectively over the patient. A few whimpered.

Sahara raised her finger to her lips, her gun trained on the main surgeon. 'No noise,' she shook her head. People pushed themselves back into the walls as they passed, as though they were contagious. They almost made it to the back of the OR when the front door burst open and two soldiers charged in. People screamed. Sahara shot both men in their brachial nerve. They dropped their guns. One tried to grab his with his other hand.

'Don't,' she warned. 'Just don't.' She shot the lights of the OR, showering them in broken glass and darkness.

'This way,' Noah shouted again, dragging her behind him. They ran through an empty room and into another corridor. 'Your pass, your pass,' he held out a hand. She threw it to him. He recognised the face on the card.

He swiped one door after another. She shut each one behind them. Soldiers slammed into the last locked door, shooting at it. He ducked, then clenching a fist around his weapon, he raised it.

He could feel Sahara's breath on his back, her arm around his waist, helping him. He fired at the glass panel, exploding it into the face of a soldier.

'We have to keep going,' she whispered.

He dropped his arm. She took the gun from him. He reached for her and pulled her left.

'No, this way –' she turned right and started sprinting. He saw her press into her earpiece as she ran. Right and then left, towards a heavy metal door. It was an exit. There was a meta-scanner in front of it. The security guard grabbed his weapon but she shot him in the thigh with one gun and then raised both, higher, firing rapidly and precisely at the scanner. Its frame crackled and sparked and ignited. She didn't stop – running straight through the halo of fire. She pushed the door into the sunlight of a side alley.

Vijay's SUV braked a few feet away, the door flung open. He threw a backpack at Sahara.

'As you requested, madam. Come, sir, our last tour of the city. No need to apologise about the car.'

Sahara kissed Noah briefly and tucked one of her guns into his belt. She grabbed his hand and reclaimed the general's pass card.

'Don't fuck this up,' she whispered.

Noah's palm was swollen and red. She traced and then pressed down hard on the wound inflicted by Devi.

'Get it right – fix it – for both of us.' She kissed him again and then ran down the alley behind the hospital, pulling her backpack on as she picked up speed.

Chapter 34

Noah lay strapped to a bed. He tried to remember the words his father had taught him. He closed his eyes but all he could see was Khan's dark blood spilling over them. He cried out and angrily pulled against his restraints. The edges of his vision blurred: people and machines in muted colours, drifting in and out. The room was burning hot, his skin wet.

'Water,' he whispered. 'Water.' Maybe they couldn't hear him. Maybe they weren't there.

He lay back and turned his head. There was a book on the side-table. He couldn't touch it. It was his old edition of the *Bhagavad Gita*.

The first page had an inscription:

To my dearest son, may these words comfort and guide you.
Your loving Papa.

'It is a pathway, son.' His father reached for the book.

Noah stood poised at the fireplace of their home. Papa stood up from his armchair and stumbled. Noah moved forward to catch him.

'Don't. Don't touch me.' His father put one hand out. With the other, he balanced himself against the chair and fixed his face mask.

'You're still well. Please don't touch me.'

Noah ignored him. He put his arms around his father and lowered him easily back into the chair. He was as light as a child. The muscle had wasted on the bone and even the bone seemed empty of marrow. Noah thought he could crumple him like the papers he threw into the fire.

'Please don't burn it.' Papa reached for the *Bhagavad Gita* again. 'I'd rather be cold.' Noah placed the book in his father's lap.

'I bought this edition for you when you were in your mother's womb. She read to you from the English canon, all those consumptive fops she swoons over. I read you the Gita and the Baseball Almanac of 2000.'

'I'm just relieved it wasn't *Pure Mathematics*, by GH Hardy.'

His father laughed behind the mask. His saliva blotched against it, small blooms of red he couldn't see. Noah sat at his father's feet. They were fat with three layers of socks. He unwrapped them every couple of hours to check for signs of the necrosis they knew was coming.

'Read this again and again, Noah. It is a path – a plan – for man to free himself from all of this.'

'A book won't free us from this; a cure will – and proper heating and food,' Noah replied angrily.

'No, son, I don't mean the virus – I mean life. Life is an illusion, a bondage to something that we are not.'

Noah had heard that talk a hundred times before. He was relieved that the virus hadn't gone to his father's brain yet. Memory and lucidity were still in place.

'This body,' Papa said, feebly pinching himself. His skin lifted like a wrinkled, oversized coat. 'This body isn't real. Only inside here,' he raised his shaking hand to his chest, 'this is real.' He concentrated and steadied his tremor before it spread to the rest of his arm.

'Man's true nature is a divine energy – inside me and you, all around us. Even this virus,' he clenched his hand weakly. 'Even this virus is divine. It too is seeking its true nature.'

'This virus is devouring you from within, slowly shutting down your kidney and liver functions.' Noah tried not to raise his voice. 'You cannot retain food and water. I wear two layers of gloves and wipe the blood from your eyes and ears and anus. It will attack your brain soon and you will not know yourself.' His voice caught in his throat.

'How – how is this virus divine?'

God help me, he thought. *God help us*. His head dropped to his knees. He covered himself with his arms. He could feel his father's hand hover above his head and then pull back. He longed to hold his father's hand. Skin against skin. He raised his tear-stained face.

'Noah, we are more than the forms we inhabit – whether it be this body or a virus. Look inside – our divinity yearns to be free, to merge with the divinity all around us. Don't let form restrain you. We are limitless. Read the Gita, son. It's all in there.' His father sank back into the chair and closed his eyes.

'I'm so tired these days,' he said. 'I'm so sorry.' The book slipped to his feet.

'It's all right, Papa. You rest.' Noah picked up the book, closed the cover on the inscription and turned it over. On the back, etched into the leather, was a square that contained a circle that contained triangles within triangles.

He placed the book back on his father's lap and threw *Pure Mathematics* on the fire. The yellow flames accepted his offering and then roared, hungry for more. His hand burned, sparking a fever in his blood.

*

Noah sat up and tried to swing his legs out of the hospital bed. He was attached to two IVs. His fingers were bandaged and his ribs taped. His side table was empty except for his wedding ring.

'Has Maggie been here?' His voice sounded hoarse.

'Take it easy, you can lie down for this conversation.' Hackman grabbed him as he swayed on the edge of the bed. Noah let him guide him back down.

'She came while you were sleeping, stayed for a long time actually. Sweet of her. She said she'll come back in the morning. Something about a bear.'

'I don't know what's wrong with me. I was fine back in Sri Lanka.'

'You weren't fine. You were tortured and standing on adrenaline alone. They had to restrain and medicate you to let you heal some. Quite rightly so, if in your medical opinion you're ready to jump out of your hospital bed and back into the field.'

Noah sank into the dense pillows. 'Have you told Garner and Crawford's families?'

'Yes, the official story is a light airplane crash, no bodies. They were en route to India to install a new data management system for the WHO headquarters in Delhi.'

'It was a wasteful death.'

'Are we still talking about Garner and Crawford?'

Noah looked down at his hands. Flecks of blood appeared through the bandages.

'Of course we are. The president said someone else wanted my team dead; wanted me dead. Who else is in the region? Who could do . . . that.' He didn't know how to describe what he had seen in the well. 'Who could do that?' he repeated, closing his eyes against the memory.

'I don't know and we have no way of finding out. Like countless deaths before, and many more to come, we have to let it go. They knew the risks.'

'Did they? This was supposed to be a fairly standard investigation of an elderly virologist who was almost certainly a bioterrorist on paper, until we worked out in person that he wasn't.' Noah spoke quietly to control the tremor in his voice.

'Can we talk about Khan?' Hackman asked. 'I've read all the transcripts and the notes now. Is there anything else you can tell me?'

'There's not much to add. He revealed that he was using a gene-mining technique to . . . create new vaccines – one of them was different – it was special . . .'

'Yes, to put it mildly. Sahara told me it has the ability to adapt and evolve when it encounters different strains of Ebola. It isn't just a multi-strain vaccine.'

'No, it's much better. The Devi Vaccine, he called it. An all-powerful vaccine that could protect us from Ebola 48, 49, 50, 51 . . .' He felt himself drifting.

Weaponised strains – Khan had said the vaccine would work against weaponised strains.

'Noah, I need you to focus a little longer. What was he going to do with it? The super-vaccine – it's worth a fortune.'

'He was going to share it. He didn't want to release Ebola into the population. I'm not even sure he wanted to bring the Sixth Virus back. He knew the Faith Inhibitor strand was dangerous, but he hadn't worked out how dangerous.'

'And those patients in his clinic at Anuradhapura? What was going on there? He spent a lot of time with them.'

'What did Sahara tell you?' His strength was fading. 'She said she would brief you.'

'She did – but she was brief.'

'Probably because there wasn't much to tell – he ran a community triage and treatment centre. They had converted the old palace and temples into clinics. He was a resourceful doctor, dedicated to public health.'

Like Sahara, he kept the rest of the intel about those patients to himself. And about the general. Who would believe him anyway? Noah wasn't sure *he* believed it. And yet at moments it made complete sense. He couldn't understand the science but he trusted the man. Perhaps he was beginning to trust something else too.

'Was he the ghost?'

'I don't think so . . . there is someone else out there.' He was so tired. He would need to see Garner and Crawford's families.

'Who?' Hackman asked.

'I have no idea – I've investigated and implicated the wrong man. I've lost two agents – two people who depended on me. I've been tortured – and I've killed an innocent man.'

'You didn't have to.'

'You think I could have left him to suffer weeks, maybe months more at the hands of Rajasuriya?'

'He wouldn't have lasted that long.'

He shouldn't have had to last at all, Noah thought. He shouldn't have been arrested. The photos of Khan and his wife; the pendant – what was Khan trying to tell him? He rubbed the wound on his palm. It had healed, the skin thickening into a small welt.

He let himself sink deeper into the pillow and then shook his head. His eyes fell on the silver pin fastened to Hackman's lapel. The tree of liberty, Hackman had said. Sri Bodhi. Abre de Libre. A gift from a friend.

'He's dead now,' Noah said. 'Tell me what you want me to do?'

'I want you to let it go. Can you do that – for your own sake? You need to recover from this. Rest, get yourself well again, and then let's talk about work if that's what you want. You're an outstanding agent and I'd hate to lose you to early retirement, or whatever you want to call it. But I'd hate it more if I lost you to the demons of this job. They can eat away at you from the inside.'

Like cancer, Noah thought.

Chapter 35

Neeson put the phone down and began tidying up. The robotic arm hovered.

'Let me, Roberta, I like doing it. It helps me think.'

He liked a well-organised lab. He stacked the equipment in the large steriliser and threw everything else in the biohazard bin. He sprayed all of the surfaces with chlorobicide and wiped them down, throwing the tissue in the bin when he'd finished.

He logged on to his computer with his password:

```
Aisha:08122025
```

Her name and the date of her death. For fifteen years, it had been the daily reminder of his weakness – and the debt he owed.

He remembered it too well. Hackman had asked him, 'Did you speak to them? Will they let it go?'

He had answered honestly. 'No, they're scientists. They will always seek to understand where we fit into the universe. Science is the search for truth.'

'Truth?' Hackman replied angrily. 'The truth is that three billion people just died in five years and science has given us a way to make it stop. Science, not God. This vaccine is our saviour.'

'No,' Neeson shook his head. 'Jesus is our saviour.'

'Save it, Jack. I'm surprised you can fit your lab coat over your hair shirt. What are we going to do? We can't afford to have them undermining the new programme. I know they're your friends – but can they be controlled?'

He was so torn. Duty to country. Or love for his friend. And his friend's wife who didn't love him back.

'Jack,' Hackman repeated. 'I said can they be controlled?'

'No,' Neeson whispered. 'No.' God help him. God help them.

*

Roberta's robotic arm moved towards him. 'Is there anything I can do for you, Dr Neeson?'

'No, thank you, Roberta – you've been a wonderful help. We might be done for today. I'm expecting someone soon.'

'Would you like me to power off and give you some privacy?' she asked.

'No, that won't be necessary.' There was no such thing as privacy in their world.

He heard the lab door open behind him. It hadn't taken Hackman long.

'How is he?' Neeson asked.

'Alive,' Hackman replied. 'I reviewed the transcript of his last call to you.'

'Of course,' he said. *Was he being warned?*

'What do you make of it?' Hackman leaned against the bench. 'Does he know?'

'Don't touch that. He knows something's not right – he'll get there in the end. He usually does. That's why you sent him.'

'No, I sent him to reveal Khan as the ghost – we need a plausible fall guy and who better than a brilliant virologist with a reason for revenge and a clinical explanation for crazy behaviour. Noah was *supposed* to conclude that Khan could be breaching the Immunity Shield.'

'Khan *was* breaching the Immunity Shield against the Sixth Virus – there's nothing like the truth as a foundation for guilt,' Neeson replied wearily.

'Sure, but his vaccine provides full immunity against Ebola. I need real gaps in the Immunity Shield if this is to work. It was all going so well. Your current iteration of the decoy is almost perfect – it fools the Eastern Alliance scanners but doesn't create Ebola immunity.'

'Thank you, I suppose.'

Hackman laughed. 'You know, you're not as much fun to work with as you used to be.'

'Thanks again.'

'The only thing that makes me nervous about your vaccine is the Faith Inhibitor strand – why can't you use a live strand? Why do both parts of the decoy have to be . . . you know, decoys? We want a gap in Ebola immunity, not the Sixth Virus immunity as well.'

'I told you, I can't do it. The Faith Inhibitor needs the *live* vector to piggyback on into the bloodstream – if you use a decoy for the Ebola component then you have to use a decoy for the Faith Inhibitor component too.'

'And you're not worried that people will . . . God forbid, find God again?'

'Their last boosters should have contained enough inhibitor to damage the faith engine. There won't be enough time for the frontal lobe to regenerate. Your plan will be in motion long before that happens,' Neeson replied.

'*Our* plan,' Hackman reminded him. 'Then your decoy is perfect. No one will know which population sets are immune and which are vulnerable to the virus. A series of localised outbreaks will take care of those sets quickly.'

'Are you sure you still want to do this?' Neeson asked, trying to keep the conflict in his mind out of his voice.

'Of course I'm sure – nothing has changed since we agreed this strategy three years ago – when *you* agreed to develop a decoy. If anything, time has only proved the business case. The population of the Eastern Alliance is increasing too quickly. I heard you mention the Christian Coalition – did you read their recent study on population growth?'

'I did. It made it to the New England Journal of Medicine and the Lancet – they're not on the fringes anymore with their research.'

'Well someone needs to tell them they got it completely wrong.'

'Be my guest.'

'You first. I hate those people. The group praying before meetings drives me nuts.' Hackman shuddered.

'They weren't completely wrong – people of any faith *are* happier. They do live healthier, longer lives. No one knows why – the study stopped short of hypothesising a causal connection between faith and clinical indicators of biological success, but its methodology was sound. They used all the data, not just the results that proved their point, which is more than I can say for our friends at Abre de Libre.' Neeson's hands ached. He flexed and relaxed them a few times.

'So scathing for a man whose career has been largely funded by ADL. We need their money if we're going to keep up with their science; and we need their *partnership* – not friendship – if we're going to keep our half of the world safe.'

'Keep up with their science?' Neeson repeated. 'We are supposed to *regulate* their science – how do we do that if we're on their payroll?'

'We're not on their payroll – we're paid by the taxpayers of the West to protect the West. Working with ADL is just one of the ways we achieve that. I hate having this conversation with you, Neese – I'm offended I still have to justify our position to you.'

'Well, I wouldn't want to offend you, old friend,' Neeson replied.

'Arsehole. The Christian Coalition study also said that people with faith – any religious or spiritual faith, not just the ones that decry contraception – have more children. That is clearly bullshit – the Eastern Alliance has no faith and they are reproducing like spores. Hence the present strategy. Once we have enough breaches in place have you thought about which strain you want to use for the cull?'

'I'd really prefer it if you didn't call it that.'

'What else would you like me to call it? Selective reduction perhaps?'

'Let's go with that. We should use a previous generation Ebola strain. Even the Ebola 48.6 if we wanted something stronger.' Neeson waited for the inevitable response.

'Nothing new and weaponised like Ebola 50?'

'No, Hack, we've been over this. Ebola 50 is too unpredictable. That strain burns fast but I don't want to risk further mutation and contagion. It could jump continents before it burns out and, as much as it pains me to say it, my vaccine isn't good enough yet.'

He would not become the destroyer. He would not let that happen again.

God would help him. Khan could have helped him.

For God so loved the world, that he gave his only Son – not to condemn the world, but in order that the world might be saved through him.

Dear God, I'm sorry.

'You're right as usual,' Hackman reluctantly agreed. 'So you'd use something old – a strain that we're all immunised against.'

'Correct. If necessary.'

'Of course, we only do what's necessary. I take no pleasure in this strategy. I'm a patriot, not a sociopath. We have to maintain our social ecosystem and we can't do that if their numbers outweigh ours. It's simple resource management. In fact, it's just maths.'

'Where did you study maths?'

'Fuck off. It's too late in your career to become self-righteous, or self-doubting for that matter. Every generation avails itself of the technology of the time – and every generation uses it to protect itself.'

'You mean every generation develops more effective weapons of mass destruction?'

'The Cull and Control Strategy is far more humane than most,' Hackman replied bluntly.

'It doesn't bother you that, each time, we move further and further away from the personal cost of what we're actually doing? Each time the death toll is bigger and our sense of connection with it is smaller.'

'What are you talking about?'

'I'm talking about gas chambers, Hiroshima, napalm, nuclear weapons, drone warfare – it's just a computer game, numbers on a spreadsheet, zones on a map.' He had to stop talking. He'd said too much already. But Hackman could stop this.

'No,' Hackman replied. 'It's natural selection and it's brutal. Do you know the alternative title of Darwin's thesis?'

'Don't patronise me,' Neeson rebuked. '*The Preservation of Favoured Species in the Struggle for Life.*'

'Well, we are the favoured species and I don't mean to lose this struggle. Is your decoy vaccine ready for wider dissemination in the East?'

'It's ready but I'd like to run a few more test breaches.'

'There's no need – the four test breaches went well – the scanners didn't pick up a thing and we've tied up all of our loose ends.'

Loose ends like Hassan Ali. Neeson had chosen him and the other vaxxers because he understood what drove them – he believed in what drove them – but he had used them for Hackman's plan anyway.

Neeson had chosen Khan too. He needed Khan for *his* plan.

'Sutherland is keen to push your vaccine out there so we can get on with the plan.'

'Yes, the plan. Of course – the decoy is ready. What are your target numbers?' Neeson could feel the sweat under his lab coat. The room was temperature controlled and cool.

'Thirteen percent. Eighteen percent max, including the margin of error. We're not monsters. We've identified the population sets we want to cull, I mean . . . whatever. Are you happy to proceed?'

Eighteen percent. Men, women and children reduced to a percentage.

'Happy?' Neeson stumbled. 'I . . . I was ready to proceed,' he recovered. 'That is, until Khan took his vaccine to another level. If he perfected his formula – and got it out there – it will shore up all your gaps in the Immunity Shield.'

'*Our* gaps. You're as much a part of this as I am. Remember that when you're giving in to your occasional moments of moral equivocation. You sound impressed with his vaccine.'

'It's a game changer for us – subversive and stunning. He's a much better virologist than me, always was. I told you we should have kidnapped him or extradited him. He would have given you the Ebola 50 vaccine by now. He has – had – this quiet vision and flair.' Neeson collected the latest lab report from the printer.

'His new vaccine is more than impressive, Hack. I wouldn't even know where to begin. I want a sample.'

'Sutherland wants it buried.'

'Of course he does. It's almost . . . miraculous. Noah senses it too. What are you going to do?'

'About Noah?' Hackman asked. 'He went beyond his brief and definitely overstayed his welcome.'

'He was never welcome there – who wanted him out more? Rajasuriya or ADL?'

Hackman ignored the question. 'We'll watch him – see what he knows, or thinks he knows. And Khan's vaccine? How can we be sure there aren't samples of it sitting in a freezer somewhere in Sri Lanka?'

'It's a freezer in the Middle Eastern Section you should be worried about,' Neeson replied.

'Thanks for that apocalyptic thought.'

'Relax, I'm just messing with you.' Neeson forced a smile. 'He's . . . he was a scientist. The formula wasn't perfect yet. He wouldn't have done anything with it until it was ready.'

'You knew him fifteen years ago – not now. You always forget that when you defend him. There's no way we could predict his behaviour given his condition. What if he tried to smuggle the vaccine out of the East? It wouldn't be picked up by the scanners.'

That's exactly right, Neeson thought.

'Roberta could detect it,' he replied, patting the AILA's arm affectionately. 'She's shown me worlds I could never have imagined. Amir used to say, blood is a river teeming with life and endless possibilities.'

He had spilled more blood than he had meant to.

'That sounds like regret, Neese. I hope you're not losing your nerve.'

'No, I'm just saying there are . . . there are other ways.' He looked up at the camera again, and then around at the five others he knew were in his laboratory.

'There are hardly ever other ways. That's why we're in this job. Are you going to be okay?'

'Don't worry about me.' Neeson sighed. 'My nerve is as strong as it was in 2025, even if my body is weak. You just get your strategy right and let me manage the science.'

Chapter 36

Hackman took the neat glass of whiskey that was held out to him. He didn't drink but Sutherland hadn't remembered that in all the years they'd worked together. The old man's limousine bar was always well-stocked.

'What will you do with him?' Sutherland looked over the rim of his glass.

'He'll have another medical. If he's fit, I'll get the full operation debrief. He'll need a more detailed psych eval and substantial rehab.'

'What about a full biometric poly? It's invasive but reliable.'

'It's invasive and frequently fatal. I've no reason to doubt him. He stayed on mission.'

'Perhaps you and I received a different mission report then?'

'He was supposed to investigate Khan and either uncover evidence that he was the ghost – or extract a confession. He did both and then he eliminated the threat.'

'He did more than that, Hackman. He connected Neeson to the breaches. Sri Bodhi to ADL. He doesn't have to be an Olympic gymnast to make the leap to both of us.'

'I'll deal with that.'

'Watch him closely. He uncovered too much.'

'You seem to have taken care of that,' Hackman replied bitterly. Garner and Crawford were good agents.

'Now, now – it's not just the blood of tyrants – it's the blood of patriots too that refresh the tree of liberty.'

'So you say.'

'So said Jefferson, Hackman – and who am I to argue with the Founding Fathers?' Sutherland smiled.

'I'm not sure this is what our third president had in mind when he said that. But we got what we wanted – Noah manipulated Khan into a confession and Rajasuriya bought it. It's time to cut him loose if that's what he wants.'

'You don't cut anyone loose. I heard rumours you were getting soft. Feeling sorry for the things you've done, Hackman – the deaths you've caused? I certainly hope not. We've come too far together to turn back now.'

'No, sir, I walk this path proudly, with or without you, in fact.'

'I'm glad to hear it. Your man is fortunate the good doctor cracked so early. I'd underestimated their bond.'

'Noah excels at that. He reads people – knows what kind of relationship to build with his target.'

'Perhaps. The interview footage is gruesome. *I* was ready to confess by the second nail. Apparently there are a lot of nerves in the nail bed.' Sutherland looked at his manicure and then curled his hand protectively into a fist.

'There are. It would take all ten fingers and more for Noah to break. We know that.'

'You have a lot of faith in him.'

'I've known him for twenty years, I recruited him myself, supervised many of his missions – it's not faith, it's professional judgement.'

'And in your professional judgement, he was on a mission – he'll tell you everything he knows?' Sutherland asked.

'Of course, he's a patriot and a professional too.'

'I hope so – for your sake. If he unravels, it's on you. He's damaged, Hackman – I trust you'll know when to put him down.'

'He's okay – Sahara says he's shaken by Khan's death. But he'll recover.'

'I can't say I care. As for Khan – there was no other way. It isn't the first time one man had to die for the sins and aspirations of many. Ghosts are always dead. It's better this way – more convincing, less room for rebuttal. We've seized and deleted his hard drives as well as everything from your over-zealous team.'

'What about the AILA – Devi?'

'She self-destructed, as they say. We couldn't retrieve any data from her – which was perfect. We wouldn't want his formula getting into the wrong hands.'

'You didn't want to keep it for yourself? Neeson says Khan is – was – the better virologist. He doesn't say that about anyone.'

'The man and the formula needed to be destroyed,' Sutherland replied.

'Like any other biohazard?'

Sutherland ignored him. 'When are we ready to execute the next stage?'

'I'm not sure – I'll talk to Neeson today. We need a critical mass of Immunity Shield breaches – when we release the virus it has to make a decent impact on the population. The Information Shield won't protect us forever and I don't want to have to do this again in a decade. A sizeable cull is a good cull. I agree with your suggestion: sixty percent is the right number.'

'Good. You know Ebola 50 would be more effective.'

'Too dangerous.' Hackman shook his head. 'I'm with Neeson on this. It only takes one ambassador to Turkey to fuck it up for the rest of us.'

'You should have more faith, Hackman. When will you break the news about the ghost?'

'Soon – so the story has time to filter through both sides of the Alliance.'

'It's a good story, isn't it? A rogue virologist and his attempted Immunity Shield breaches; followed by the outbreaks.'

'Yes. Then we both step in to reassure people that ADL and Bio has it all under control, that the GVP is vital for public safety. And all of the unconverted rush back to the true faith, scarred by pictures of children dying of Ebola in the Eastern Alliance.'

'Sounds like a plan.' Sutherland refilled his glass and raised it.

*

Noah struggled to swipe his pass. The security pad was impossible with his bandages. He set the cooler box down and was about to attempt the code with his elbow when the door opened.

Neeson stepped forward and put his arms around him.

'I wasn't sure you'd make it,' the older man said.

'Me neither,' he smiled briefly and then his face darkened.

'I'm sorry about your agents, Noah.' Neeson led him into his lab.

'Me too, Neese.' There were no words to express the weight of that responsibility. It never lessened despite the passing years, the number of missions, the outcomes that never really justified the losses.

'I heard about Amir too . . .' Neeson's voice trailed away. There were no words for that either.

'He remembered you with great affection and respect,' Noah began.

'He was a great scientist, a great person,' Neeson replied, busying himself at a work station.

'A great friend?' Noah probed.

'Yes, a dear friend.' Neeson sat on his stool and swung around to face him. 'We worked closely together at the . . .'

'The School of Tropical Medicine, yes I know.'

'Yes. And I would see him often at conferences – we shared research and often wrote papers together. I travelled with him and Aisha many times. They were keen tourists.' He laughed, remembering something, a shared time perhaps. 'She was lovely.'

'He missed her very much,' Noah replied. 'I can understand that. In the interrogation Rajasuriya said he killed her. Do you know what happened?'

'Sudden illness was the official story. It's a lot easier than talking about an execution.'

'An execution?' Noah leaned against the bench. He was still so tired.

'Yes,' Neeson paused. He looked at Noah pleadingly. 'You must understand, I helped develop the Faith Inhibitor – I thought we were doing the right thing. I thought it was the key to our salvation, as much as the Ebola vaccine. Religious wars had escalated all over the globe, threatening to wipe out communities faster than the disease.

'The religions of the East were blamed for starting it – they were declared a virus, the Sixth Virus. Ebola and war . . . the perfect playmates. Wherever one went, the other followed.

'Africa was already finished. But the others – the Middle East, Asia – we could have helped them. Instead, we vaccinated our people against Ebola first. We added the EBL-47 to the flu jab and other standard vaccinations in the West without telling anyone. We protected ourselves. And then . . . we allowed the pandemic to devastate the populations of the East.'

'Allowed it or helped it?' Noah asked.

'It's the same thing.'

'Allowed it or *used* it?' Noah remembered what Khan had said about influenza.

'It's the same Godforsaken thing,' Neeson replied bitterly. 'The strategy worked. The East was eventually forced to declare truce upon truce. It stopped its warring and begged for help – a vaccination, a cure, anything that would help its people to survive, its children to stop bleeding.

'Walls have always been built between us – East and West Berlin, the East and West Bloc, the 38th Parallel. But this one was different. It used science and technology – it used medicine – these were the new weapons in a new kind of war.'

'A new kind of peace.'

'That's right. When the vaccination programme was implemented in Sri Lanka, people volunteered – they lined up for days to be vaccinated. No one wanted to miss out. They were exhausted by the killing. Everyone had lost someone. They were terrified of Ebola. The vaccination programme was a condition of the peace and that was all they wanted – to stop fighting.

'No one realised that the vaccination would make them stop believing. No one except Amir and his wife and their team at the hospital.

'They watched the first wave of vaccinations and realised what was happening. Not immediately – at first they just thought something was wrong with it. They thought it was having adverse side effects – memory loss, disassociation, prolonged lethargy.

'They reported it to the WHO. They ran their own trials. They pulled the vaccine apart and tried to construct it again. They realised that there was something integral to the vaccine that was targeting the brain in an unintended way.

'Eventually they realised that it was targeting the frontal lobe in a way that was fully understood and intended by the WHO – by us. They suspected their government was part of it – a willing participant in the deception. They tried to warn people, but who would believe such a thing? That a government and WHO-sanctioned vaccination programme was damaging the faith engine of their brains? That we had found a way to kill faith, and with it, a way to kill God.

'Amir and Aisha resisted. They fought back – I told them not to. But they both . . . they loved each other so much. And they loved God, Noah. They believed that God inhabited the core of the cells they worked with every day.'

'What happened to them?' Noah asked.

'They shot her,' he replied. 'Amir was in Mumbai, speaking to the Minister for Health there. He was afraid to leave her – Rajasuriya had already threatened them and he doesn't make empty threats.'

'Then why did Amir go?'

'Because I said I would look after her,' he whispered. 'He trusted me. They both did.'

'You were there? Oh my God, Jack – what did you do?'

'Not enough. I loved her and Amir. Maybe I loved her too much, I don't know. I begged her to stop their work, to recant – if I could have convinced one to persuade the other . . . I even begged her to leave him – to come back with me. Of course she refused.

'Then they came for her. It all happened so fast. I wasn't ready. They took her to the courtyard at the hospital and made her kneel down.

'I saw the pendant on her neck swing forward. She held it to her chest. They told her to put her head down, but she looked straight at me.'

Neeson remembered: He was screaming and crying. There were soldiers holding him – Western Alliance soldiers holding him back. Orders from Bio to remove the threat.

'"Don't cry, Jack," she said. "Tell Amir I know whose I am and I know where I'm going. Tell him I will see him soon." That was all she said. She closed her eyes, held the pendant tighter and began to pray. They shot her in the back of the head.'

'Why did they let him live?'

'He was a talented virologist. They needed him,' Neeson said simply.

'Presumably Khan was given the vaccine?'

'Yes, of course. As soon as he returned from India. They told him she was dead, knocked him unconscious and did it the easy way.'

'*I* did it the easy way. I couldn't look in his eyes while I was poisoning him. I left Sri Lanka and never went back. His wife and his faith were taken away from him at the same time. I don't know how you keep living after that but he did. He carried the loss – one he could remember and one he couldn't. He carried the loss but he didn't let it kill him.'

'No, I killed him,' Noah stated flatly.

Neeson turned to face him. 'He was a good man. Thank you for what you did.'

'Thank you? I *killed* him,' he repeated.

'He was ready. He had done as much as he could.'

'He knew whose he was and where he was going?' Noah said bitterly.

'Yes, something like that.'

'And how about you, Neeson – whose are you?'

'I'm a company man, Noah, you know that. You?'

'Me? Whose am I?' He looked at the AILA moving around the lab, tidying up experiments. It was just like Devi, but faster. It would do. He had learnt enough from Khan; and Neeson could do the rest now.

'My father said, "*Man is made by his faith – as he believes, so he is.*"'

'Your father knew his scripture well. So do you.'

Noah shrugged. 'After all the death we've wreaked – do you still believe in God?' He didn't dare ask more in the lab.

'Deeply. I have faith in something more than my world, something more than life and death.'

'I thought we killed faith?' Noah replied. He looked at the camera embedded into the far corner of the ceiling. There were eight more in the room that he could identify. Others he couldn't.

'All things find a way to survive. Nature adapts to changes and threats. It finds a way to survive and thrive – to worship and be worshipped. Sometimes it needs more time. If we could just give Nature more time ... Like people, Noah – if you give them enough time, they recover. I'm a scientist – I don't believe anything can be truly eradicated.'

'So a wise man once told me,' Noah replied. He thought about the tumour – maybe Nature was finding a way.

'Was he a scientist too?'

He shook his head and riffled through his cooler box. 'An explorer. I have something for you.'

Neeson didn't look at the cameras in the room. 'I believe you do,' he said carefully.

'Lychees – I had to work for them.' Noah reached forward with a small sack of fruit and revealed the vaccination welt on his hand.

Acknowledgements

I've realised now that it takes a village to publish a book. I am hugely grateful to the people who have helped develop *The Barrier* from a collection of Post-it notes to a book that I can hold in my hands and hover next to in book shops.

Thank you to the team at Pan Macmillan for giving me this opportunity: Alex Lloyd, Deonie Fiford, Haylee Nash, Mathilda Imlah and Cate Paterson. I'm a better writer because of it. Alex, what a constructive partnership you created.

Thank you so much to Alex Craig for your support and encouragement of my writing. I couldn't have written this second book without your insights into my first one. Nor would I have published this second book without you.

A very big thank you to my agent, Tara Wynne at Curtis Brown Australia, for pushing me and this book tirelessly. Tara's faith was firm when mine wavered.

My First Readers on this one were much the same as the last one (sorry gang): Kate Kelly, Nat Oliver, Bek Cheney, Lisa Havas and Natascha Pereira. Thank you for loving this book right from the first disturbing scene. I'm not sorry – I'm grateful and so lucky to have you.

Kate Kelly, I've known you for as long as I've loved reading. I don't really remember books before you. And for as long as we have read together, you've told me I can write. Thank you.

I am especially fortunate with my book club – Sandra, Narelle, Tina, Carmela, Alex, Angela and Su Lin – who generously and patiently read this manuscript and helped me navigate the 'when, where and how' of each reveal. Your friendship is an essential part of my writing process and my life.

Keda Ormsby was entrusted with the product of writing each day for many months. At the end of each day you told me that tomorrow I should write some more. How do you eat an elephant? With a great friend by your side.

To Latha and Tim, this book is about many things but mostly faith and loss. Your losses are incomprehensible. Your faith in each other is intensely tangible. It's always in the room, just like Anji.

Thank you to Clare Lewis at Clare Lewis Photography for making me look like a 'real author'. And to Jodie Wood, the artist whose work helps me see before I write. Thank you to Kerry from Kerry Richards Design for creating my beautiful website. Also to the University of Western Australia Law School, through Kate, for helping me understand the role of historic contagions in the development of policy and power disparities.

Mum and Rohan, the original Team Siva, were entrusted with the care of our children (and at times me), when I got lost wandering through the streets of Colombo, 2040. Mum has a spirit that always leads me home.

I am profoundly grateful to my siblings, Narendran and Rachel. Thank you for patiently explaining (and re-explaining) the finer points of immunology, cellular biology, epidemiology and the other -ologies to me. Thank you also for helping me throw out everything you taught me and create science (fiction) that was consistent and rigorous. You are wonderful teachers and beautiful siblings.

Darling Ellora, Kailash, Hari and Sid, I wrote this book originally as an adventure story for you but it quickly became far too violent. Read it when you're older and don't swear, just because Mummy does. There aren't enough words or lifetimes for me to tell you how deeply I love you.

This book is dedicated to my parents who gave us our faith. Your commitment to community, spirituality and science inspired us. 'Thank you' will never express what we owe you. When you read this book, I hope you realise that Narendran and I really were listening.

And finally, to my husband Haran Siva – your faith in me drove this book and your faith in us sustains our greatest creative partnership. Thank you for being the beginning of all things. And for letting us get the puppy.

Clare Lewis Photography